Book of Never

Throne of Leaves

Ashley Capes

Throne of Leaves
(Book of Never: 8)
Copyright © 2021 by Ashley Capes

Cover: Illustration by Lin Hsiang
Design by STK Kreations
Layout & Typeset: Close-Up Books

ISBN-978-0-6453605-4-7

www.ashleycapes.com

Published by Close-Up Books
Melbourne, Australia

For Brooke

Chapter 1

Never lit his lantern with a spark of crimson-fire then set it upon the nearest shelf, deep orange flickering to red across the walls – amber luminescence mixing with the blood. When he trailed a hand along the stone and quartz, the same thrill of Amouni magic lingered.

Unsurprisingly, the library in the Amber Isle had not changed. Its resin-coated shelves were protected from the elements, the words in each heavy book protected by quartz pages. He let the liquid fire flare a little, raising his arm to add enough to read by.

Now that he'd found and unlocked the five-pointed puzzle that revealed two more hidden tomes within the walls, it was time for success… at last. He'd found no other hidden stores of knowledge, not even in the mural room.

He lifted the first heavy tome free. *The Forgotten Ones.* "Please," he murmured as he turned each weighty page carefully. Even a single clue about Arkenon, God of the Malecaphera would be enough.

But he did not have to read much before Arkenon was mentioned… as a footnote.

It is claimed in The Origin *that the Malecaphera worshipped a dread God – Arkenon. Others believe this may have been another name for the Grand Poise. Whatever the truth, few relics of the religion remain, save for what is preserved in the Temple Trivium.*

Never lowered the tome.

Finally.

A clue. It might not be reliable, but it was more than he'd found so far. While the book raised several questions and held unfamiliar terms, the biggest problem was clear: such a Temple might no longer exist, let alone still hold supposed traces of the ancient religion mentioned in the book.

Steel clattered from somewhere within the isle.

Sea-creatures again? Never closed the book and set it down with a sigh. During the first few encounters since his return to the isle, nearly two weeks ago, he'd been gentle enough but if they were seeking him once more, they weren't going to receive a warm welcome.

Or they would receive an *exceedingly* warm welcome.

He strode through the passages – some lit by the shimmering quartz veins, others his crimson-fire – following the leaf symbols until he reached the many-chambered altar room with its domed roof and amber walls.

There, the sea-creatures shrank back into the openings.

None challenged him and the floor was empty, red and green smears upon the altar just as dark as when he'd last checked the room.

Never let the globe of crimson light flare, covering his entire forearm a moment, and the sea-creatures scuttled farther away, the smack of webbed limbs echoing somewhere from the sleeping chambers above.

It didn't seem to be the creatures at all.

Which meant the sound must have come from somewhere else... beyond the hidden door, which stood open, exactly as he'd left it? Had one of the sea-creatures headed down toward the jewel pit?

Another crash of steel against stone.

From just that direction.

"Surely not."

Never quickened his pace but cut the crimson-fire before he reached the passage. No need to give his position away... if he hadn't already.

But when he reached the sea of pale blue fire flickering from the jewel pit, it illuminated a woman dressed in a leather vest and pants beneath a yellow cloak. The light gleamed on glass buttons that had been sewn into her jacket – a constellation. Her blonde hair bore a streak of woven white ribbon. Quisoan?

She knelt at the far end of the jewel pit, one hand upon her knee, skin pale, muscles defined by the hard shadows thrown by gleaming jewels. Her lantern and pack lay nearby, and bulged with enough provisions for a long stay, it seemed.

Some of the way along the path between the glittering gemstones rested a few scraps of shredded steel and a handful of jewels.

Something she'd tossed forth, no doubt.

The Guardians were still.

That she'd reached the Amber Isle alone suggested she

was capable enough, and she'd obviously not been fooled by the trap either. More than a typical treasure hunter then.

"The guardians within are faster than you or I," Never said when he reached his side of the pit.

She rose with widened eyes, steel-tipped staff extended.

But her gaze quickly narrowed. "Who are you?" Her accent seemed to suggest she *was* from a Quisoan tribe but her cloak, belt and boots were more of Marlosi design. And there was her use of a staff, not a typical Quisoan weapon.

It was also clear, even frowning at him, that she was beautiful. Very beautiful. That hardly meant he could lower his guard. "I am Never, a traveller."

She did not lower her weapon. "Sounds like you know the isle well."

"A little better this time around," he said. "Hunting for treasure?"

She did not answer.

Never sheathed his blade. His crimson-fire was but a heartbeat away if needed, unlikely as that was, considering the jewel pit between them. "Could I offer some advice?"

"Only if it's how to deal with whatever's lurking beneath those jewels."

"Gladly, but this pit is not the only threat here."

"Those creatures? They pose no threat to me."

"I don't doubt that, since you've made it here, but I imagine your boat is missing by now."

She pointed her staff at him. "What have you done to my boat?"

"Not me. The sea-creatures will likely have sabotaged it by now; they did the same to me last time I was here."

"Is this some trick?"

"Not at all," Never said. "If you don't trust me, see for yourself. But if you want to do that, you have to leave any jewels behind that you're carrying. You've seen what the Guardians can do."

She shook her head. "I cannot give them up."

"Then you cannot pass."

Her jaw clenched. "I *must*."

The word was a hiss of determination rather than desperation that might have suggested greed. Hard to really be sure. Whatever her purpose, there was no point pressing her. And more importantly, what reason existed to simply let her die?

None.

The Guardians had to be stopped again.

"Give me a moment."

"Do I have a choice?"

"Trust me if you can," Never said as he strode down the passage. Once out of sight, he lowered his voice. "Guide."

A figure robed in gold with arms bare appeared, the head of a stag regarding him this time. A familiar, flat voice. *Master.*

"I asked for the Guardians to rest. Why are they moving again?"

They cannot rest always. You created them to always watch.

Never sighed. "Make sure they are resting now."

Yes, Master.

Never strode back to the jewel pit and crossed the walkway. "It is safe to leave. See, nothing attacked."

The woman's expression of doubt eased a little and while her first step was hesitant, she continued with only a final glance at the pit of jewels.

At the other side, she paused and her suspicion seemed to linger. "You don't seem interested in the treasure. If you can stop those... things like you say you did, you could have taken it all."

"Treasure isn't only found in jewels," he replied.

"No?"

"Knowledge," Never replied with a faint smile.

"I see." The Quisoan woman hoisted her pack and appraised him moment, her distrust seeming to fade just a little. She started down the passage. "Thank you, stranger."

"Huna ic sanwe vidawon," he said. *Stars watch over you.*

"Keda," she replied after a slight pause.

And you.

Chapter 2

Never stood upon stony earth beneath a darkening sky, where the five-pointed leaf had once glowed. The soft crash of waves was a distant melody, reminding him of when he'd first visited the Amber Isle long ago. He nudged a small stone with the toe of his boot. Long ago? Hardly decades... but so much had happened that the memories weighed like years.

The ground lay dark, no hint of any bright Amouni symbol visible where the sea air reached him upon a cool, spring breeze. He folded his arms. Would night need to fall for the silver to return? Or would his own tattoo trigger it sooner?

There had been another treasure in the hidden books at least – an explanation for the tattoo.

And it was time to test what he had learned... if he could.

Reaching the isle had not been as difficult this time, thanks to his wings, but every hour, every day he spent upon the island was more time for King Oleksan to poison the land on his path to Arkenon.

Or whatever his end goal might actually be.

The decay that lay in Oleksan's wake left wide swathes of wilted grass and plants, spotted with black and yellow, or drained to grey; melted snow or twisted stone and a terrible, lingering scent of honeyed mould. The bones of animals caught within were frames of powdery grey, some having taken on a faintly purple hue, all without clear pattern. An entire village in the Vadiya mountains had been swallowed up by the bleak decay too, with no trace of survivors, just crumbling stone and withered wood.

Mounds that had once been people.

A true terror had been unleashed upon the world. The chill it left lingered, and Never clenched a fist, changing the birch patterns on his skin. "And I should have stopped it happening."

Footsteps approached and he turned.

The treasure-hunter appeared from Javiem's cave, staff in hand, a frown upon her face. She moved easily, even with the weight of her pack, which now doubtless included more than a few diamonds. "You were right about my boat – assuming you weren't responsible yourself. It's gone."

"That's how they add to their number, by trapping people here."

She leant on her staff, her expression of suspicion returned. "You don't seem very worried."

"I'm not."

"Why?" She edged across the space between them, closing enough to strike with her weapon if she wished, though it didn't seem likely.

Instead, she set her pack down and lifted one of the Amouni texts free, the heavy quartz catching the slowly setting sun. "You have no boat of your own and you're not interested in the jewels. But if these books are what you came for as you claim, you have no way to take them from the isle. Unless you plan to fly."

"They are invaluable, true."

"Stop avoiding my question."

"I suppose I am," Never said with a nod. "Have you come to seek my help?"

She set the book down. "I have an offer."

Never raised an eyebrow. "Are we negotiating?"

"Yes. You can obviously escape this place somehow," she said, then took a breath. "Take me with you when you leave. I will repay the debt with something rare and valuable." She gestured to the white ribbon woven into her hair. "I'm betting you know what this is."

He nodded. The weave was part of a rare Quisoan gift, usually used to restore or help things grow. Many tribes carried traces of the gift, but the powerful Weavers he recalled from his youth were able to do more, even improving their own physical strength. "That is generous."

"That's not all I'm offering," she said, a fierceness appearing in her gaze. "I'll kill you if you try to betray me."

"Seems a little much, to be honest."

"Not to me. Do we have a deal?"

Never regarded her a moment. Speed was important. He *was* ready to leave for now, but carrying books *and* the woman such a distance? Fatigue would wear him down. But if the Amouni symbol was anything like the Guide's power to travel a river course, then surely yes. It shouldn't matter who or what he brought along.

It was untested magic, however.

But since the Amber Isle contained no river and nor could Guides travel the ocean, leaving the woman behind was a death sentence.

"We do, but here are my terms," he said. "First, I'll take one diamond. Second, tell me why you came here, and third… your name. Finally, I want you to keep what you learn about me to yourself, mostly for your own safety."

The treasure-hunter folded her arms. "Are you trying to impress me?"

"Well, you should be impressed already, considering how I saved you from the jewel pit."

She fought a smile. "Get me off this island and I'll be impressed."

"And the rest of my terms?"

"My name is Rikeva," she said. "And I was here for the Sea God's Eye, or anything of great value, it didn't really matter. But I have enough jewels now."

"A classic motive for visiting this place, but why risk your life by doing so?"

"Ask me again when we're safely away from here."

Never shrugged. "Very well." Once more, it probably didn't matter so much, truly – he didn't need to know in order to save her. It *might* have helped decide if she was a threat but it didn't seem likely.

She reached into an inner pocket, withdrew a large diamond and tossed it across the space between them.

Never caught and lifted the jewel to the light, orange refracting in a pleasantly dazzling way, then lowered the precious stone. It would certainly be useful. "Thank you."

"Are you sure that's enough payment?"

"It is."

"I'm surprised you didn't ask for more." Rikeva shrugged. "I can't figure you out, stranger."

"Call me, Never," he said. "Ready to leave, then?"

"Very well... Never. I am curious as to where you've hidden your boat."

Never bent to place the jewel within his pack, wrapping it in a spare cloak so that it would hopefully not scratch the quartz books.

"I have a different method in mind, but you have to take my hand and trust me, as it will be unusual." And untested in the current Age too, since Snow hadn't seemed to be using symbols... "Can you do that?"

"No boat? I'm starting to regret our agreement."

Never glanced at the sunset – hardly anywhere near midnight, but surely dark enough for the light to appear within the stone. Darkness was no requirement according to the book, but it might go some way toward convincing her. He strode across the open area but the exact location of the five-pointed leaf was hard to recall...

Silvery light rose from beneath his boots.

Rikeva joined him. "What is this?"

"The magic we'll use to escape." He flipped a knife into one hand and used the point to prick his forefinger, then knelt and traced the outline. Hissing gold followed his movements and a shiver ran through his body – part from the Amouni magic, part excitement.

After so long, the truth. The symbols *were* for travel and as Ascended, he *could* use them. Since the *forasa* symbol activated as the book described, success was all but guaranteed.

"There are no Quisoan or Marlosi arts or magic like this."

"Agreed."

Rikeva was not precisely frowning, but her expression still suggested concern. "This has to be dangerous."

"Not for me."

She folded her arms. "How does it work?"

Never pulled the neck of his tunic down enough to reveal the top of his glowing tattoo. "This symbol and my blood allow me to use the *forasa* symbols. I can take us to the nearest symbol on the mainland."

Some of the doubt was easing, replaced by what might have been creeping awe. "You're claiming such a vast power?"

"I am," he said. "And that's part of why I want you to keep my secret."

"I don't even know if I believe it," she said, but still nodded. Up close, a light dusting of freckles was visible across the bridge of her nose.

"Then I'll make sure everything is clear for us to travel," he said. "I just need a moment."

Never closed his eyes and almost instantly lines of spreading silver stretched before him. Like branches, they were connected to scores of buds or pods, each giving the impression that they might flower. Few ended without other branches shooting off, the majority offering connections in various directions, suggesting he could move to and from most *forasa* symbols to most others.

The nearest was presumably somewhere on the northern tip of Marlosi... yet some were so faint, so distant that they were just vague, feathery touches against his mind.

Other lands? Beyond the farthest reaches of the ocean...

Or just the limits of his current position on the isle?

"Is it ready?" Rikeva wore her pack now, staff looped through the straps. "What do I need to do?"

"It is," he said, stepping away from the symbol. And hopefully that was the truth. "Just take my hand. And don't let go."

The Quisoan woman held out an arm. He took her hand with a nod. Calloused but warm. A little thrill passed through him. How long had it been since he'd actually touched another person, even incidentally?

But the isolation had been worthwhile, especially if the *forasa* worked – researching the Burnished King and the dark god would be swifter, more so even than what he could manage with wings.

Never stepped back onto the five-pointed leaf.

Silvery light glowed from the throat of his tunic, blazing bright enough to blind him. Rikeva's grip tightened before the light changed to a golden flare.

Chapter 3

When the piercing light cleared, Never found darkness lit only by a glow beneath his feet and a few slivers of warm light from above. A cave or cavern?

Rikeva's knees gave out, and Never caught her as she slumped. "Are you all right?"

She groaned as she rubbed at her temples. "I think so... for a moment there I was sure that my joints were being pulled apart. I couldn't move." Rikeva removed her pack and stood, testing her legs a moment. "Are you sure that's normal?"

"It is." Or at least, there was a possibility. Perhaps for those without Amouni blood, travel was more difficult. No way to be sure since she was probably the first person without Amouni heritage to use the *forasa* symbols in centuries. "Forgive me for not mentioning it. It passed quickly, right?"

"It did, I suppose." She moved slowly, tentatively almost, as she searched the room. "It looks like we're not on the Amber Isle anymore, as you promised."

"Is that grudging approval, I hear?"

Rikeva chuckled. "Maybe once we're out of here."

Never set his own pack down and examined the room. As his eyes continued to adjust, what looked like a shrine resolved before him. A low, rectangular altar set before a tall alcove. Within, stood a robed figure carved of stone, wings folded around the body. The face was welcoming, a soft smile on the lips.

Amouni, obviously.

He leant closer, running a hand along the side and back of the altar, and then the statue, but found no hidden switch or lever.

"I think this used to be the entry," Rikeva said.

Never joined her at the wall opposite the shrine where a triangular pattern in the floor led to a pile of rubble, the larger pieces jammed with smaller chunks to create a solid slope, sealing any escape.

Rikeva kicked the rock pile. "Looks like we need to try another symbol."

"Perhaps. That might depend on where you plan to head from here. We're in the foothills of the Trieta Mountains. The next nearest is probably closer to the Twin Villages."

"Wrong direction."

Never grinned. "Then get ready to keep another secret. Maybe take a few steps back too."

Rikeva did so and Never drew a dagger to make two small cuts to his hands, then let the crimson-fire free. A gasp echoed in the shrine but he focused on the rubble – best not to hold back, since the extent of the cave-in was not clear. Hopefully he wasn't about to overextend himself because the fire needed to be *quite* hot.

Searing flame shot forth in a bloody flare. It splashed across the cave-in's surface but he narrowed the streams. The beams of crimson-fire soon changed as he forced more heat into the fire, then more until it became a pinkish white. Rikeva retreated toward the statue.

Never did not let up – stone was melting, a tunnel forming swiftly.

Perfect. And yet, he did have limits. Hopefully the cave-in wasn't going to test them; it all depended on just how deep the cave rested beneath the landslide. But he kept the crimson-fire roaring until all resistance ended.

He let the flames die away, saving some strength for possible surprises, and sucked in a few deep breaths.

Little tendrils of steam rose as faint light entered from a long tunnel – something they'd have to crawl along once the melted stone cooled.

"You're the one they talk about, aren't you?" Rikeva asked, staring at him, voice a little hushed. "The Winged Hero of the War."

He sighed. "They do say that, yes."

She shook her head in what might have been disbelief, but instead she thanked him and murmured to herself. "There is hope."

Never couldn't prevent a frown as he moved to the altar and sat, dragging his pack up beside him. He found his flask and took a long drink. Despite the weariness that settled across his limbs, he was by no means exhausted – a relief.

"I must ask you something, Never."

He nodded.

"My horse is back at the lighthouse and I cannot afford

to return so far; I don't have time. Can you truly fly?"

"I can." There seemed little point keeping that secret now; she knew most of them already. But whatever her next question... well, the answer he gave would depend on what sort of delays it might create. Even with his new-found speed, thanks to the *forasa*, visiting a town or city and gathering information was his first priority.

"Will you take me south to Red Ridge?"

Red Ridge. An old settlement and not a single step out of his way... in terms of direction, at least. "I will."

She made a fist but gratitude filled her voice. "Thank you."

"Who are you trying to save?" he asked, certain of his guess before he spoke.

"My family. My tribe – all of the tribes."

Never lowered his flask. "The decay?"

"Yes. It destroys all it touches, plant, tree, animal or woman," she said. "None know from where it came but it appeared overnight, bursting from the very earth, cutting through the camps. Other tribes have been afraid to count the dead."

Never pushed down a surge of guilt. Too long searching the isle. "But someone is trading in a cure?"

"No. It can only stave off death, we hope long enough for a cure to be found."

"I am seeking the source," he said. "And I will end whatever it is."

"In time to save the tribes?"

"Yes." Determination filled his voice.

Her expression did not reveal what she thought of his claim. "A mighty promise. Even for a war-hero."

"Not the moniker I'd choose, but I know."

She moved to the tunnel and extended a hand within, and obviously the stone had cooled enough, since she retrieved her pack, shoved it in and crawled after. "It's not too bad."

Never followed with his own pack. The passage was tolerable, even if the surface hadn't fully cooled.

When he crawled free, it was to meet a darkening sky above and thick shadows between trees of sweet-scented pine, their needles almost purple. An overgrown trail led down, eventually no doubt, toward level ground but the *forasa* seemed fairly high in the hills. The faint echo of water reached him from somewhere nearby.

Melted stone spread across the edges of the old landslide, one which seemed as much solid earth and stone as anything else. An old slide, then. Who knew how long the shrine had been buried?

"How does this work?" Rikeva asked. "Because I think I might be expecting too much. Can you carry me *and* both our packs?"

"I doubt it," he said. "But we can take the river."

"Without a boat?"

He nodded. "More magic."

"Oh."

Never led her down the path, pushing through undergrowth to an animal trail when they neared the water. Old pine needles met piles of wide, grey leaves from the Boar Shrub, some floating by on a twisting stream that leapt and bubbled between tree roots.

"I'll call for help," Never said before lifting his voice. "Guide?"

A figure flickered into view, knee-deep in the water, its

blue robe unmoved. Rikeva started, reaching for her weapon as Never apologised. "More of my secrets. He can help us travel."

"I see."

The head of a fox regarded him impassively. *Master.*

"Take us close to Red Ridge."

Of course.

Rikeva glanced between Never and the Guide, eyes a little wide. "Well. How does this one work, then?"

"About the same." Never held out his hand as he explained. It seemed she was quickly growing accustomed to Amouni magic. On the outside, at least. "It'll take us near enough that you shouldn't have to travel too far on foot. Expect darkness and streaking colours, this time."

"Thanks."

Once again, her hand offered a welcome warmth.

He reached out to the Guide then and darkness fell, followed by streaking purple, white and blue.

No sooner had it begun than it seemed the ride was over. Never found himself standing on the banks of a stronger river, though its name escaped him. Darkness had fallen now, so some time at least had passed, but there was enough light to make out a nearby crossroad with its weathered signpost.

"I'm dry," Rikeva said, running a hand through her hair. "Didn't expect that."

"Better than the *forasa*, at least."

"Agreed." She reached up to untie the white ribbon but Never raised a hand before she could finish.

"Keep it, please. The jewel is plenty."

Rikeva lowered her arms. "Are you certain?"

"I am. Orunawe." *Gratitude.*

She smiled. "In my tribe we say *Orunawea*. You sound like you spent time somewhere in the south?"

"We followed the Twin Blade constellation."

"Ah," she said as she checked the ribbon in her hair one last time. "Thank you again, Never, Winged Hero of the War."

"Good luck."

Rikeva offered a wave and set off at a jog, heading toward the crossroad and a winding path which led into the hills. Somewhere beyond waited Red Ridge, something of an oddity in Marlosi, as though a God-sized shovel had carved a hunk of land free – different to the Cracked Plains, since it was not barren.

Never watched the Quisoan woman for a moment before letting his wings burst free and leaping into the darkness above.

Chapter 4

The muted, yellow fire of a town glowed below Never as he tilted his wings. Warm spring breeze flowing across his skin was almost enough to make completing an extra circle of the town worthwhile, but instead he found a nearby stand of trees and thudded down.

Not the best landing. Easy enough to blame the weight of the pack if anyone had seen him but he was alone on the outskirts of the small town. Hard to recall, but it was likely Cagila, being only a little further south than the mighty crossroads at Golden Plains.

Hopefully, it would boast at least one inn since a bed would be *most* welcome.

Once he had information.

Never strode through long grass beside the road and then along the paved surface, nearing the town swiftly.

Cagila was not large. No wall encircled it, but there stood a clear division between stone and mud brick homes, with a wooden shack in turn sitting on the outskirts. Most chimneys bore striped weathervanes, dark and moving only gently.

The sweet scent of night-blooming Wisamin swum through the night to reach him, and he drew in the scent but no-one else was out enjoying the air. Windows were shuttered, golden candlelight slipping free but no sounds from within. Even up ahead, past a shadowy well, no raised voices of laughter or anger, no singing, no music.

The entire place seemed empty.

But it was not, for he glimpsed shadows moving behind the curtains.

At the inn's painted door of blue, the hush of lowered voices reached him. Were most people within then? For safety? Some manner of town meeting? He climbed the single step and pushed the door open.

Inside waited a cosy common room, stone walls covered in bright cloth hangings and light from the fireplace, but when all heads turned to face him, their eyes were wide with concern. Perhaps fair, he was a stranger, but toward the back, two of the locals even slipped into a passage. Whether it led to their rooms or outside, they moved quickly indeed, tunics of banded yellow and red fluttering as if caught in a gust.

The warmth in the common room seemed bolstered by the scent of beef and spices but few faces seemed to be enjoying their meals; small groups sat huddled over their plates or cups – men, women and children alike. Empty tables were dotted about, as if more folks usually ate at the inn of an evening.

Before Never could step within, a short fellow stood and approached with a glare. "Stop. Where have you travelled from?"

Never frowned. "Petana." Which was close enough.

Apparently, a favourable answer, since at least some tension left the room. Most of the people returned to their meals, a few waving for the man to sit. "Let him in, Yogan," the innkeeper said from where he leant across the bar, his white beard reaching easily to his stomach.

By the glowers Never received, others did not seem to agree with the innkeeper, but they did not give voice to their concerns.

Yogan spun. "He could be lying – like the other one!"

Murmurs of assent rose.

The innkeeper straightened. "This is my inn and he is seeking shelter."

A third speaker stood, a woman with a streak of grey in her dark hair. "But Cagila belongs to all of us, Uncle."

"I know that, Ginara."

"I do not mean to cause suffering here," Never said with raised hands. "I only seek news. And rest."

The woman continued. "Then answer, do you have a thirst? Difficulty moving your limbs? A grey pallor to the eyes?"

"No." He glanced at the closest table of patrons. "And as for my eyes, you can no doubt see them from your seat."

One of the men nodded. "It's true."

Ginara exchanged a look with Yogan. The short man seemed angry still and worry was clear in her own eyes, as though the proof she'd demanded was not enough to overcome her fear.

A new figure appeared from the hallway; robed in the pale yellow of Pacela, sprig of juniper sewn over the breast bearing two branches. The man blinked upon seeing Never, then moved to the centre of the room. His frown was deep.

"It is our duty to help this man, surely?"

Yogan spun. "Like we took in that other one? Look what happened there, fool!"

The old innkeeper folded his arms. "Father Maheo has healed plenty of us. If he says so, the stranger stays in this inn, Yogan. *My* inn. I hope you remember that."

"Fine." Yogan pointed at Never. "You're leaving tomorrow, right?"

Never raised an eyebrow. "Lucky for you I'd already decided that, friend."

"We aren't friends, stranger," he snapped.

"Consider me convinced."

Maheo the priest raised an arm, a friendly smile on his weathered face – though he was not so old. "Come, sit beside me, traveller."

Never joined Maheo at one of the empty tables, setting his pack at his feet. "I appreciate the welcome."

"Of course." As the muted conversations resumed, the priest lowered his voice. "I wish it had been a better one, Hero."

The earlier blink from the priest had been one of recognition. "Have we met, perhaps?"

"Not precisely, but I recall you from Temple," he replied. "I admit, I am relieved to see you here."

"By the sounds of things, I should be relieved to see you. You've had success helping the people of Cagila?"

He nodded. "Some. Three here have recovered under my care. Two in neighbouring villages."

"That *is* wonderful."

The priest glanced away a moment. "Well... I am one of few that Jardila has found since the land was cursed.

Pacela has blessed some of her servants with knowledge and skill with healing in the past... but it is not clear why some of us have been found to possess a higher aptitude."

"But this sickness cannot be stopped by other means? Does anyone know the source?"

The priest sighed. "There are rumours of cures but the few I have examined were false. We suspect something in the south. Let me show you." He called to the innkeeper. "Lorenza, do you have your map?"

The fellow bent beneath the bench a moment, then brought over a scroll tied with faded red ribbon. When he unfurled it upon the table, it was from beneath brows drawn together in a look of warning. "This is no piece of scrap, hear? Don't either of you go messing it up by marking it."

"Of course, Lorenza." The priest used his finger to trace a line that started in the Folhan Ranges then ran east, curving up to loop around Olecsa. Next it ran straight toward the Evache Lakes in the far south, from which a Quisoan tribe had taken its name, and that was where the priest stopped. "This is the path it seems to have taken. Some believe it is an attack by Vadiya, bitter about losing the war. Others a curse from various gods and yet more talk of Pacela turning her back on us, but all reports suggest that it stops at the Lakes. Or that there is *something* there," he said as he tapped the three lakes on the map. "At present, the curse hasn't spread everywhere but far too many towns have simply been swallowed by the decay."

The Evache Lakes... why there? What did the Burnished King seek? And even with all the death and suffering so far, things could get *far* worse. "I will go there tomorrow. What of the illness itself, tell me what happens?"

Maheo rolled the map carefully. "It seems that close exposure to decaying fields and even buildings can be enough. Certainly, ingesting food that grows too near or drinking water tainted with the decay. Thus far, I do not personally believe the sickness can be caught from another person but the decay creeps across the land steadily if not swiftly, spreading forth from the tainted highway it has created." He paused, closing his eyes a moment. "I am so thankful that you have come."

Somehow, the man's trust was both a heavy weight and equally inspiring. "I will find a way to stop this," Never promised.

The man nodded, wiping at his eyes.

"What about a cure? I have heard that some medicines can stave the illness off for a time."

"Yes. Some old remedies that include venom from the golden viper seem to offer temporary relief – sometimes only a matter of days, however. I have heard that there is someone near Red Ridge who has had more success but for those I saved here, it was due the Goddess' gift."

Never only nodded. Nothing should be ruled out, but whatever magic the priests could wield, it probably did not come from the long-absent Gods. Not that it mattered. Only that it worked. "And the people here were infected due to... food?"

"No. They were forced to flee the cursed earth in the south."

"Lucky you were here, then."

Maheo spread his hands. "High Priestess Jardila sent us out the moment she knew – so I'd like to think her wisdom and compassion had a larger role, Amouni."

"Never is fine," he said with a smile. "And that sounds about right, your leader is certainly both those things."

"I do not wish to speak out of turn, but she would no doubt appreciate your thoughts on whatever you discover in the far south."

"Absolutely."

Footsteps approached the inn – someone running. Murmured conversation within the common room hushed once more, shoulders tensing and parents moving their children closer.

When the door burst open, a young man with wide eyes called for the priest. "It's the traveller. Father, something is wrong."

Maheo stood. "Tell me."

Yogan slapped his table. "He's not coming here."

"I will go," the priest said without even glancing at the fellow.

Never joined him, Yogan's warning not to get too close following them. No-one tried to stop Father Maheo, his status or ability was obviously enough to assuage even the most vocal in the inn of whatever doubts they harboured.

In the darkened streets, the priest led Never over well-trodden paths and beyond the ring to the wooden home on the edge of the small town. When the priest paused, hand on the door, rasping breaths snuck through the wood. "Have you witnessed the very worst cases?"

"No."

"I fear I can do nothing for him now – the decay had nearly covered the poor soul already, when I left to take a meal."

"I will help if I can."

Maheo opened the door with a creak to reveal a lantern turned low beside a figure on a bed. It was barely enough to see a... shape lying there, water barrel nearby.

The traveller's breathing was strained and tiny creaking sounds came from... his body, combined with a dry scent, like old stone – it filled the space despite an open window.

Maheo brightened the lamp a little. "Stevan, I am here."

Never's vision adjusted; Stevan was a gaunt man, skin seemingly patterned with thin fractures, not unlike crumbling stone of grey... but his eyes were feverishly bright.

An unsettling mix.

"Father... please... end this." His voice was a rasp of desperation, constricted as though his jaw no longer moved properly. "I am... still suffering... it does not end."

Never swallowed. What could possibly save the man? It *was* worse than he'd imagined, even after seeing the ruined villages and stone ghosts that remained. Was this something that even Amouni blood could not change? Never drew a blade and sliced into his palm before joining the priest by the patient's side, waiting with a handful of blood.

Maheo knelt but did not step too close, raising a hand to halt Never. "The floor," he said softly.

Never squinted. There too, decay spread – dry, lichen-like colours covering the floorboards, spreading from where they ran down the leg of the small bed. Did it almost sparkle in the lamplight?

The priest leant closer, murmuring something before he paused – then he inhaled, breath rasping.

As he did, a grey smoke rose from Stevan, drawn into

the priests' lungs.

Never took half a step forward but Maheo shook his head. He leant to one side and coughed a hacking cough. Something splattered against the floor.

Was that the gift from Pacela? To draw forth the maladies himself? And what was the cost to Maheo?

"It's no use, Father," Stevan said. And though his cheeks regained much of their colour, enough for him to speak clearly, the grey returned steadily.

Maheo wiped at his mouth, discarding the cloth. "Forgive me, Stevan. I had hoped..." "Let me try," Never said.

The priest nodded and Never leant over to let his blood drip onto the skin of Stevan's arm...

The dark liquid disappeared, soaked up almost too fast to trace.

And nothing.

Never tensed but the gasping from Stevan did not change and nor did his skin, no matter how hard Never glared. Another curse left behind by the Gods, or his ancestors, whoever – he could not heal this... unless the man ingested the blood?

But when Never explained and tried again, there was no change.

"Please," Stevan said after what seemed a long, long time. His arm trembled, grinding like slate, as if to reach out for someone, for anyone, and now his eyes no longer burned and instead, had turned to pale grey orbs.

"Forgive me," Priest Maheo murmured again, but this time extended his hands over the man's face. Wind stirred, slipping into the small room, and the lamp flared in a small burst of gold...

Stevan's breathing eased to silence.

Father Maheo's shoulders slumped then. "He is at rest."

"You eased his pain."

"Yes... but it was spreading so fast." The priest looked to Never, hopeful. "Never, I do not know if it is true but I have heard stories…"

Never placed a hand on his shoulder. "I can burn this place to ash, yes."

He swallowed. "Can you control the fire once it starts?"

Twin globes of crimson-fire sprung up around his hands. "I can."

Chapter 5

By the time Never departed the inn the next morning, doubts from the people of Cagila about exactly how he'd controlled the fire so perfectly were dampened by relief. Even Yogan seemed happy enough overall, since the spread had been stopped.

The crimson-fire had been enough to deal with an isolated part of the decay, but would it stand against a Plague King? Worse, nothing had been enough to save Stevan the traveller – a person so many in Cagila had reduced to something to be shunned, isolated, and eventually destroyed. Fear drove their actions. Stevan had posed a threat but did that mean he didn't deserve compassion?

Maheo and a few others had granted that – mercy too, with a display of Pacela's power that Never could not recall being possible. Not that he'd ever truly paid much attention to the religion, or any of them for that matter, save to plunder their myths for clues about his 'curse'.

Bitterness lingered as he followed the road out of town, dust stirring with each step.

Powerful wings and rejuvenating blood, crimson-fire, a long lifespan, knowledge of a dead language, a hand like birch – none of it could reverse what the Burnished King was spreading. Answers *had* to lurk somewhere but he'd already spent too long searching... other towns were surely faring far worse.

And Oleksan was doubtless hard at work –

Something small struck his back.

Never turned, hand on the hilt of a dagger but it was a young girl in a blue smock, running toward him with waving hands. "Wait, please!"

"Do you throw pebbles at most people who visit your town?" he asked, even as he smiled down at her.

The girl's cheeks were a little flushed, as though she'd run hard, chasing him some distance from Cagila, and her eyes were wide with worry. "I couldn't catch up and I had to find you before you left. I'm sorry, Mister. I had to run *really* fast."

He didn't mention that calling out from the beginning might have worked just as well. "Is something wrong?"

"Well..." She hesitated. "You left your pack with the priest... so I didn't know when you were coming back and I really needed to speak to you. And he said you'd be able to help." She was talking fast, still trying to catch her breath.

Never knelt and unhooked the water flask from his belt. "Here."

She took a big drink and smiled. "Thanks."

"So, take your time. What's your name?"

"Gia."

"Can you tell me what's wrong, Gia? Did Maheo send you?"

"No, it's my doll." She pulled a rag doll from where she'd stuffed it down the front of her smock. It was multi-coloured fabric, with beads for eyes, bright flaxen hair and a big smile. "Can you fix her? He said you could."

He hesitated. "I'll try."

"Thank you!" Gia thrust the doll forward.

Never took the soft toy. "Wait, who said I could...." He trailed off.

Something *old* had taken residence within the doll.

That was awfully clear now that he held the toy, far too heavy for its size. A gaze fell upon him too, ice-like, boring through his chest to clench itself around his heart, a presence that had little curiosity and a vast impatience, an iron will to destroy.

Scurry on, Amouni, toward yet another colossal failure.

Never clenched his jaw against the pain and the presence, the somehow-rotten voice ringing in his mind. "Who are you?"

"It's the one who said I had to find you. He said he'd leave Kat, if I did," Gia explained.

Oleksan, known as the Lord of the High Peaks, the Relentless Wave and the Burnished King. The doll remained motionless in his trembling grip. *And I offer a warning; you must realise that I am the tide and you are drifting wood before me.*

"Save your poetry, Oleksan." Had the King come to strike? His power was nothing to dismiss, even at a distance... yet if the creature wanted to attack, why bother speaking first? Why reside within a ragdoll? Why send a child to do his bidding?

Each pitiable step draws you nearer to a soon-to-be-forgotten grave. Abandon this path and go not the way of your ancestors.

Never lowered his voice. "Is that all?"

You will see, in time.

And then the doll was merely a doll. Just soft, beloved fabric. Never exhaled heavily as he handed Kat back to Gia. "All better now."

Gia hugged Kat, then threw her arms around his neck. "You did it!"

Never almost smiled. Perhaps things weren't so dire, for the Burnished King might well see him as a threat since he'd chosen to take the time to taunt instead of attack. As Oleksan claimed, time would reveal the truth of his actions.

"I'd better get home now," Gia said.

"Before you go, will you make me a promise?"

She nodded.

"If he uses Kat to speak to you again, go to Father Maheo at once."

"I will." Gia set off at a half-jog, half-skip.

"What an age to be," he murmured as he started walking again. To have such abandon and joy... impressive during such troubled times.

Without any real rivers to speak of nearby, the best choice was the *forasa*, returning north. For the moment, it seemed no travellers were abroad, though it wasn't too early for people to be on the road either. Would all roads be quiet thanks to the spreading decay? After Gia's happy voice, the soft swaying gold of the wheat seemed awfully quiet.

But whether or not a stranger would witness his flight, it was time to make up some ground.

Never let his feathers slide free and launched himself into the air, pumping his wings hard to climb. Much easier without the pack and, save for lingering traces of worry following him from Cagila, the flight was already enjoyable. A fresh breeze to contrast warmth from the still-rising sun coupled with a sense of action, of closing in on his goal.

When he eventually landed at the cave mouth, Never half-dove through the smooth tunnel into the shrine, where he leapt upon the silver symbol.

Branches and pods spread before him in bright lines.

He skipped over many. More than he'd expected to find, and for some reason, something had changed... the pods bore names. Amouni words; names for places, some familiar and others not – Isacina wasn't so different, Ijakenna, but much further south waited the Blue Mirror Lakes. Lovely enough for a name, and doubtless referring to the Evache Lakes, but to be certain he'd have to visit.

Never reached out and the light flared to gold.

When the glow cleared, grey replaced everything, smothering with a pungent scent of rotting wood so strong that he gagged.

Flee!

Never slapped a hand over his mouth and nose as he stumbled forward, feet crunching through whatever he charged across – puffs of dust rising with each step, and too late, the grey cleared in time to reveal a wall.

He crashed through the rotten timber, tripping across the rubble beyond and thudding to the ground.

The wall had been *far* too brittle.

Never climbed from the clouds of dust with a clenched jaw. The decay was everywhere! He charged through the jagged ruins of a building and into a sunlit street where he dusted off his clothes, pausing to spit, the very taste somehow just as grey as the dust. Was he already poisoned? His Amouni blood hadn't reversed the decay for Stevan, but could it be *resisted* at least?

Or was that a fool's hope?

He was already covered in the decay. Running had been a poor first instinct. Probably too late to fly. Would it make a difference now? Or should he try to protect his wings?

Adrenaline surged through his veins.

He sprinted along the street for open space, somewhere, anywhere, passing low stone walls and bleached wood, all of it seemingly ready to shatter at a touch. Inside the buildings, and sometimes spilling into the street was a powdery debris... things that were once furniture and clothes, other possessions?

And human-like shapes. Stifled beneath the weight of an endless decay.

He slid around a tumbling well and then between two homes to find a modest palisade, it too worn down as though centuries had hit it in a single moment.

Such was the force of the Burnished King's passage.

Had anything been spared?

Never charged between the barricades and skidded to a halt upon the withering grass of the hills – there! A pond within a stand of olive trees. Nothing like a lake, but deep enough.

He whipped off his cloak and boots, but at his belt both hands had transformed into clubs. "Idiot." Never forced himself to slow down and was soon flinging his tunic aside too, and then his pants, and once naked, he waded into the water at last.

Weeds swirled around his calves as he strode to the

pond's centre. The cool water only covered half his chest, but it was enough. Never sunk down, dunking his head and thrashing about – even shouting to wash out his mouth in a rush of bubbles.

No way to know if it would be enough but it was better than nothing, and travelling in tainted clothes was out of the question.

Never surfaced and wiped at his arms, pulse easing with relief. He sloshed his way to the bank, where the grass was still green and healthy. And while the trees and pond lay in the decay's path, where it spread from the crumbling town, it was not moving visibly.

He spread his arms to let water drip from his body.

"What a fool," he muttered.

Obviously there had always been a chance that any *forasa* symbol near the Lakes would be in the path of decay. The reward for haste was so often disaster.

Would his luck hold?

Testing the strength of his Amouni blood had not really been on the cards but if the answer was favourable... The best thing to do was keep a close watch on his skin, or a loss of flexibility in his limbs.

That, and find new clothes.

The pile of discarded garments was already paler, as if being leeched as he watched. "Damn." His knives were likely ruined as well.

At least – so far – he didn't sense anything attacking his body.

Across the grassy stretch before the mounds of grey, the small town remained painfully silent. Just like the mountain village in Vadiya. Nearer the road, at the edge of the stumps of buildings, stood the remnants of what was probably a horse and cart.

And inside, how many had died?

No-one deserved such a cruel fate. Never glared along the withered path left by the Burnished King where it wound into the hills.

Oleksan had to be destroyed.

Chapter 6

Never hovered high above the green hills, a mighty streak of decay running through them, draining colour from all it touched. At times, the trail of withered grass and blighted earth ran parallel with the highway, but it cut across just as often. In the end, both paths met an enormous wall that encircled the entire lake system along one side, leaving the dark of the Folhan Ranges as a barrier to the west.

Penned within, three lakes glittered, brilliant blue in a picture of calm.

No sign of any King, of any troops, any magical disturbance or even hints of movement within the fishing villages that clung to the shores either – and nor were the buildings pale and deathly, instead each appeared untouched.

A puzzling detail.

But the wall was what he studied, angling his wings to catch shifting currents – it was almost enough to forget the chill that ravaged every inch of his exposed skin.

Mist clung to the barrier, enshrouding it in wisps and swirling trails, some sections so heavy as to be pure white.

Elsewhere, a simmering darkness behind the mist was clearer. Was the wall made of earth or stone? Something else, something unnatural?

He swooped lower, closing enough to see more of the shimmering surface not unlike dirt-covered scales.

An arm of mist shot forth.

Never banked, and the streaking tendril flew wide, clutching at nothing. He swung around, beating his wings to put some distance between himself and the wall once more, but there was no second strike.

Had the Burnished King sensed him somehow?

Was the veil sentient?

If nothing else, the vast wall and its strike further confirmed how important the Lakes were to Oleksan. It also suggested that the Temple Trivium waited somewhere below. In years of wandering, there had not been any reason to go diving; no rumour or legend suggested anything of value lurked below, but Oleksan had rushed into Marlosi and headed south, and he was clearly not encouraging visitors.

"I'll be seeing you again," Never told the Burnished King as he turned away.

There was little he could achieve without more knowledge and without help – a lot of help.

He ascended high enough not to be seen but details below were still clear. He needed a new town, since the *forasa* at the withered village was too risky. A detour to a place with clothes would have to be the first order of business, then came finding a river or a *forasa* symbol.

Heading north offered towns and smaller cities before the Broken Plains and in turn, the city of Olecsa – but that destination would be a last resort. Another option would appear first, like the collection of fishing ports and hamlets a little further east, nestled by the Sol Seas, if needed. Once, early in the search for a cure to his 'curse', a rumour of twin Sirens with magical voices led him to that coast... of course, finding nothing had been no surprise.

At least the people there had been mostly friendly.

Yet he did not have to travel so far as the Broken Plains before spotting a town resting in the shadows of a long depression – and by the giant, striped pavilion in the centre, it was Jonvai.

Cheer did seem lacking however, as scores of campsites and temporary structures of wood and canvas surrounded the modest walls. A shanty town had encircled Jonvai.

With the poisonous path of the Burnished King lying not so far southwest, perhaps it should have been no surprise. Those who'd sought refuge in places like Jonvai would be full of doubts and fear, with no idea when or even *if* their homes could be restored, their lives returned to. Their needs would probably put a strain on the people of Jonvai, resentment and violence would spread, and all thanks to the Burnished King.

The same tragedy would be occurring in plenty of other places.

"Maybe everywhere, if I fail."

Never began his descent, seeking a good rooftop. The tallest building would be the best choice, considering the afternoon still offered plenty of light, but the bigger homes didn't tend to leave washing unattended, strung across lines between homes or upon poles on the rooves.

And surprising someone inside, naked save for his

feathers, on his way to steal their clothing, wouldn't win him any favours.

Never tilted his wings toward the pavilion.

If there was a place anywhere in the small city that a man wrapped in black feathers would not draw too much attention, it would be the Sabre's circus, with her performers, animals, costumes and illusions.

He circled overhead, squinting down at the yard behind the bright, striped pavilion of pink and white. Animal cages lined high walls of stone and wood, leaving space for a wide, grassy clearing with pens and storage sheds. At present, there was no-one moving around – the cheers and music from within the pavilion meant most performers would be busy.

Good.

He swooped down between two empty cells, feet slapping against the hard earth as he landed, and glanced around. Only one figure, someone shovelling feed from a cart, his back to the yard as he laboured.

Never wrapped both wings about his naked body and approached the pavilion – a large tent flap granting access to an empty ticket stand. Further within, a single figure stood obscured by the glow and cheers from the performance.

A distracted attendant was most welcome. Never crept to a curtained-off area, slipping along a narrow corridor to a dressing room where he found racks of clothing – costumes, really. Unguarded... and all unsuitable, truly, but *unguarded* was the more important detail. "So be it," Never said as he reached for a pair of pants that were criss-crossed black and white.

He stepped into them with a grimace – they fit well enough, but there was nothing close to unobtrusive for his torso either; bright feathers of pink, red and blue or yellow tunics lined with glass beads. Perfectly reasonable for performers... but not quite hardy, traveller's garb.

Voices neared.

Never snatched at something purple and slipped from the pavilion.

Outside, he strode to his previous hiding place between cages and knelt to struggle his way into the... silken blouse. Never sighed. It was not a good fit but at least he hadn't torn it, though a flash of guilt gave him slight pause; it was a precious item to have stolen.

Movement on the wall above caught his eye – just a grey cat coming to settle nearby. It rested its head upon forepaws and stared down, yellow eyes bright. Too bright? Its tail swung gently; it did not seem fevered or feral.

Why didn't you visit me, Amouni?

He froze. The putrid voice in his mind had come from the cat. Oleksan once again. "That was a large wall for someone who claims to want visitors."

Then be assured that I can send someone to greet you. The animal did not break its gaze.

"Namely?"

Simply wait. Or run and be found anyway.

Never straightened. "Too afraid to come out yourself, then?"

Alas, my responsibilities are many. But stay vigilant and you may even see my servant approach; he may not speak but I am assured of his commitment to your destruction.

The cat shuddered into stillness then, eyes closing as its

fur turned mottled and then deteriorated further, reduced to a powdery heap. Far too quickly, the whole animal had become a mere pile of dust.

And unlike the last visit, this one left a chill.

Exactly what had been sent out and from where?

Chapter 7

"Never! What are you wearing?" Gia asked when he'd returned to the quiet streets of Cagila. She'd burst from one of the homes as he approached the inn, hair flying, trailed by an older sister perhaps, who hissed at the girl to stay inside.

"Surprised?" he asked Gia.

She grinned up at him. "I like it."

"Gia, come back right now," the older girl said, waving at her with a frown.

"Fine." Gia turned as she ran back. "Kat hasn't said anything again, so she's still better."

He smiled and waved; good news was a welcome change. Maybe Gia wasn't under threat... Oleksan could obviously use whatever was convenient for his taunts, but maybe not people? So far, a ragdoll and a cat...

Although, the animal had not survived being used so.

Inside the inn, suspicious eyes were mostly absent – more than a few townsfolk had been working in the fields as he'd entered Cagila, or sweating and swearing as they raised barricades, but Father Maheo and Lorenza met him with smiles, offering a drink.

The men also offered a pair of confused expressions at his attire, though neither questioned it and the innkeeper soon went about organising provisions. "Thank you for this," Never said when he accepted his pack, the unpleasant weight reminding him of the quartz books. Books which needed further study.

Maheo nodded. "How did you fare in the south?"

"I did not learn much. There's a mighty wall enclosing the Lakes and it seems to be aware."

The priest blinked. "Aware...?"

Never explained the mist and then the taunts from the Burnished King. "There's definitely a purpose to the wall, perhaps protecting a sunken temple that I suspect may be important to his plans, but I don't know if it's actually located there. Or what its purpose would be."

"Still, that's something. What of the people?"

"The fishing villages appeared untouched, and I'm not sure what that means. I hope it means everyone is alive and well but I couldn't get close enough. The decay is still spreading from the path and from the wall, creeping but unrelenting."

"But you have ideas how to stop it? Your crimson-fire?"

"Is one idea, yes," he said. "But I wanted to ask about the cure you mentioned before. Something to the south?"

"Yes. The Quisoan tribes were first to report its use but the supply is limited. Apparently someone is, well, hoarding it."

Never frowned. "At a time like this?"

"So the rumours say."

"Then I'll investigate on my way to Isacina."

The priest's expression hardened. "If it is true, change

their minds, won't you?"

"You have my oath." Never finished his drink and lifted his pack as he stood. "Keep fighting here, the people need you."

"I will."

Never made his farewells and once he'd strode far enough out of town, he changed clothes, rearranged his pack then took to the vast blue of the skies once more, the flow of air streaming over him, pleasant.

Below, small figures still toiled the golden plains; the further from the streak of death the more measured their work seemed, while in other communities, fires had been started in the fields, leaving charred lines of ash like a barrier before the decay, as growing columns of smoke climbed swiftly.

Would it be enough? He did not descend to investigate – perhaps on the way back, maybe even with some hope in hand.

For now, the truth behind Red Ridge.

And whatever he found, Jardila and the temple would be the next stop. The High Priestess would have valuable information about fighting the plague, considering what Maheo could do. Just as important, hopefully, more lost lore on Arkenon, God of the Malecaphera, or the Burnished King and perhaps the Temple Trivium.

If his luck held.

The crossroads and river where he'd left Rikeva rolled by beneath him now; time to get a lot closer. Never banked over the hills, diving low enough to skim the treetops. Overhead, the shrill cry of a falcon was answered from the trees below, glimpses of movement between the leaves.

A winding trail led to an expansive gorge where cattle and horses spread across green pens in the valley. And though they'd been given a vast amount of room to roam, they were still fenced off, sturdy constructions with feeding stations and even a pair of dams.

Walls of undulating, deep orange rose above the animals – the Red Ridge, so called for its colour at sunset – and a ribbon of road that had been carved from the wall led up to a plateau. There, a grand mansion waited. It spread across three storeys, dozens of rooms and plenty of outbuildings. Even from a distance, the marble seemed opulent, red tiles almost blending with the walls of the gorge.

The mansion looked down upon the pens but also something that was doubtless a more recent addition – a blockade complete with spiked barriers and sentries leaning on their bows. Half a dozen armed men in mismatched armour stood at a checkpoint. Behind them in turn, a row of tents. These were not uniform in colour, shape or size either.

Plenty of hired swords to protect the cure.

Or, just as likely, to intimidate the seekers – those who had travelled to gather in small groups before the barrier.

Close enough now, Never landed on the road with a grunt. The pack pulled him off-balance at first, but he was soon striding toward the guard post, which was still not all that close. Even so, someone might well have witnessed his landing.

If so, he'd deal with any questions when they arose.

At the barricade, the range of people seeking help became clear. Farmers and villagers in their straw hats, small groups of Quisoan tribes wearing familiar leathers, and a young family of Hanik folk huddled together. There was even a pair of Imperial Soldiers, both armed with sword and spear, but only one who wore cloak and breastplate.

The other fellow was being supported by the first man, and when Never reached them, the illness became clear on his bare arms. Grey and healthy, tanned skin sat side by side and when the fellow moved it was only slowly, as though his limbs weighed too much. Despite the soldier's suffering, based on his companion's expression – grim determination visible beneath the helm, not fear – the soldier did not seem to be contagious.

And so it seemed that, just as Maheo warned, the decay spread from the earth, from food and water, and not when someone touched a victim. Yet there was obviously a point when the decay took over enough to move from a person to objects or buildings themselves, considering the hut on the edge of Cagila.

Could the supposed cure prevent that?

Other seekers bore similar afflictions, some simply laying upon blankets beneath the sun or peering from behind tent flaps of their own as he passed.

All in all, some two score people sought salvation.

Or at least, sought something that could 'stave off death' as Rikeva had described whatever was being produced at the mansion.

Never approached a group of the Quisoa – the Cloaj tribe, considering the fishing nets peeking from their saddlebags. Most of the adults sat with twin boys, whose large eyes were dull from fatigue, skin greying. "Doita al," Never said, using the Quisoan greeting.

"Doita," a woman replied, after a moment's hesitation –

perhaps at Never's Marlosi heritage.

"Have you come seeking medicine for another?" the oldest of the Cloaj asked, his bushy eyebrows giving him a stern appearance, though his voice was soft.

"Answers as much as anything," Never replied. "It must work at least for a time, since people come here?"

A nod. "The twins have not succumbed, thanks to it."

The woman had folded her arms. "But like everyone here, we are bleeding to pay for the lives of our loved ones. And it is not a complete cure."

"How much, if I might ask?"

"Beqona sells a single vial for two gold pieces or equivalent."

Never muttered a curse. Just as Maheo warned. Enough to purchase a horse in most parts, or provisions for weeks just about everywhere. No wonder Rikeva had sought such a fortune at the Amber Isle.

And no wonder Maheo wanted the merchant punished.

"We sell possessions and barter, put our horses to stud, whatever we must. We have no choice," the old man said.

"Even so. This Beqona clearly profits from the suffering of others."

"But we know this works," he replied. "We must pay that price."

Never looked at the guards and the barricade. "Not for long, if I have any say in it."

"He is well-protected, young man."

While little at the barricade was an impediment for his wings, nothing about it was sign of a generous soul either. "It doesn't look like speaking to this Beqona is easy."

"No." The woman pointed beyond the guard post, to

where a small figure in a green hood approached, striding along the path with a large wooden box. He was accompanied by a hulking figure who carried an axe strapped to his back, the blade wide as a human torso. "The Bean Counter and his muscle. If you are lucky, you will receive a token."

"Then there is order here, not just the threat of violence?"

"There is certainly both," the old man said. "Someone tried to leap in front of another, to steal a vial. He was beaten near to death and received no medicine."

"Never?" A familiar voice spoke from behind.

Rikeva stood behind him, eyes a little wide. She still carried her staff and a long dagger was visible beneath her yellow cloak, but the white ribbon was harder to spot this time, as she'd tied her blonde hair up into a high ponytail.

Some men straightened when they saw her, and Never couldn't be certain that he hadn't done the same. Was she more beautiful somehow?

"Did you manage to convince him?" he asked.

She frowned up at mansion. "I cannot say for sure. The Bean is supposedly bringing Beqona's answer today."

"You've had to wait all this time?"

She shook her head. "I took several doses to my tribe but Beqona limits how much each person can take at one time. Despite his prices, he has some small sense of fairness, I suppose."

"Or he wants to enjoy having more and more people dependent on him."

"Equally likely," she replied. "If so, what are we going to do about it, hero?"

Those from the Cloaj tribe exchanged glances but did not ask any questions; perhaps their curiosity was not so strong as the hope that something could change. Rikeva's expression was once again just as determined as when they'd first met.

"First, I want to see this medicine," Never said. "Let's talk to this Bean Counter and his minder."

"And if that doesn't work?"

Never flipped a dagger into his hand. "Then I'll just have to *introduce* myself to Beqona."

Chapter 8

With a brisk wave, the Bean Counter gestured for the next in line to approach, an older woman who had been tapping her foot and running both hands over her forearms the entire time. Of all who waited, only five had been called to the guard post and its sturdy table, though the remaining seekers in the makeshift camp did not seem to resent this by their patient or sometimes lacklustre expressions.

"That's because we have these," Rikeva explained when Never asked, holding up a small token – just a square piece of wood with a painted number. "The guards hand them out each morning."

"I see. Seems like it does a fair job of counteracting possible panic, then."

The Imperial soldier before them glanced over his shoulder. "Usually. A few times the mercenaries had to intervene. Once, I caught someone trying to steal our token," he explained, his voice hardening. "Didn't have the heart to give him a good thrashing, but I didn't bring Yanjo all the way down from the garrison for someone to take our place."

"So this cure works?"

"They call it *soma*." The soldier turned now, perhaps glad to tell his tale. "All I can say for sure is that Yanjo doesn't grow worse when he takes it, thank Pacela. It's costing us everything we have but when he first fell ill, nothing else worked."

"What about the Empress or the High Priestess? I heard that some priests can cure people?"

"Supposedly," the man replied. "But I couldn't wait for them to arrive. Empress Crisina is sending the army along the Plague Line; I saw field infirmaries being built but I think we all know that the bigger problem is how the decay poisons the fields and wells."

"Number two, approach," came a weary voice.

The soldier gave a nod and strode to Bean's table. Beqona's servant seemed corpse-like this close, pale skin and dark shadows round his eyes, his shoulders hunched in his dark vest. The mercenaries gave only cursory glances over the line and the camp, but the Thug stood with his arms crossed, mighty weapon still strapped to his back. He stared down at Rikeva, his bent nose giving him the look of a brawler, though it was the hairless nature of his face that caught Never's attention. No eyebrows, no beard nor hair upon his head either. "The big guy seems interested in you."

"Thinking about the jewels, I suspect," she replied with a shrug that caused a faint rattle from the gemstones within her pack.

"Number three," came the call from the Bean Counter.

Rikeva led Never forward, passing the Imperial soldier, who started back to his fellow at a half-run.

"Token, please," Bean said without glancing up from a ledger before him. Beside his book rested the large wooden box and within, set in precise rows, thin vials of white liquid nestled beside one another. It seemed unremarkable, but appearance was no indicator of effect.

Rikeva handed the scrap of wood over. "Does Beqona have an answer?"

The man nodded. "He will see you after the delivery – Idth and I will escort you there."

"Us," Rikeva said, gesturing to Never.

Bean squinted. "And he would be?"

"Additional assurance that there will be no misunderstandings up there," Rikeva replied.

"Just so long as you both understand your position when you do," Bean replied.

"And what would that be, little man?" Never said with a grin.

The Bean Counter's quill quivered but his expression remained composed. "Of someone about to speak with the most important man in the whole of Marlosi."

Never whistled. "Looking forward to that."

Idth narrowed his eyes but did not speak. Rikeva had one hand on her hip. "I'll be impressed when he accepts my offer."

"Then please, take your share of soma and wait by the large tree."

Rikeva accepted the vial and led Never through the guard post to the nearby elm with its spreading branches and mixture of green and yellow leaves. His skin seemed to sigh once he reached the shade but on the other hand, it didn't deter a handful of flies that found him.

"I'd better explain exactly what I'm trying to do," Rikeva said as she handed the vial over. "I don't really know what's in this, save for some common minerals from Beqona's mine, water, and something else. But I could not make it grow in quantity, I know that much."

Never raised the soma to light that slipped through the leaves. The pale liquid was not so thin as water. "I didn't know there was a mine here."

"Maybe it's new? But it's blocked by the mansion. I've seen the entry – the carts are moving pretty steadily."

"Hmmm. So, what did you offer him, specifically?"

"To carry a portion of costs for his grimy little operation in order to bring the price down. Either via the jewels themselves, or by hiring more hands to work the mine and increase the supply."

"Assuming he agrees today, what about your own stores of this?"

"It's not unlimited," she replied with a small sigh. "And what we're paying for is only a stasis, not a cure. I know that, but it's all we have for now."

"A fair point," Never said as he pocketed the vial. "But you can't rely on me to fly you in and out of the Amber Isle each time Beqona gets greedy for more diamonds. Which he will."

Rikeva grinned. "No. What I need you to do is fly that vial to Isacina so someone can learn what it's made of, and maybe make something better from it too – an actual cure."

"That I will gladly do," Never said with a nod. "What about our merchant friend, then? You've met Beqona, will he keep his word here?"

"I have. But now that you're here, Never, once again, I

want to come to an understanding. I could use your help; greed is one thing, but I need Beqona afraid too. Petrified."

Never nodded slowly. Rikeva was not someone to be crossed, it seemed. "You lead your tribe, don't you?" If so, she was perhaps young to do so – near enough to his own age, and thus no elder.

"Yes. But you don't have to worry; they're in good hands."

"Then all that's left is to wait for our escort, it seems," he said as he leant against the trunk.

"You have no terms this time?"

"Just what we've already agreed to," he said.

"Thank you, Never."

When the Bean Counter finally finished parcelling out the last of the day's medicine and approached, it was with a curt gesture for them to follow. Bean strode ahead and Idth took up rear guard as they started toward the ascent.

"Beqona seems quite lucky," Never observed as he examined the red walls on their ascent, old tool marks still visible. "To have a mansion above a mine."

Bean sniffed. "Master Beqona would disagree – luck is not the same as recognising and maximising opportunity."

Disaster and suffering as *opportunity*? Never took just a moment to imagine the impact of his birch hand crashing into Bean's jaw... and instead, glanced at Rikeva, who was scowling down at the little weasel. "Then your master is obviously clever enough to see the value in Rikeva's offer, that's a relief."

"That's not for me to decide."

"He's called me to his home," Rikeva said. "That fact alone speaks of his interest."

Bean did not answer then, and it seemed Idth smiled, but

the expression had been too brief to be sure.

At the top they found a broad arch of marble that granted access to a stone path crossing a lush green lawn. Steel frames allowed yellow flowers on vines to enshrine grand double doors, which were in turn being engraved with tendrils by two craftsmen. One set his chisel and hammer aside to pull one wing of the door open as the Bean Counter led them closer.

Bean offered no thanks as he passed into the mansion.

Never inclined his head to the artisan.

The mansion's interior was much the same. More marble-cladding and plant life in fine pots, but Never witnessed little detail as they were ushered along the polished wooden floors at a brisk pace.

And it was not long before they reached a set of doors opening to a paved courtyard. This had been adorned with hanging plants of green, yellow and pink. Almost a riot, but it suited the red silks that Beqona had draped across his slender frame.

He smiled from a wicker chair but did not rise, gesturing that they might sit – his dark hair, unshaven cheeks and bright blue eyes created a sinister look, though his features alone ought not have been enough to evoke such an impression.

The true tell was what Never had already learnt about the man.

"Be comfortable. I have arranged for refreshment." His voice, brimming with arrogance, further confirmed Never's initial reactions.

Rikeva took the only chair, leaning across the table. "I can wait until we have spoken, Beqona."

Never stood beside her, as Idth assumed a similar position just behind his master. Bean had already scurried away, it seemed.

The merchant chuckled. "As expected. Very well, without delay. I have considered your proposal and I accept your offer to finance expansion of the mine."

"And the price per vial?"

"Even with the impressive fortune you offer, I cannot do both," the man said with a sigh.

"I can bring more jewels."

"Then I will consider the new possibilities offered."

Rikeva lifted her pack onto the table. Jewels clinked. "Reduce the prices for the people who need the soma now. I will bring more so that you can expand the mines – once I see the change."

"Hmm." Beqona brushed at his silks. "Sounds almost like a demand, rather than a counter-proposal."

"Then you know I am serious."

Booted footsteps approached from the hall outside. "As am I, my dear."

Chapter 9

Never did not reach for his blades, nor ready the crimson-fire; but tension crept into his limbs as mercenaries encircled the room, hands on hilts. Most wore leathers or breastplates, older garb but all well-cared for – professionals to the last.

Even so, escape would be no real problem but at what cost? Could he protect Rikeva at the same time and do so without souring any chance of her reaching an agreement with Beqona? Had the greedy little worm already accomplished that himself?

If so, there were always other methods to attain the proper result...

By Rikeva's clenched jaw, she was not impressed. "And what are you demanding now, with your lackeys?"

"This is merely a statement," he replied. "And a hope that you reconsider."

"Thanks to this little display, I'm considering taking this fortune directly to the villages and towns."

He nodded. "Understandable. It would, however, be a shame if I were then forced to raise the price of soma. It is expensive to both mine and concoct."

Rikeva leant back in her chair as she folded her arms. "If you had no intention of negotiating on good faith, you didn't need to waste my time."

Never stepped a little closer, lowering his voice but keeping his words audible. "He's obviously not bright enough. Let's just take the High Priestess' offer instead."

Rikeva concealed whatever surprise she might have felt at his lie with a nod as she reached for the jewels. "An excellent idea."

Beqona rose. "I urge against haste."

Never smiled as Rikeva lowered the pack. "Sounds like you're aware of all the success Pacela's servants are having."

"I admit that your original proposal is not without mutual benefit."

"Say it, Beqona," Rikeva demanded.

He narrowed his eyes as he spoke. "I will subsidise the price of soma now and expand my mining force with your next delivery."

"Then we have reached an accord," she said.

"We have, Rikeva of the Doerin." He drew the pack across the table and handed it to Idth, who again seemed to wear a faint smile. Beqona dismissed his mercenaries with a scowl and a wave.

"I will deliver more jewels as soon as possible," Rikeva said as she started toward the exit.

Beqona did not reply, and Never did not follow at once.

Instead, he slowly drew a knife and raised his hand, making a small cut before returning the blade to its sheath. Idth had straightened upon sighting the weapon and Beqona appeared confused. "What are you doing, fool?"

Crimson-fire burst into a liquid globe around Never's

hand, casting wild shadows as he pointed at the now flinching merchant. "Hear me well, toad. Truly unpleasant things will certainly happen if I hear that you have broken your word."

"Who are you?" he asked as he shoved his wicker chair back.

"Is that your answer?"

"I've given my word, I swear it!"

Never glanced to Idth. "Any objections?"

The big guy shook his head.

Never killed the fire with a snap of his fingers and strode from the room where he found Rikeva waiting beside blossoming violets. "Think he'll keep his promise?" she asked.

"I'd be more than happy to make sure," he offered as they walked toward the bright light of the exit.

"Time will tell, I suppose."

They passed into the slowly darkening sunset and started down the slope with its deep wagon ruts, picking up the pace as they did. The evidence of wagons was not something he'd noticed before, but then, needling the Bean Counter had seemed quite important.

Rikeva paused before the bottom. "Never, I have a question."

"About Isacina?"

"I want to help find a cure. I *can* help you," her voice grew firm. "Take me with you."

There were obvious advantages to doing so; she was strong, determined and clever, and her gifts as a Weaver would be useful too. Not just the strength she could call upon, but the way her very body could, at a cost, imbue ribbon with vitality. At the very least, they would not likely go hungry if she used her gift upon edible plants.

The problem was *beyond* Isacina, when he'd have to face the Burnished King... the risk would be great. "If you don't mind using the *forasa* again, I'd welcome your help."

She smiled. "I'll just have to get used to it."

***

Once again, Never found himself crawling into the darkened Amouni shrine via the tunnel his crimson-fire had made. He'd shoved his pack through first, letting it thud to the floor before him. When he climbed free, the *forasa* leaf was already glowing silver. Perhaps it didn't need more blood now that it had been awakened.

"How close will it take us?" Rikeva asked when she joined him.

"I'm hoping a lot closer, like inside the city itself. Let me check." Never stepped onto the symbol and closed his eyes – the mass of branches, buds and their Amouni names appeared, and there, north and west, nestled beneath the Folhan Mountains waited Ijakenna, or Isacina.

And this time, the longer he focused on the location, the more detail he was rewarded with. The image of a much taller city, full of spires and domes, of narrow beams used to support pod-like buildings of glass and steel as much as stone, and a city viewed from the plains that suggested the *forasa* symbol waited beyond the walls, as at the Lakes.

The palace seemed to bear a *forasa* too... only, far beneath the dungeons, within a labyrinth of enormous steel pipes and glass tubes. More Amouni secrets? Or something else? In time, a visit beneath the palace would probably not go astray.

There was a third choice. A cobblestone square, somewhere inside the walls, perhaps where theatres lined the streets. Isacina would have changed over the centuries and so the *forasa* might lie within a different district today, but it seemed the best choice of the three options.

"Directly into the city, this time," Never said. He extended an arm. "Ready?"

She gripped his hand. "Ready."

The silvery glow grew, swiftly blinding – and before his vision cleared, water splashed down upon him. "What?" Never started forward but his legs met resistance – knee-deep water, and the deluge was not growing any gentler.

When at last his vision recovered, he had his answer.

Coins glittered at his feet, clear water rippling from a steady fall. A fountain; they stood within one of the city's fountains. Less disconcerting than if they'd appeared inside a waterfall, but the result was the same, a steady drenching.

Rikeva had already passed through the screen of cascading water.

He joined her to find the fountain located within a large market square. Shadows at dusk, cast by the tall stone buildings, many four or five storeys high, reached the centre of the square. People in their banded clothing went about their business with the usual bustle, moving from stall to stall or crossing the square, some strolling with meat skewers in hand.

Here, the strips of colour were more patterned, with

the bands on robes and tunics spiralling together or even splashing, sometimes augmented by coloured belts or sashes. Some men walked the streets with naked torsos and coloured scarves. Lingering post-war exuberance? Or the influence of Hanik fashions from the west?

Cheerful voices and lively music from one of the theatres offered a counterpoint to the welcome he'd received from the waterfall.

"Not what I imagined, Never," Rikeva said as she climbed free, shaking her arms and legs. Sprays of water flicked across the cobblestones and nearby, a couple who'd been sitting hand-in-hand slid away with some grumbling.

"Nor I," Never admitted as he glanced up at the statue in the fountain. Saint Tirasali in her flowing robes, sword belted at her side, arrow in one hand and a horned owl resting upon the other.

Never joined Rikeva and from across the square, where a row of colourful fruit stalls stood, a pair of city guard approached, breastplates bright in the sun, frowns suggesting they were distinctly unimpressed.

The heavier one was shaking his head when he arrived. "You're both old enough to know better, surely? The Fountain of Saint Tirasali is not a place for frolicking; it's a precious landmark."

"Not to me," Rikeva murmured.

Setting aside the somewhat depressing general lack of cheer from the guard, her comment had not been an offhanded one, considering Marlosi's dark history when it came to the tribes.

Never spoke before the guard could reply to Rikeva's comment. "Of course, we appreciate the reminder."

"Well, see that you conduct yourselves with a bit of decorum."

Onlookers had already slowed and some came to a halt, one noblewoman even raising a bouquet of pink and red flowers to her face as if to protect her from the very sight of such impropriety. "We shall do precisely that," Never said.

The guards returned to their post with another warning, and once they were out of earshot, Rikeva chuckled. "I don't remember Isacina being so staid."

He grinned. "Neither do I. Fashion seems to have changed a little."

"You don't like it?"

"Too early to say."

She wrung out the ends of her hair, white ribbon still mostly in place. "Will we have any trouble seeing the High Priestess?"

Never turned to the spire, rising above the rooves in a pale spiral. "No. Jardila will welcome us."

"What about the soma? Can she really use it to find a cure? Or create something else?"

"I'm confident after meeting Father Maheo," he said. "It might be as much magic as medicine involved in the process. Either way, since I'm going to destroy the source of the plague too, maybe that will make a difference," he said as he set off.

"You found something?"

"Not much." Never described the wall at the Evache Lakes. "I just need to find some sort of weakness before I face him."

Rikeva missed a step. "*Him*? Never, do you know who

is responsible for this?"

"I do. Have you heard of Oleksan?"

"No."

"To sum up, an ancient evil has escaped – exactly like a fairy tale, you might say. He was known in Vadiya as the Burnished King; Disciple of a plague God. That's who I was researching on the Amber Isle," he said, then hesitated. "Oleksan escaped a mountain tomb after someone stole my blood to break the Seals. And so I have to stop him now; *I* have to atone for that."

"Wait," she said. Her expression of worry had eased. "Are you sure about that?"

"About what?"

"It sounds like you think that you're responsible for the misdeeds of others."

"I..."

Rikeva smiled. "I'll help you, Hero – whatever it takes to save my people. But you don't have to bear the crimes of others as your own."

"Thank you." She suddenly seemed more forgiving than he'd come to expect. Or perhaps it was just that much harder to be gentler toward his own failures. And still, welcome as her help could be, there was a great risk the closer they came to the Burnished King.

She chuckled. "Try not to sound surprised."

Never lifted both hands in a gesture of apology. "No, your help is most welcome."

"Good. Any ideas, then?"

"They all revolve around my Amouni forebears. It seems I'm a threat, so far as the Burnished King believes," he said, explaining the taunts and the lack of direct attack. "But I'm going to need to learn a lot more before I return."

"But we're working on the cure first, right?"

"Maybe they'll be the same thing," he said. "Let's see what the High Priestess has to offer."

Chapter 10

In welcome contrast to occupied Isacina of the past, the square resting beneath Pacela's Spire was now clear of weeds and its four silver statues polished to gleaming. More, twin sets of stalls offering medicine, herbs, charms and clothing stood manned by priests and priestesses in their pale-yellow robes, all working to help the poorer folk of the city.

Above, Pacela's Spire rose in its spiral, bright wings and glass in windows seeming to both collect the fading sunlight *and* reflect the lamps from within. Somewhere inside waited all the artefacts he'd stored. A great need had arisen, but would any be of use?

Rikeva stood with hands on her hips as she looked up. "I hope you're right about the High Priestess."

"She's not our only option, but as I said, I'm especially confident after meeting Father Maheo."

"Who else would we seek? Back to the Amber Isle?"

Never scratched at an unshaven cheek as they reached

the stout wooden door and its closed hatch. "Perhaps. There are other writings, other libraries – there is a place in Kiymako, among others."

Rikeva nodded, apparently happy enough with his answer.

He knocked upon the door, his birch hand making for a sharper sound, though he hadn't been rough. The wooden panel slid open soon after, revealing a pair of white eyebrows, followed by pale blue eyes as the priest seemed to stretch up to see.

"Welcome to Her Spire," he said, a mild Hanik accent echoing – somewhat unusual, since few folk from outside Marlosi took to Pacela's religion. "We will be conducting the Spring Ritual tomorrow evening, should you wish to return then."

"Actually, we need to speak with the High Priestess about the spreading decay," Never said.

"The Stone Plague?"

Perhaps a fitting name as any for the curse. He nodded. "My name is Never, if that makes it easier to interrupt her."

The old man's eyes widened a little. "The hero?"

"Only if I can put a stop to the illness," he said, not having the heart to ask the man not to call him hero.

The sound of bolts clanking free followed, and the door swung inward to reveal a short priest, three sprigs upon his robe, standing in a darkened entryway. "Please, if you would wait in the antechamber, I will send word at once."

Never followed the man's gesture to an archway where he found a simply appointed room of stone. Bench seats faced a modest statue of Pacela in her robes, standing within a field of wheat, carved in soft detail. Bunches of actual wheat had been arranged at her feet as a further gesture.

He let his pack thump to the floor and sat with a little groan.

"Is something wrong?" Rikeva asked, sitting nearby. She had not glanced at him, instead staring at the statue.

"Just thinking of all the stairs in this place – it's awful."

"Hmmm."

Never followed her gaze to the statue and its serene expression... and yet, the marble actually wore a leer.

He stood. "Something is wrong."

Rikeva joined him. "Do you mean the statue? It's not so bad, surely? I mean, her expression seems a little odd, as though the sculptor wasn't skilled enough, perhaps but is that such a bad thing?"

"No. It's leering at us."

Appreciate the time I spend with you, Amouni. It is never easy to visit the dominions of other deities.

He glared up at the stone face. "Feel free to leave."

Rikeva gripped his arm. "What's going on?"

"He's here – the Burnished King."

Your companion has an intriguing darkness about her, I am amused to discover.

"In the statue?" she asked. "Never, I see nothing. Are you sure?"

Nevertheless, I would furnish you with a future. All you need do is deliver something to me, a certain Memory Seed. We both know it is here. Deliver the seed to me and the wind will no longer howl for your blood.

"I would sooner destroy it."

The leering expression darkened to a sneer. *Then if we*

cannot reach an agreement, you will be obliterated. Await it, Amouni.

And then the statue was no longer a grotesque mockery of its former self. Kindness returned to the gaze, her smile serene. "He's gone." Never sat once more, tension lingering in his body as he glanced around the room. "I'm fairly certain, at least."

"What happened?"

"He appeared as the statue and offered to spare me if I gave him a Memory Seed – it's an Amouni relic. I have no idea what it could be used for."

"Nothing good if he has it, right?"

Never nodded. "One more thing that needs to be investigated. Wonderful."

On the other hand, Oleksan's claim about darkness within Rikeva was not credible. No, she cared too much about her people; she wanted an end to the Stone Plague. Her determination was not darkness. It was a strength... the Burnished King was simply sowing doubt.

Another of his taunts, and a new approach for a King without the means to do more, perhaps. And giving the taunt credence was exactly what the Plague King wanted.

No chance.

"If he keeps appearing through other forms, I think it means that he can't simply strike us down from afar," Rikeva said. "As for the future?" She shrugged. "He doesn't seem to be at his full strength now. We need to stop him before that happens."

"Agreed."

"It's a big ask for just the two of us, you know."

Never smiled. "I have some friends we can call upon."

***

High Priestess Jardila was lighting lamps in her audience chamber when they arrived, soft yellow robe and dark braids swaying as she passed before the images of Pacela. In addition to those he recalled from his last visit, such as the Goddess tending to forests and fields, or blasting away shades with golden light, there was a new image on the fountain, one of Pacela cradling a blazing sun, a small, winged figure flying against it.

Flattering?

Or a little irritating to be depicted as merely working under her direction?

"Where have you been, Never?" Jardila asked.

"It's wonderful to see you again, too."

She sighed. "Apologies, that was curt. But my question stands. Something terrible is happening. You're aware of it, yes?"

"That's why we're here." Never introduced Rikeva, who nodded.

"Please sit, both of you. Refreshments are on the way but I'd like you to tell me what you know while we wait." Jardila led them to her seedling-shaped table, taking the chair before the half-circle that had been cut free – again, much like his last visit. Once more, he could not quite place her musical accent. Perhaps it related to Pacela's chosen rather than a specific region of Marlosi.

Not the most important problem to be solved.

She tented her fingers before her face, elbows leaning on

the table, the tattoo of the tree within its circle visible on her bare shoulders. "What have you discovered so far?"

"Few Amouni texts speak of Arkenon, God of the Malecaphera."

Jardila nodded. "The Dread God is not unknown in our own ancient writings, though not considered anything more than myth like Harpies or The Devourer. Please continue."

"Was Oleksan, the Burnished King, also mentioned there?"

"A King of Disease from the east, who was said to follow the dark path of the Malecaphera."

"That's who has spread the creeping decay. He seeks something in the Evache Lakes, perhaps a return of this Arkenon. A 'Temple Trivium' is also mentioned but I need to read more."

"There are texts you should see," the High Priestess replied, slight frown upon her face. "But first, have you been to the Lakes at least?"

"I have. There is a wall of decay enclosing them – Oleksan has warned me from standing in his way."

"We all stand in his way, whether he likes it or not," the High Priestess said.

Never smiled. "Of course."

"What more of his purpose?"

"Well, there is something here that he desires," Never said, explaining Oleksan's visit and attempt at bribery.

"He was here?" Jardila rose. "I did not sense that at all."

"He did not linger, if that allays any of your concerns," Never said.

"Hmmm."

"We have brought this," Rikeva said as she placed a vial of soma upon the table. "I'm not sure how it measures up to what some of your faithful can do but it stays the sickness."

Jardila tilted the soma, letting the white liquid slide within the glass. "Taken from the cad to the south?"

"Yes. Can you discover anything more about it?" Never asked. "Rikeva already knows most of the elements but Beqona mines something important to the make-up of what he calls soma."

"Anything that may help is welcome; we will learn what we can, yes," she replied. "What else can you share with me of its effects?"

"The loss of movement and the... drying of people is eased but not reversed," Rikeva explained. "The way the skin changes colour, this can prevent that symptom too, but so far we don't know how long it works. The doses vary, but for most of my tribe a portion of one vial offers stasis for at least a week."

"What about the earth or objects that people touch?"

"They don't seem to pass it on if they take the soma."

"I see."

"What of your own gifts?" Never asked Jardila. "Father Maheo said you've sent priests across Marlosi, but their numbers are few?"

"Sadly. I pray for more, but not enough have been found to have her blessing."

"Then it's a recent change?" he asked.

"Yes. Pacela provides, Never."

Proof that the gods had not abandoned the lands? Or wonderful coincidence? Either way, a little *more* help would be welcome. And even better, help which didn't put Her faithful at risk.

"The land around Olecsa suffers most; we still do not know why," Jardila said. "The Empress has sent troops to fight the spread but even after the fire, traces often remain."

"What of your fire, Never?" Rikeva asked.

"It made a real difference at the village of Cagila."

"That is heartening," Jardila said.

"If nothing else, at least we know there are only two problems to solve. Putting a stop to the source – the Burnished King – and saving people from what he has already done."

"Both will require more knowledge than we currently possess," the High Priestess replied as she rose, vial in hand. "Once you have eaten and rested, I will send for someone to escort you to our library. There are old texts there that may be of use, written in ancient Marlosi. I will ensure that your guide can translate. Work on that and I will focus on the soma for now."

"I might be able to read it myself," Never said.

Jardila nodded. "You might at that."

"What about more help?" Never asked. "Empress Crisina?"

"I will call upon the Empress, yes," the High Priestess replied. "And I hope you can seek your own powerful allies, Never."

"The very instant we're done here."

Chapter 11

The acolyte came to a halt before one of the rooms, moonlight from the window casting his hesitation in stark relief. "Ah, is this... ah, suitable for you?" He glanced to Never and Rikeva without seeming to address either.

Rikeva grinned. "Two rooms for now; we'll be sure to let you know if anything changes."

The priest flushed but Never thanked the poor fellow before the acolyte could apologise. "Please tell the High Priestess we appreciate her hospitality."

"Yes, yes, I will." He was already a few steps down the carpeted hall, mumbling something about returning with their guide in the morning.

"So, what are our rooms like?" Rikeva asked as she followed Never into his.

The lodgings for guests were unchanged – still plenty of room for his pack and other items with both a clothes-rack and wardrobe, the same soft yellows and greens in the fabrics, moonlight and air streaming through the open windows.

When he sat upon the bed, glancing around for the bath

in an adjoining room, Rikeva strode to the window, staring down. Never rummaged through his pack, first removing the Amouni texts and then seeking an apple, still a little hungry after their delicious but less than filling meal. He crunched through the skin, sweetness following. "See anything interesting?" he asked around mouthfuls.

"It's an impressive view, but I want to be moving again."

"Hard to feel that sense of taking action while waiting around to read books, right?"

She smiled back at him. "Well, at least we can start early tomorrow. Do you think we'll find anything?"

"I do. Even if it's only a single clue."

"I'm hoping you're right." Rikeva turned back to the view.

He joined her by the window. "Is someone keeping a supply of soma heading for your tribe while you're away?"

She nodded. "I left enough jewels behind to hopefully keep everyone alive until we return." Rikeva regarded him with a hand on her hip. "Am I so easy to read?"

"Well, it just seemed like threats from an enemy would bother you less than the suffering of those you want to protect."

"Perhaps," she said. "It's nice to hear."

"How many?"

"Nearly a quarter of my people. It's hard to stop worrying."

He placed a hand on her shoulder, the leather warm from her skin. "We'll find a way to save them."

"Is that another promise from the Winged Hero of the War?"

"A promise that I won't give up trying, at least."

"I'll take it." She moved from the window and started for the door. "Sleep well, then."

"You too."

The door clicked closed behind her and Never returned to the bed where he re-read a few pages of the Amouni texts – the second book, *A History of the North Spear*. Even more than *The Forgotten Ones*, it seemed an unusual text to hide away.

That fact alone seemed suspect.

Most pages were an account of a tribe that resisted Amouni rule for only a short while before being swallowed up by the ancient empire. Some of it detailed accounts of troop movements and skirmishes, and a deciding battle where the leader surrendered.

The final line of the tome might have mentioned the Amber Isle itself.

And by the very thinnest of margins was the Second Seal on the Isle preserved in spite of the forces unleashed that night.

Was it truly the Amber Isle? And if so, what did the Second Seal refer to? He'd not found any hints of such a thing before... Was the book even referring to the Amber Isle? A northern people and the word 'isle' was hardly conclusive evidence.

Never rubbed at his eyes before setting the book aside. Better to rest and start tomorrow with a more convincing alertness.

Once he'd bathed and climbed into the bed, Never closed his eyes, a pleasant heaviness coming across his limbs. But no sooner had he settled than a stone clicking filled the darkened room.

Never rose, breath held better to listen.

Something crossed the starlight from the window – a small figure neared, tapping claws keeping pace. Never reached for a dagger, on loan from Jardila, and drew it from beneath the pillow. He slid the point across the back of his hand, crimson-fire blooming.

Flickering red and orange revealed the startled eyes of a possum, its soft, grey face frozen as it started up at him.

And with the animal came the now familiar chill, the fetid voice.

How sweet unbroken rest must be, yes?

"I find it hard to believe that whatever you sent to hunt me is this poor creature."

Assuredly not.

"Then leave, *Your Majesty.*"

I'm sure you will grant me delivery of another message – after which I will return to my most pressing business.

"The Temple Trivium?"

The possum's head tilted. *Then your ancestral memories are not completely void? Interesting, for one such as yourself. But yes, though the Temples will likely be your last sight, should you actually survive so long, I am sure you will be swept up by the magnificence.*

"Raising sunken temples all alone?"

You are seeking information about the lives of the fisherfolk, I presume?

"Why not?" Or at least, *any* information that could be gleaned. And if Oleksan wanted to boast along with his taunting, there was no need to stop the fool.

It is possible that at least some will survive; I give you that much, Never.

Never straightened. How had the Burnished King learnt his name? Had the possum been lurking nearby during the conversation at the window with Rikeva earlier? At other times? Could Oleksan listen from afar? Never forced a new concern aside long enough to answer. "I'm flattered you took the time to learn my name."

Such a moniker certainly serves to conceal your heritage – even Awakened, as you are. The possum turned back for the window. *I feel compelled, perhaps by pity, but your search for a cure is doomed without siren shells.*

"You're telling me what I need to combat your poison?"

Insomuch as you have now learnt that the final ingredient belongs to a long extinct mollusc, yes, I am. Understand, the suffering of others, especially the Amouni, grants me much pleasure.

Never stood. "And what will you feel when I succeed in spite of that?"

But the possum only leapt up to the windowsill and disappeared into the night.

He nearly chased it, but stopped.

Before the night ended, there was another place he needed to visit. A place that would offer more hope for a cure than any claim made by Oleksan.

***

Never kept to the shadows of Beqona's mine, the dust-covered overalls he'd 'borrowed' from a now-unconscious miner granting him access to an underground of dark, earthen walls tinted red. Or orange, whenever he passed an infrequent lamp. It was an otherwise well-constructed mine; support beams and good tracks for the largely empty carts that rumbled by.

Even at night, the mine was, if not bustling, certainly still awake and working; distant thumping and clangs came from deeper within. Even so, it had not taken long to find an overseer speaking to another miner, voice lowered but not exactly whispering.

"... nothing much we can do. The yield is still just too low," the miner was saying as he ran a hand through his hair, leaving behind a smudge of dirt.

The overseer sniffed. "It doesn't matter. Master Beqona said to keep going. He's made his decision."

"Even without the *hizre*?"

"Those are his orders."

The miner actually took half a step back. "But will the soma even work?"

"Those are his orders," the man said. "Just keep working. We're still being paid, aren't we?" He stomped off further down the mine.

Never slunk back into the dark – he'd actually raised his pickaxe and moved toward the men where they stood in the light, jaw clenched as someone's life hung in the balance...

No. A better target waited within the mansion.

He spun on his heel and crunched along the passage, passing few other miners, most of who only nodded. They seemed unaware or unconcerned with the news that despite the lack of the precious and mysterious *hizre* mineral, they would still be producing soma.

Soma, which was soon to be worthless.

Any weariness Never might have felt after a long day, or the thought of the flight back to the *forasa* later, vanished as he climbed up and out of the mine and into the night air. There, he somehow resisted the urge to hurl the pickaxe to the hard earth.

Instead, he dropped the tool into an empty cart with the others and started toward the miners' quarters – little more than a group of sheds that stretched along the earth. But he did not enter, slipping around behind them before launching himself into the air. He flew to the mansion and hovered before an out of the way window, where he used crimson-fire to melt glass and latch alike. Once again, the urge to unleash his anger threatened to overwhelm him.

"Save something for Beqona," he told himself as he walked the polished wooden floors, seeking light from a bedroom or study, *something* that would suggest the merchant's location.

But when he did find the man, it was in a darkened room.

A large bedchamber adorned with functional furniture and plain blankets – no hints of rich colours or silks were revealed when he flared the crimson-fire. From the bed came a groan, and Never called more light, so that when Beqona finally rose, hair a mess, it was to a room of red.

The man gave a shout of terror. He pressed himself against the wall, clutching at his blankets.

"I am giving you just one chance," Never snapped. "Do not sell useless soma."

Beqona swallowed. "I... wait, wait. Surely I can offer you something? A share in the profits?"

Never tore a knife free and flung it across the room.

The blade thudded into the man's chest. Beqona slumped, eyes wide in shock and pain, but Never strode to the window without a word to the dying worm. Footsteps thundered toward the bedchamber.

No need for stealth now.

Never sent a ball of crimson-fire forth. It shattered the window and he reached for the ledge as the door crashed open. He glanced over his shoulder to find the hulking shape of Idth in the doorway, club in hand, his blade missing. The bodyguard's own surprise was evident by his hesitation as he stared between the corpse of his master and Never.

"If you want to survive this night, then do as I say," Never said.

Idth nodded slowly.

"Do not follow that man's path. Give the rest of the true soma to whoever asks, and accept no payment," Never said. "Do that, and I will not return to take your life."

"You have my word," Idth replied, and it seemed he sneered down at the corpse of his former master.

"Good answer."

Chapter 12

Never shifted in the comfortable library chair as he opened up the shields on his lamp then lifted the scroll, squinting at faint words written across the bottom. A strong, musty scent was his reward – it wasn't precisely unpleasant and of course, knowledge was often hidden within the long folds of time.

"Are you sure you have enough light?" Rikeva asked from across the table, leaning over a stack of books. Her surprise at his description of last night had worn off, her spirits even raised with the news about the *hizre*, even with its apparent scarcity. Even so, Jardila would now be seeking it in every mine.

"Point taken." The Spire's library had been lit quite generously.

Between the stacks, lamps were set upon the stone walls and above, generous skylights, while on their table alone two other lamps burned. More, their guide, Father Henros carried one of his own as he approached, yet another tome in hand.

He placed it before Never with a shake of his silvery head. "I'd offer to translate again but I assume that by now, you're quite fluent in ancient Marlosi."

"Perhaps not to speak, but I'm reading it well enough now," Never replied.

Henros rubbed at the bridge of his nose. "Remarkable. In any event, let me keep looking," he added as he returned to the stacks.

Never lifted the blue-bound book and began turning the pages, gently of course. So far, Rikeva had more luck researching the siren shells. It seemed they had indeed once existed in the eastern oceans but like so many desirable things, they were now lost – in this case fished out of existence. None had been seen by sailors for centuries, and the last reports were from a village by the name of Solmi in the Ramakki Islands.

Even with a *forasa* symbol located nearby, Never couldn't summon much desire to visit. Oleksan would have ulterior motives. Was there something he wanted there? Something he could not reach for some reason, but that an Amouni could? Hiruso had played a similar game in Kiymako.

Or was it just an old-fashioned trap?

At best, the islands were probably a ploy to waste his time.

"Anything else of use?" Rikeva asked as she flipped one of her books closed with a sigh.

"Not truly," he replied. "Another mention of Holy Fire that could be used to drive away the 'dark ones that appeared from the mountains' but that's vague."

"But these books are supposedly copied from older ones,

from about the right era too, aren't they? That's what got you and Henros excited before."

"They did."

Father Henros had suggested the Holy Fire came from Pacela but Rikeva was convinced it spoke of his own crimson-fire. Convenient if true... but it wasn't effortlessly effective against the decay back in Cagila. It had taken some time to burn it away.

"Then what's changed?" she asked.

He slid the book to Rikeva, who shifted closer. He caught the scent of citrus from her hair and somehow, her closeness seemed *very* close, arms near to touching. "The Holy Fire is 'borrowed' according to this," he said. "But from who? The Goddess? If I compare the crimson-fire then it is very much a part of my heritage; I wouldn't describe it as borrowed."

"All right, then let's find that other book your Amouni slates mentioned. *The Origin*?"

"We might be forced to do that," he said.

"Forced?"

If there was another place where Amouni texts could be stored, it was Father's despicable chambers in Kiymako. Rikeva had detected his reluctance easily enough. And yet, why hesitate to return? Awful memories or not, answers might well wait there.

A new figure approached their table, this time Jardila. She carried a large tome in gloved hands, yellow ribbon marking several pages, and was trailed by an attendant. The High Priestess paused at the table, letting the young girl spread a cut of dark fabric across the tabletop before placing the large book down. "Here."

"I want to offer a quip about how careful you're being but

I think I'll just express my gratitude instead," he told her.

"Good," she replied with a smile. "Because bringing the Memories of the Order here *is* convenient – for you."

"It is," he said. The flights of stairs were not insignificant. "What did you want to show us?"

"This." She began to turn the pages, moving each carefully.

Never noted the Amouni who had saved a child from the storm-lashed ocean as the pages turned but did not catch glimpses of the other images she'd shown him upon his last visit. Instead, he saw a group of priests tending to a garden and a stand of juniper, but when Jardila stopped, it was upon something less pleasant.

Streaking shadows tore through a burning orchid.

Embers gnawed away at the base of each tree while flames danced through the canopy, fallen shapes covered the ground, the antlers of a stag gleaming in the orange glow. The figures seemed to be flying, and in their hands they held burning brands.

The art style was a little less detailed compared to others, giving the impression of a haze, doubtless a purposeful choice.

"What if those are not wings?" she asked, gesturing to the figures. "Now, the following page describes Amouni and their servants ravaging the land to control resources, to prevent others from breaking free of dependence."

He leant a little closer. "You think the Malecaphera and Amouni were working together?"

"Not that, no. I meant to say, there is more to this painting. It bears a title; Marlosi artists were especially proud, and so both the name of the artist and title of the image are preserved." She turned more pages, stopping near the end where a list of names waited.

Mostly references to other books and their authors, but Jardila gestured to a smaller list without letting her fingertip touch the old paper.

"Seigona, *The Poisoning of Nesasika.*"

Nesasika did have a vaguely familiar ring to it... a *forasa* might clear things up as to what part of Marlosa it referred. "Nesasika could be an Amouni name rather than Ancient Marlosi."

"It may be nothing," she said. "But considering the Stone Plague, I think it possible that the painting could also bear the word 'aftermath' and still hold true. We know fire slows the spread, we know your crimson-fire is stronger. Perhaps this image depicts Amouni *helping*."

He nodded slowly. Why not? There was every chance that her interpretation was true, and that the book found an image that suited its larger agenda. Or, a probably accurate history, considering the Amouni.

"Should the rest of your searches prove fruitless then this name is a starting point," Jardila added.

"Thank you," Never replied. "This definitely helps. If Kiymako bears no fruit, then that is what we'll do." Asking Ayuni about the Fire of Heaven and the possibility of 'borrowing' it was surely now the best path... but first, the Memory Seed had to be dealt with.

***

In the sealed chamber of stone, Rikeva circled the silver

man with its moulded shape, details scarce but the sense of potential and vague awareness had not faded in any way. "What is this meant to do? Or be?" She paused before the slight face. "I can feel something but it's so faint."

"It's left over from a time when the Amouni ruled the lands," he replied. "But I don't know what it's for, no-one does. Maybe it won't be of use at all."

"What about the marble, then?" She joined him at the long table, taking one of the heavy wooden stools. One was arranged before record books, observations made about the silver man by Pacela's chosen over the centuries. Large gaps existed in them, as interest waxed and waned, and no real clues lay within. Never had taken the other stool, which rested before a single book and other smaller items.

He lifted the crystal marble and the wooden figure reclining within. "This fellow has warned me of danger in the past."

"Then let's take it," she said. "What about the Memory Seed?"

He picked up the golden Memory Seed too. "Whatever ancient Amouni lore resides in here, whatever Oleskan wants, well, I'm hoping there's something useful for us instead."

"And the book?"

He ran a finger along the green bindings. The *Hor Pyrilh*, or in the Marlosi language, The Human Maps. "Something my brother once used for dark purposes, to change the bodies of the people who followed him, but I suppose I can't dismiss it right away."

"Do I want to know?"

"I don't even know if I want to know the extent of it," he replied.

"All right, perhaps I should avoid it too. What about the necklace and fang? And is that a sword hilt?"

"Memories, now. Gifts from my time in Kiymako, but I don't know how to restore their abilities. They probably won't be of use," he added. "And that is a hilt, yes. I melted down the blade in case it fell into the wrong hands."

Rikeva scratched at her head a moment before gesturing to the Memory Seed. "Then why don't you start with the one useful thing here, while I organise some supplies."

"We won't need much," Never said with a nod as she started toward the exit. "I'm expecting a short stay in one part of Kiymako and a warm welcome when we visit the Phoenix."

She paused. "The Phoenix is actually real?"

"You're skipping over my little joke?" he asked. Rikeva frowned at him. "Fine, yes. She is real. Ayuni's also my half-sister, so she'll help us."

Rikeva stared a moment longer before shaking her head. "You somehow manage to keep surprising me, you know."

"Well, I'm running out of them, if that puts your mind at ease."

"Not quite sure I believe that," she said as she closed the door.

Never turned back to the Memory Seed.

Was it a blessing or a curse that he was not able to return to the Memory Tree and seek more Amouni secrets? It had not been so long truly, since he climbed the silver branches of the Tree with Snow, the passion that danced with madness burning in his gaze... the tree crashing down to end his suffering. "And change mine," he said softly.

And still Never hesitated.

Was every memory going to add a potentially deadly hesitance to his actions? Never lifted the Seed and stared within.

An Amouni in silken tunic, wearing black gloves, stood before a large group of what seemed to be students – she was explaining how to maintain the runes within a supporting buttress, using a small model of silver and blue.

The words and methods made little sense to him but the lesson seemed to be a mixture of building and architectural advice... and it was not a long lesson, finishing once she had demonstrated the disproportionate power the runes offered.

Cold comfort, perhaps, that investigating the Memory Seed earlier would have earned no reward then... at best, it was a relief to know that the Burnished King could not use the Seed for anything, surely, even if he got a hold of the Amouni relic.

And yet, if Oleksan wanted the Seed, there was no other choice.

Never dropped the golden relic and crushed it beneath his boot.

Chapter 13

A steady stream of smiling acolytes and young priests passed Never as he descended the Spire's worn stone steps. They were all chattering about training in the Upper Hall, some engaged in good-natured arguments about who was more handsome and dashing, or more beautiful.

"Say what you will," one lad said. "But Instructor Lina is the one for me, no doubt."

Never paused. Rikeva and Jardila were probably already waiting for him below but supposedly the Empress had been delayed. The Upper Hall was not so far above either... an easy decision. He joined the flow of youngsters and climbed back up several flights to follow them along a passage lined with windows. Each opening offered a view of the city below, plenty of red tiles, white walls and a few chimneys puffing smoke into mild spring air.

The two youths were still talking. "Father Halona said the High Priestess is so impressed with Lina's idea that she's considering making it mandatory."

"Really? I doubt Old Man Gelvi will like that."

"Well, after the invasion I don't think too many will agree with him."

"Good point."

The sound of shouts and clacking of wood against wood neared as he reached the Upper Hall – which was meant for worship based on the altar and benches, all of which had been pushed to the edges of the room. The large statue of Pacela was even draped in white cloth. To shield her from the violence? Never hid a smile.

The cold stone floors had been covered in softer, woven grass mats as acolytes and a few priests and priestesses moved back and forth through basic patterns, swinging their wooden blades.

Those who'd come to watch rushed to the bench seats, already half-full, but Never stayed by the entryway.

Older priests were encouraging and admonishing where they moved up and down between the pairs, black tunics worn over their robes, some carrying their own wooden blades but most unarmed, correcting posture or stances, footwork or grip.

A familiar face worked in the same role, not too far distant, her dark hair tied into a braid and her movements swift and sharp; gaze bright as she demonstrated a parry for her students. Quite the contrast from when he'd first met Lina atop the Spire, her voice soft and her wide eyes mostly downcast.

Even from a short time observing, it was clear that she was doing well, another welcome contrast to their first encounter.

Between bouts she stopped to take water from a flask, surveying the hall, and when her eyes found him she straightened, then smiled as she raced through the students. "Never, you're here!"

"So it seems," he replied with a grin.

Lina almost bounced on her toes. "It's so wonderful to see you again."

"And you," he said. He gestured to the students. "I hear that you're behind this change."

"I am." Her cheer faded a little. "After the invasion... I just wanted to do more. So that we could protect ourselves. But not everyone agrees with me."

"With Jardila supporting you, I'm sure they'll see the value."

"Thank you, Messenger – ah, Never," she said, a slight flush coming to her cheeks in a glimpse of the old Lina. Those nearest had stopped training, whispers growing. Lina shot the students a glare, and they resumed sparring.

"Would you rather we spoke in the hall, perhaps?" Never offered.

"Good idea." Once they stood in the comparative quiet of the hall, she looked up at him. "Have you come about the rumours?"

"Rumours?"

She nodded. "They say that you've appeared in the city and that you're helping people, only sometimes they say you're too violent, or that you steal half of what you retrieve."

"I what?"

"I don't believe it – I didn't for a single moment, but that's what's being whispered," she said. "Supposedly, if someone has been wronged, they leave a message by your statue and soon enough, you appear with your wings, ready to help."

An imposter? Never frowned. Someone was going to

discover who the real Amouni was very, very soon. "Lina, I need to put a stop to... wait, you said I have a statue? Here in the city?"

"Yes, since after the invasion – it's magnificent. Everyone knows what you did for us."

"Sounds like my work isn't done here," he said. "Are there any hints as to where the imposter hides?"

"Not that I've heard, sorry."

"I'll find him soon enough," he said with a grin, then started back down the corridor. "Keep up the good work, Lina."

"I will," she called after him.

When he at last reached the bottom of the tower and exited into the square – flying down would have been much easier – Rikeva and Jardila had been joined by a fellow in thigh-length satin robes of blue, open at the throat, the tunic beneath a rich red. His expression was sour enough to curdle milk. Flunky or functionary? The fop had a dozen Imperial soldiers, these men looking like Steelhawks with their overabundance of weapons, from spears to swords and some with axes too.

Before Never could speak, the noble pointed. "There. Arrest that man, Captain."

Never raised an eyebrow as the soldiers advanced. "I suggest you do not try that."

"What is the meaning of this?" Jardila demanded.

The fop did not answer and his men did not halt either. Never removed a dagger and drew blood, letting the crimson-fire flare. The globe of bloody flame quickly engulfed his forearm. "Are you sure about this?" he asked the soldiers.

Now they stopped, and even the fop flinched.

Never met Rikeva's gaze. She had one hand on her staff and he nodded, looking to the noble.

With barely a step she'd taken him hostage, staff locked across his throat.

The wide-eyed noble was still able to speak, since he shrieked about his name and station, though the words were not clear. Half the soldiers had spun to face their leader, while the others kept their weapons trained on Never.

"If you could shut up for just a moment, Siro, we might be able to talk," Never said. "Why do you think I need to be arrested?"

Siro glared. "Your pretence of ignorance is an insult. You are responsible for dozens of crimes against nobility and merchants across the city. You are not a hero – it's clear you're nothing like Empress Crisina."

"Ah, the imposter," Never said, going on to explain for Rikeva and Jardila.

The High Priestess snorted. "Have those rumours started again?"

"They're more than rumours! We have proof, and now we have the miscreant himself," the fop hissed.

"Your optimism is inspiring, Siro."

The clack of hooves on cobbles preceded the arrival of a carriage, one that was somewhat worse for wear at first glance. But when it rolled to a halt and a pair of soldiers emerged, flanking a young woman with fiery red hair and wrapped in a heavy, dark cloak, there seemed a certain artifice about the carriage – its handles did not rattle and the flaking paint revealed firm wood beneath.

The woman's eyes widened almost imperceptibly at the

sight of the crimson-fire, but she raised her voice. "Sheath your weapons, all of you."

The soldiers complied, each going to one knee. "Empress," the captain said.

Siro was silent, but his face remained red with outrage – or maybe it was a lack of air? "What about this one, Empress?" Rikeva asked, keeping her grip on the staff.

"Even poor, eager Siro, yes." The hilt of a blade was visible beneath Empress Crisina's cloak, and when she pointed to the fop, she was wearing leather gloves. "Siro, you are *very* clearly mistaken. These soldiers will accompany me and you will return to the palace and await my summons."

Rikeva let him go and the man, whose cheeks had drained of colour now, bowed before scurrying away.

Never let the crimson-fire vanish as Empress Crisina approached. Up close, her youthfulness was clearer, but tempered with a sadness to her eyes, likely changed by whatever horrors she had seen during the invasion.

"I finally have a proper chance to thank you for everything you did for our city – our nation," she said with a smile.

"I'm sorry I wasn't able to act sooner," he said.

"I hope your modesty does not hamper your efforts now, Never of the Amouni," she said. "High Priestess Jardila tells me you will be fighting the Stone Plague while she works on a cure, and I offer you whatever assistance you might require."

"Thank you, Empress," he said. "I do, in fact, have one request."

"Please."

"If you could lend me some soldiers, I'd like to deal with

the imposter before I leave."

She issued the order to the captain, whose name was Luche, then turned back to Never. "Do show mercy if you believe the culprit worthy."

"I will."

Together, the High Priestess and the Empress entered the spire, speaking softly, attended by the two bodyguards and several priests.

Rikeva joined him with a chuckle. "That was... interesting."

He grinned. "I agree. I'd like to delay our trip to Kiymako a little, do you mind?"

She shook her head. "It won't take long to reach Kiymako with the *forasa*. And the soma won't wear off so fast. They shouldn't be suffering yet."

"Well, this won't take long either."

"How can you be sure?"

He nodded to the soldiers, who now waited for his instructions. "Siro's men have probably done a lot of the groundwork for us."

"Then let's find out."

Chapter 14

The broad thoroughfare that led from the huge, gleaming dome of the palace took them eventually to his statue where it rested in a familiar location.

"Well, here we are, it seems," Never said as he paused before Ashina's mighty oaks – or, at least, the memory of them... now, their blessed shade was gone. And the absence of the oaks was not the only change.

In place of the ancient trees rested saplings and new grass, bright flowers, and in the centre of the open space, his statue had been placed upon the trunks. And while the regrowth was another welcome sign of Marlosi washing away the invasion and occupation, the statue really was something less pleasing.

"I'm surprised you wanted a detour to see this," Rikeva said with a grin. "It's an accurate likeness, I'll admit."

It didn't look so different; traveller's garb beneath a dark cloak, wings spread in a magnificent display and daggers in both hands. His hair was a little longer, and his cheeks *very* clean shaven, and the artist had given him a noble, even kind expression.

A generous fellow.

Never sighed. "Part of me regrets the curiosity."

"If nothing else, you should thank the artist. It is amazing work," Rikeva said.

"It is worth at least my thanks, but I wouldn't want to encourage that sort of thing."

"Why not? You obviously meant something to the artist, to the city."

He shrugged. "So-called heroes have a tendency to come crashing down from pedestals."

"Sometimes only after they've died, if that helps."

"Comforting," Never said with a chuckle. He turned to Captain Luche. "Captain, what about the people here? Any familiar faces?"

The soldier cast his gaze across the people, most simply going about their business, though more than a few stood to watch from where they ate before food stalls or at a large bakery, the scent of pastry crossing the thoroughfare.

At least one small group of people seemed to recognise Never, but were not willing to approach, hiding their whispers behind their hands.

Captain Luche shook his head. "Seems not. We've scared 'em off, but as I said before, we've narrowed down their location to two sure bets."

"Two sure bets?"

The soldier jerked a thumb to the bakery and its big windows of colourful displays, sweet pastries and breads. "One is right across the street there."

"Gutsy. The 'in plain sight' approach."

"Aye. Other one's a basement few streets over, near enough to the public graveyard."

Rikeva was looking across at the bakery. "So, you haven't tried to catch the imposter yet?"

The captain rubbed his chin. "Lord Siro says some other lord owns the place, so he's been waitin' on a bit more proof first, and I want to launch a double-strike, you see."

"Then let us take the bakery, Captain," Never said. "You and your men head for the basement and that way you won't have to personally ruffle any feathers."

Luche grinned, revealing a single crooked tooth in an otherwise straight row. "Right away, My Lord."

"No need for that," Never replied. "And do take the lead of our Empress, with whoever you find – sounds like she wants prisoners, not bodies."

"That she does." The captain set off at a jog with his men.

Perhaps a little too eager, if they had been observed from the bakery, but then, there was no hiding their intent now.

"Are just you and I enough here?" Rikeva asked. "We don't know how many friends this imposter has."

"I believe so. Why don't you check for a back exit and I'll stroll in the front, see if anyone scurries out. If it's half a garrison, leave it to me."

"Expecting that many?"

"Not really, but not all surprises are pleasant, right?"

She nodded and started across the street, circling the building. Never followed but did not take the alley between bakery and butcher, instead approaching the front door, where he let a patron exit before stepping inside.

The scent of warm bread and spices filled the room, a mother and son browsing a long counter filled with racks of bread, pies and sweet buns. The young woman behind the counter paled when he approached, wiping her flour-covered hands on the front of her apron as she greeted him. "Welcome. Can I help you with anything?"

A good sign. "Yes, I'm hoping to speak with someone – he might be upstairs. Supposedly, he looks something like me."

"Ah," she began to stammer, still wiping her hands. "I'm not sure what you mean, sir."

Never leant across the counter and lowered his voice. "I might not even have to hurt anyone if you help me. I'm just planning on making a request of my 'brother'. Do you understand?"

Her eyes filled with tears and she swallowed before whispering. "Please. Nicholan is not a wicked man."

"I will hear what he has to say," Never said as he moved back, softening his tone.

She scrunched up her apron as she hesitated.

An image of the imposter was starting to become clear... or at least, Never was no longer leaning toward a large group of hardened criminals with a clever swindle. Something else might have been afoot.

"If you truly recognise me, you must know that I am not a rampaging monster. You have my word that I will listen."

"All right. You can wait in the back. I'll send Nicholan in," she said, and gestured to a passage that led to a staircase and what turned out to be a small strongroom, which she had to open with a key.

Inside waited a table, chair and several locked boxes stacked in one corner. A flash of guilt overcame him – he'd rattled her enough that she'd shown him to a room no stranger ought to have visited.

But as he waited, he drew a knife and checked on the door – it was heavy enough, with a sturdy lock. Perhaps she was hoping to cover more than one eventuality? And there was still a chance he was in a snake's lair...

Voices reached him. "... and what if he's *not* the real thing?" a man was saying, his voice strained. "He shouldn't be in that room of all places!"

"But I don't think he's lying at all," the young woman replied as their footfalls reached the ground floor.

Never took the seat.

Whispering barely reached him from the hall, and then a young fellow in tunic and apron entered, his jaw clenched, dark hair brushed with flour. His eyes darted around the room, but he held himself steady as he stopped before Never. And there *was* a passing resemblance, after all. "In the right lighting, with some fake wings, I can see it working," Never said.

"This isn't what you must be thinking," Nicholan said, and his voice only cracked once.

Never glanced at the locked boxes in the corner. "I promised I'd listen, so tell me what's going on here. And I hope it's good, Nicholan. Because even though this is the first I've heard of anyone pretending to be me, I can't say I like it."

The baker-imposter kept his arms straight at his sides, fists clenched. "The city is going to close down my old orphanage, My Lord. I couldn't allow that."

Never raised an eyebrow. "Robbing the rich to feed the less fortunate, is it?"

"It's the truth," he said. "Please. We'll find another way if you spare us."

"And your friends near the cemetery?"

Nicholan tensed. "We're all doing it for the same reasons. I know it isn't the only orphanage in the city, and I know we're causing suffering too, but without that place…"

He sighed. "After I make sure you're not lying, I'll speak to the High Priestess or maybe the Empress before I leave the city. They'll take care of the orphanage – on one condition."

"Anything, Lord Never!"

"Get rid of the fake wings and whatever else you came up with – and stick to baking."

Chapter 15

The market containing Saint Tirasali's fountain was quiet so early, allowing Never to hop into the water and splash his way to the *forasa* without bother, Rikeva close behind. There weren't many onlookers, and so only a few people would be due for a shock.

He was already sensing the shining pods as he approached the symbol, though it still took a moment to widen his 'vision' beyond Marlosi, over the mass of dark forests of Hanik and on to Kiymako, where the pods bore a faint tint of paler green.

"Nearly done?" Rikeva asked over the splashing.

"Just a little longer."

Of all the pods in Kiymako, there would surely be one within Father's hideaway... and there it was, connected to the Beshano River as expected. But the edges of the *forasa* were jagged somehow, though its presence suggested complete consistency with other symbols.

Had Father modified or moved a *forasa*?

Created one?

In any event, the *wrongness* of the Forge was clearly connected to the *forasa,* which was as good a confirmation as any.

Light blazed and a chill quiet soon replaced the fountain. Father's lair.

The domed chamber bore no sounds save the steady drip of water from their clothes.

Naught had changed. And how could it?

Illuminated by a vague light source, perhaps connected to the skylight in the Forge, each wall was still lined with tables and stools, cabinets of wood and steel too, and plenty of silvery objects he still did not recognise. Of those closest, many were crafted from silver or steel, tall and spindly, some almost like folded frames.

Once again, they were not items he *wanted* to understand.

Rikeva had started toward the paintings but Never's gaze was drawn to the Amouni weapons. They hung over squat, wheeled chests, which seemed like steps used to reach the relics. Each blade, bow, dagger and axe had been locked behind clear quartz, their poisonous power sealed... poisonous at least, to those without Amouni blood in their veins. Would taking one be a terrible risk?

Or a boon to be used against an enemy not seen for centuries?

But he did not move toward the cases, instead he raised his voice. "Guide, there is no fuel here."

A guide appeared in her purple robe, bare arms at her side. The serpent's head regarded him with flat grey eyes. *Understood, Master.*

Rikeva turned from where she stood before the paintings across the room. "Fuel?"

"Yes." Never started across the empty floor and joined her at the haughty Amouni woman with her golden wings, painted eyes visible upon the shoulders of her robes. "Behind that painting is a smaller room and a Forge of sorts. My so-called father used it to reduce people to certain qualities he found desirable. The Guides might have mistaken you for such fuel for the forge."

"Oh." Rikeva folded her arms and now seemed to glare up at the painting, before moving to the others. "And behind these?"

"I haven't thought to check."

"What about those books, then?"

Never glanced back to the table where the leather-bound journals waited. One still lay against a wall, half-open, pages twisted.

No reason to hold off on reading... but would any hold even a scrap of useful information?

"Never?"

"They're written in Marlosi, at least. I'm just not sure if they'll reference anything but my father's sick obsessions."

"Only one way to be sure."

"True."

At the table, Never took a stool and reached for an older book, sliding a few across to Rikeva. He also removed food and water from his pack and then lifted one of his father's journals with a sneer.

***

Never stood to stretch his back, pacing the room as he rubbed at his eyes. How long since he'd last moved?

Hours? Had noon come and gone?

Amongst more disturbed accounts of his father's life, there was one entry that described the man visiting Mother in the village, returning to help rebuild after a fire, but even that seemed only an act to serve his twisted goals.

Never *had* learnt that his mother was a good archer and that when Father met her, she was fond of a particular leaf-shaped bracelet, but those small details, precious as they were, did not help with the search.

Nearby, Rikeva also rose to stretch, and he could not help but notice her figure as she lifted both arms over her head, the curve of her breasts and hips... and how wonderful the warmth of her skin would have been...

A stupid time to be noticing such things.

Far too much was at stake.

He turned to the paintings instead, and approached the one hanging beside the Amouni Queen, though he didn't know for certain one way or another whether she was actually royalty.

The second painting was a forest glade beneath the blue of the moon, beams striking a glittering stream. A fawn drank from the water, gentle calm in its bearing. Perfect highlights were frozen on the water and the fragility of the leaves was clear, tufts of fur imbued with a faint glow...

Never exhaled slowly. The painting, like the others, was good. Up close, it did not seem so ancient. Had Father stolen it? Or worse, what if the man had actually *painted* the works of art?

Talent wasted.

"Never, what about this?" Rikeva was now walking toward him, journal in hand. "This here, about some sort of wolf."

Never took the journal.

The Old Wolf was especially talkative today, sharing ancient tales that I scarcely believe but suspect contain at least a shred of truth. Some may even bear further investigation, at the Isle or perhaps at the Oracle.

"Is some trace of this Oracle worth seeking?" Rikeva asked. "If they left behind writings?"

"Hmmm." Father had been to the Amber Isle? Of course he had. Did that mean he'd taken relics or texts from the library? Left something useful at the Forge? "Perhaps." On the other hand, with so many seemingly disparate clues, was it all beginning to collect into a mess rather than even a single plausible trail?

Was the Amouni book *The Forgotten Ones* correct, and the only hints would be located within the Temple Trivium itself?

"We search a little more. Maybe there's another hidden room or stowaway."

She nodded. "Any ideas?"

"You could try your suggestion and check the other paintings," Never said. "I just want to see inside those chests and cabinets first."

Rikeva reached for the frame on the fawn as he turned for the chests, only one of which turned out to be locked. The first few contained jars of long-spoiled foodstuffs which had become disturbing colours of seemingly frozen sludge – grey, brown and green, some of them covered in white and blue mould, and that too had a sense of permanence, as though crystallised.

Perhaps what lay inside some jars had not been food at all.

The lock on the final chest was unable to withstand a little crimson-fire, and it revealed an Amouni robe, the five-pointed leaf spun in silver.

Nestled within the folds were a pair of quartz keys.

Never tried both on the quartz display. Only one key fit the lock. He twisted it. The display slid open, leaving the hilt of a faintly blue-glowing sword within reach. Again, was it actually a useful tool?

Such weapons were beyond powerful.

Disastrous.

Was that what it would take to stand up to the Burnished King?

He'd destroyed enough Amouni blades to be sure he could do so again, if needed. Never hesitated a moment longer, then lifted the sword down. A familiar awareness reached him, like during the invasion, and for a time after too. Insistent, but not strong enough to cause trouble.

But the power was obvious. Holding the weapon, it did not seem there was much the Burnished King could send that would stand against the ancient sword.

"That Amouni ego, huh?" Never murmured.

He hooked the hilt into his belt and joined Rikeva, who was lifting the final painting down, and there, perhaps exactly as Never had hoped would be revealed, a small steel hatch in the wall, the shape of a keyhole clear.

"I think I can open that," he said as he joined her.

"Will whatever's inside be dangerous, like the Forge you mentioned?"

"Hopefully not," he replied as he inserted the key. "It's

small enough, at least. Perfect for a few books, I'm hoping."

Rikeva caught his hand. "Things like the Stone Plague are probably small enough to be contained in a vial or jar."

Never paused.

She released him with a sigh. "Actually, forget I said anything. We need to know, right?"

"Something worrying you?"

"It shouldn't be." She glanced around. "But this place... I think I know why you didn't want to come here. Something about it feels wrong. Evil, even."

"I agree, but I don't sense anything behind this lock."

"All right."

He turned the key and a sharp click followed. The hatch swung open with only a small, rectangular hole to show for it. But a single Amouni book waited within, its heavy quartz pages gleaming in the light.

When he drew the tome to the edge, tilted and then opened the book, he saw Amouni text of a less precise hand. Father's own notes? The lines were lists, rather than connected paragraphs or a single story... mostly just observations or clues about places and artefacts, things that the man perhaps had found in other places and hidden via a language no-one else could even read?

Perhaps Father was not the author at all...

And yet there *was* another note about the *forasa*, a trick to return to the last visited symbol – all he had to do was trace the five-pointed leaf upon his own chest.

Useful indeed.

But as Never neared the end of the book, it seemed there would be no other secrets to share, and nothing about the Burnished King.

"Well?"

Never kept turning. "Most of it is just fragments about long-lost items and places, I recognise very little."

"Then it's worthless?"

He paused as he reached the final page of the heavy book. "Maybe not. Listen to this. 'I have searched long enough to conclude that *The Origin* is no more. At least, no more a single tome. After the mutiny aboard the Skylark, several pages were lost and I am sure some stolen, taken east by the Fang. Others, I believe are now buried with Ivadr'."

"Is there more?" Rikeva asked.

"There is," he replied as he read on. "The writer goes on to wish that they all fail to achieve their hopes and dreams, or that they at least die horribly somehow, blaming their obsession with 'fragile myths about Evolution contained therein'. Well, that's a cheery final thought."

"That didn't make a lot of sense to me but if *The Origin* is actually important, it sounds like we have to find this Ivadr's grave," Rikeva said, her voice sounding heavy.

"Not much to go on, I know."

She leant against the chamber wall. "It's more than that, Never. This is starting to feel futile when I could be helping with the soma."

"I can take you back to Isacina?" Never offered, and though he meant each word, having Rikeva's help was something he'd miss if she left... and more, having Rikeva on the journey would simply be *better*.

She thought a moment. "Let's see the Phoenix first."

"Betting that the so-called 'holy fire' is our best chance?"

"I am."

Hard to disagree.

The ancient Amouni clues and hints about other books, about Seals and Oracles weren't amounting to much, especially not compared to everything else they'd learnt. "Then let's get some rest at an inn and tomorrow, I'll introduce you to the Phoenix of Kiymako."

Chapter 16

Darkness had fallen and weariness with it as Never approached the port town of Najin. It rose above a bay, glowing lights climbing over walls only to fade into the night. Cutters, rowboats and bigger ships alike were vague shapes in the harbour, sails still and decks darkened. Some few would probably have been foreign ships, now that Kiymako was slowly opening up. And if sneaking around was necessary again, it would have been easier with more visitors on the streets.

While the *forasa* had deposited them upon the outskirts of the port, it had not been near any major roads. Only now, breaking from animal trails within the silent bamboo, did they near their destination. Never couldn't help a touch of irritation – it was not such a long trek, even with many trails branching off toward the soft crashing of the black waves, but if the gate was just a little closer...

He sighed; beneath the urge to grumble lurked a spark of hope, and he quickened his step. To be moving again, finally, it was a long overdue change. Moving hopefully toward answers.

And despite a lingering hesitation, to be finally moving toward Ayuni once more.

What would she say?

Was the spark of hope actually one of nervousness?

"I'm still worried about finding an inn, you know," Rikeva said from where she walked beside him, her head swivelling from forest to the coast. "Kiymako still isn't *that* fond of visitors."

"I'm fluent in Kiyma."

"So you told me, Never. But I'm not and I'm not all that convinced. There must be a *forasa* on the mountain. Tell me we haven't backtracked."

"A little." Never came to a halt. "And there *is* a *forasa* far closer to the mountain, yes. But I know one of the inns here and I'm planning to rest – in a proper bed, after washing off any traces of my father's memory."

Rikeva glanced at him. "No beds or baths at the temple of the Phoenix?"

"Honestly, I don't know – I'm sure the village has been restored by now but it seems rude to just arrive without warning," he replied. But was that just an excuse to feed his hesitation?

"There has to be a better reason," she replied. "Are we in danger if we visit your sister?"

"No." But Rikeva was likely right. What deeper reason stopped him choosing the *forasa* near Najin? So close to Ayuni now, the last few steps seemed far harder to take. And it wasn't just nerves at a reunion. Guilt and shame lingered...

"What's that?" Rikeva asked, lowering her voice. Her staff was already in hand, and she used it to point.

A mere dozen paces away, the earth trembled, dirt shifting in the moonlight.

An arm broke free.

Never drew the Amouni sword, a faint blue glow coming with it. He hesitated, but once again, the sense of the sword's presence was strangely muted.

But there was no time to wonder further.

Other eruptions were occurring. Half a dozen at least, and from each small mound rose a skeletal figure, sandy earth trickling from tattered clothes and gaunt limbs. The nearest corpse-thing had greying locks plastered to a skull dark with mummified skin, eye-sockets too large, gaping mouth bleeding black bile.

The figures wore similar rags and while only one was armed with a rusted *sisan*, all advanced without hesitation, feet tearing at the earth as they picked up speed.

"Messengers from the Burnished King?" Rikeva asked.

"Seems so," Never said as he leapt forth to meet them, swinging his cursed blade in a flash.

It cut the first skeletal-figure in half, like slicing through silk, and he spun into another creature, birch fist swinging. Bone cracked as he caved in a skull, sending the thing stumbling back into a third creature.

Others had already flown past, but cracking and shattering bones followed behind him too, as the ancient corpses met Rikeva's staff.

Never swung his sword again and two halves of yet another skeletal warrior fell to the trail.

Almost too easy.

Cold hands encircled his neck from behind.

He caught the wrist of his silent assailant with his free

hand but could not break its iron grip. Air was already being cut off. Never twisted an arm to swing his weapon but the angle was unwieldy, a clean strike impossible.

Instead, he reached along the blade and let the edge pierce his skin.

Blood blossomed into fire. He dropped his sword and with both hands blazing now he caught the skeleton's bony grip and squeezed, harder and harder until naught but ash filled his hands.

Never sucked in air as he spun and lashed out, driving a burning fist through another dead-eyed face. He kicked the torso away and before it could rise, snatched up his blade and hacked into the creature, leaving it in thirds. The other long-buried corpses were next, though their efforts to rise were not so determined.

Nearby, Rikeva knelt atop one struggling creature's back – she jerked its arm sharp enough to snap bone, tossing it aside.

Then she snatched at the hair and skull and snapped its neck too.

The creature fell still.

He turned for the next threat... and found only motionless bodies and broken bones.

In the aftermath, the roadside was quiet, only the sound of their breathing. Was the attack finished? Never searched the road. Just moonlight on the torn earth of the trail, shadows between the pale bamboo. How far could Oleksan reach?

It could have been no-one else.

No-one else could come close to such a feat... perhaps not even the nekromant, but it didn't seem likely that Illya was in Kiymako. Nor did she have a single reason to attack.

Never joined Rikeva by one of the bodies, extending a hand.

She reached up and when he helped her to her feet, it seemed that muscles rippled beneath her sleeve. She was no wilting flower, that much he knew simply from travelling with her; she was fit, skilled, able to take care of herself – but had he not extended his birch hand, her grip might have realigned his knuckles.

More evidence of her Weaver gift. And while it was a temporary change, it was a significant one, bringing to mind stories of Weavers single-handedly fighting off bears.

"Are we in trouble now, if these things carry the Stone Plague?" she asked, her frown deep as she stared down at the ruin of what had once been a man or a woman – someone who deserved rest, and not to be used as a disposable slave for the Burnished King.

"They don't look as though they are," he said. "No word of the Stone Plague in Kiymako, either... but we should keep a watch on each other's skin to be safe."

Rikeva glanced at him, raised an eyebrow. "There are more direct ways to see me naked, Never."

He managed to grin after a bare moment's hesitation. "I'll keep that in mind."

"Are we *certain* the Burnished King sent these after us?" She nudged the ribcage of a corpse with her boot.

"Certain? No. Mostly likely, though..."

"Think he's got anything better to throw at us?"

"These can't have been his best." Even without the cursed blade, he could have seared every skeleton down to a steaming lump easily enough. Still, it was nice to save some blood for a change. "I'd hate to grow complacent, however."

She laughed. "Enjoy the victory, Never!"

"On one condition, then," he said. "If we can get to the inn right away and no-one else attacks us again, I'll do just that."

"Let's see what Nijan has to offer, then."

Chapter 17

"Ready?" Never asked as he adjusted his pack. He let both wings slip free, rolling his shoulders as he did. So often, it was a pleasant surprise to free them, as though a sensation of being cooped up was conferred upon the rest of his body, a subtle, niggling feeling that only became apparent through its absence.

"Absolutely ready," Rikeva said.

He paused. "Others tend to be a little nervous about being carried through the air."

"Really? It's exhilarating."

"Even the landings?" he asked with a grin.

"They're less enjoyable but I doubt I could do better."

"I appreciate that, Rikeva," Never said as he leapt into the air to beat his wings fast enough to hover over her. Dead leaves stirred as he extended his arms. "Let's try a running start."

"Am I so heavy?" she asked, but her question was good-humoured.

"Not at all, my lady. I'm just a little tired."

Rikeva started at a jog and though it was not graceful, he matched her speed as best he could.

"Jump on my count," he said as she increased her pace, then counted three and pulled up as she leapt, launching higher and keeping a firm hold on her wrists. Her own grip was steady as they ascended through the cool air. A few feathers drifted free as he beat hard, but Najin's walls were soon passing beneath them.

He turned to fly over the northern section of the city, toward the Green Leaf Inn... between a baker and a peddler of cheap jewellery? Of course, at night most of the tiled rooves appeared similar enough, but if his memory served, the Green Leaf was at least a little taller...

There, a familiar building – one he'd definitely seen before, definitely ran across its tiles while chasing Muka. He glided closer and when they reached the inn, Never beat his wings twice as hard to compensate for the extra weight, and Rikeva touched down with a small grunt.

He landed next, feet sliding on the tiles, but he stayed upright, hiding his wings away before returning to her.

"Not bad," Rikeva said.

"Thanks."

Together they climbed down to the street, lit by a flower-shaped lantern at the inn's entry. He knocked and waited, repeating the process twice more before footsteps approached and the door opened.

Mrs Ku stood before them in her robe, blade still belted at her side. Her eyes widened before she frowned. "Not again."

"I'd hoped for a warmer welcome," Rikeva said, no doubt basing her response on the innkeeper's expression.

"Forgive my imposition once more," Never said. The Kiymako words returned easily. "This time I won't need to cause any trouble – you have my oath."

The innkeeper raised a grey eyebrow. "Is that so?"

"It is."

"Last time you stirred up plenty of trouble."

"I'm glad to see your wonderful establishment escaped unscathed, at least."

Mrs Ku stared a little longer before nodding and stepping back. "Some of the changes you brought were for the better, I'll admit."

In the darkened common room, lit only by the pale light of the moon, she led them around tables to the counter where she collected a steel plate with triangular patterns that would match a door above. "Last room available. No objections, I take it?"

"Your generosity is appreciated," Never said as he reached for money but the innkeeper waved a hand.

"Tomorrow is soon enough. There's a place you can get your money changed in the port markets."

"Thank you again."

The woman lit a flower-shaped lamp and led them upstairs and to the room before handing the light to Rikeva and striding back down, muttering about broken sleep as she did.

Never used the plate to open the door to a sparse room. One bed, one closed window and a water barrel in the corner. "I'll take the floor," he said as he knelt and removed the bedroll from his pack.

"Very gentlemanly, but you worked harder than I to get us here."

"I don't mind, truly."

Rikeva sat on the bed. "Hmmm, why don't we settle this with a game of tira-tra?"

A game all Quisoan children were familiar with, and plenty of Marlosi ones too. Gamblers even used it sometimes when no cards or dice could be found. "It's been a *long* time."

"It's easy," she said as she lifted her hand, first and last fingers only raised, somewhat like horns. "Deer." Next, she put thumb and forefingers together. "Serpent." And finally, she spread thumb and forefinger apart – the wingspan of a Condor, which was the least realistic, but then, they were all vague by design, easy shapes for children to make.

"On whose count?" he asked.

"Mine," she said as she knelt before him. "Remember the rest of the rules?"

He nodded. "I think so." The aim was to match symbols. If your opponent made the same shape as you did on your turn, you won. The game rested on the notion that you could call whatever animal you wanted, while making another with your hand, if you so wished. Snow had often tried to double bluff, calling Deer while making the symbol for Deer. "I'll call first, then."

"Just a moment." Rikeva leant a little closer, her blue eyes meeting his. "Lock eyes first."

So close, the scent of citrus reached him again. "Huh?"

"No 'reading', right?"

Some tira-tra players became good at predicting what animal would be shown by reading body language and the way their opponents moved their hands. Locking eyes was a common counter, but it wasn't usually done with faces so close together.

"Right."

Rikeva counted to three and he spoke when she finished. "Deer." At the same time, he made the shape for Serpent.

"Check," Rikeva said with a smile.

He glanced down and her hand revealed the Condor. No win, no loss.

"Your turn," Never said and began the count.

Rikeva kept her gazed locked upon his. Was there a message beyond the game itself? She'd not been shy so far, at least, when it came to words.

"Deer," she said on 'three'.

Never glanced down and his hand showed the deer – as did hers, and he smiled. "You made that look easy."

"Don't worry," she said as she moved to the bed. "We can practise tomorrow."

"I don't like my chances, even with practise."

Never arranged his bedding and removed his boots and tunic before taking a final drink from his flask. Next, he stretched across the bedroll and almost groaned – the lamp. He reached out to douse the light.

In the dark, his heartbeat was a little too swift.

He held his breath – what if he rose and joined Rikeva? Had she made it clear? Or were the signs just signs he wanted? And he *did* want them to be true. That was not really a surprise, either.

Still holding his breath, Never rose to a half-sitting position.

No.

Maybe she'd been trying to tell him something, maybe it was just a ploy to win the bed, but misreading any so-called 'signs' was the kind of mistake that would make travelling with Rikeva too uncomfortable. He'd already come to depend on her and more. He'd promised Rikeva a cure. That had to be his priority.

Never lay back down and closed his eyes.

Chapter 18

When Never woke to a face-full of sunlight, he turned from the window with a muttered curse, wrapping the pillow around his head. Even that was a little too much effort, considering his tongue was twice its usual size.

Once his eyes adjusted, he rose to an empty room.

The bed had been made but Rikeva's pack remained and her staff leant against the wall nearby. Had she gone to relieve herself? Never moved to the water barrel and splashed his face before doing what he could about his torso, water dripping all over the place.

He dressed but before he could seek her, the door opened and Rikeva entered. "Don't worry about the room," she said. "I've paid, just a small gemstone but it was enough."

"Mrs Ku understood?"

"Of course. No-one misunderstands money, Never."

"Right, stupid question."

"I forgive you." Rikeva smiled as she collected her things. "If you don't mind skipping breakfast, I think we should try that symbol on your chest."

Never sighed, exaggerating the sound. "I'm beginning to feel like a chariot. Or a horse."

"Not at all, you're faster than either."

"Faint praise but I'll take it." Never buckled his pack then removed his tunic and unsheathed a dagger to prick his finger. Without the silver glow he had to estimate as he drew red lines across his chest, but barely halfway through the symbol the familiar five-pointed leaf began to glow – gold this time.

Rikeva hopped closer, grabbing his pack as she reached out – just in time to catch his hand and be engulfed in the light.

When the glow cleared, the soothing green of the forest was revealed, ridges of the surrounding bamboo glistening with a faint damp, still mostly protected from the rising sun. There were no hints of any shrine by day, just old loam in a small clearing.

The scene was likely more picturesque in last night's moonlight, but Never switched focus to the branches and their pods. He moved between them until he found the mountains and a *forasa* that might have been the Vale of Lights near Ayuni's village, and one even closer still, but he didn't reach for either.

Doubt and desire from the night before had faded, replaced by the hesitance Rikeva picked up on before their stay in Najin. Guilt and shame. How easily they'd held him back before and how doggedly they clung to him now.

He hadn't visited Ayuni since fleeing the shrine of the Phoenix in a bitter state that now seemed quite childish. After all, Ayuni's own words were clear. *I need my brother.*

And her smile had been sad – too sad in his memory,

as though she knew he would not keep his promise to return in good time. His stomach seemed to twist, as if fully acknowledging the guilt lent the emotion new strength.

All that time spent desperate for family and he'd put off seeing her again, for far too long.

Would she forgive him?

"Is there trouble with the symbols?" Rikeva asked.

Time to face up to his mistake. "No. I think I have one that will take us directly into the cavern."

She took his hand. "Sounds perfect to me."

Light engulfed them once more.

When it faded, Never found himself within a familiar, stretching stone cavern that was no longer completely open to the elements – a lattice-frame of wood and vine stretched above now, fiery orange flowers budding across the green tendrils.

It protected an enormous egg of stone, rearing several storeys tall, the sides gleaming in the growing light. The egg in turn stood within a new garden. And where once it had been ruled by weeds or emptiness, the place was now restored. Paved paths lined with moss that grew in neat lines, curving away to stands of young bamboo or maple, where white benches had been arranged in circles.

All stood empty as Never led Rikeva closer to the egg, its dark surface beginning to glow as a stone door slid open. It revealed the short, darkened passage leading to the nest, and Never paused within.

Ahead, more low stone benches were arranged to face the magnificent nest. Even from a distance, the detail on the black marble gave the impression of real twigs and the occasional soft feather. Still a work of art.

"Never?"

Ayuni stood in the garden, eyes wide.

She still wore her pink and white silks, only now a soft blue had been woven into the pattern too, perhaps a river running between flowers? She even wore a blossom in her silky dark hair.

She was just as he remembered, but she had grown too, both in height and in her sense of calm – her doubts had faded and a wisdom beyond her years now rested in her dark eyes, an even preternatural grace to go with the sense of vast power.

But it receded when she threw down a garden fork and ran across the stone. She leapt into a hug, smiling through tears. "I'm glad you're finally here."

He swallowed. "Ayuni. I'm sorry."

"You can make it up to me by staying a little longer this time," she said, and her words were too gentle for a rebuke and more generous than he deserved.

"I will," he promised. Then blinked. "You're not inside. I thought..."

"I'm still bound to the Shrine, but I can move freely around this place, Never, even to the village, just as Mother could," she said.

"I just assumed... Well, that's a relief."

Ayuni smiled then looked to Rikeva. "I'm sorry, I should have introduced myself and welcomed you," she said, speaking Marlosi. Her accent was light. How long had she been practising?

"It's an honour to meet you, Great Phoenix," Rikeva said.

"Please do not worry about any formalities," Ayuni

replied with another smile. "Come, let's sit."

Ayuni led them beyond the egg to the trio of stone huts; one of which he'd visited to collect the fire-stone necklace, but now the homes had been restored, new glass in the windows and whitewash applied to the walls.

Beyond, on a lower tier, more homes waited. These too had been repaired and some expanded with more lattice and gardens, greens and pinks everywhere, the soft chirping of birds from the branches.

Yet most surprising were the tiny streams that ran between the homes and beside the paths, appearing and disappearing into walls and beneath the walkways, often lined by strips of moss. Blossoms floated along the water too, though it wasn't clear from where they came.

Inside one of the larger buildings, Ayuni seated them around a long table lit by stretching windows. The walls had been lined with shelves and books, maps and paintings of other places: the snows of Vidya, the pale forest of Hanik and plenty of the warm colours common to the Marlosi plains.

"Sister Sikoka brings them, to help me travel," Ayuni explained. "But I am not so regretful as she believes, and learning the languages is fun."

"Your Marlosi is good to my ear," he said. "Are you learning Hanik also?"

"I am," she said. "Though my progress there is slower. But it is not just the duty of my role, I enjoy it too."

"Is Sister Sikoka here?" Never asked. Few, if any of the homes suggested anyone was living there, despite the improvements.

"No, she is in the village below, working with everyone

else," Ayuni said. "Biyo should be tending to the crops while others are still expanding the entryway – we've been working on making the village more accessible but progress is a little slow. I want to build more homes too," she said, then folded her hands together. "But I shouldn't keep you from what brought you here. It wasn't just to visit, I know."

"Then you know of what's happening to the east?" Never asked.

Ayuni nodded. "Bad news flies on swift wings. Tell me what you know, then later, I want to hear about your travels too."

"Gladly," he said. "About the Stone Plague, we've searched ancient texts and found suggestions of a 'Holy Fire' that might have been used to fight it off. It made me wonder about your own Fires of Heaven."

"That is actually familiar," she said. "I can almost remember..."

"You can remember?" Rikeva asked.

She nodded. "Over the next decade I will continue to absorb the memories from generations of my family, from each of the Phoenixes who lived before me."

Rikeva lowered her cup. "That long?"

Ayuni smiled. "There is a lot to learn. Even now, I might need a little time to sort through the memories."

"Can we help somehow?" Never asked.

"No, but don't worry. Even if they're not clear, I know there is a line back to my ancestors, to a time where a Phoenix faced the Malecaphera. Let's eat first. Then we can see if the Fires of Heaven are what you have been seeking."

"Does that mean you'll have to lend Never your power?" Rikeva asked.

She nodded, and it did seem that there was a trace of sadness to her bearing. "I'd love to help you myself..."

"You will be," Never said, reaching to place his hand over hers.

"Thank you, Never."

Chapter 19

"Immolation?"

Never rose from one of the white benches in the garden with Rikeva and Biyo, Ayuni's attendant, who stood in the black robes of a monk, his once sombre expression now more calm. No other monks or villagers were present, obviously still hard at work elsewhere, but the shrine and village seemed less empty now, even with one additional person.

"Nothing so dramatic," Ayuni said with a smile.

"So... what does that leave us? Will I have to eat an egg or something?"

She laughed now, a sweet sound. "No, not that either."

"Really, Never?" Rikeva asked, her tone quite disapproving.

"Maybe I'll stop trying to guess, then."

Ayuni rolled up her sleeves. "I have something in mind that's far simpler and it should work, considering your Amouni bloodline."

"Here, My Lady?" Biyo asked. "Are you rested enough?"

She nodded as blue and green light glowed around her, flickering as a pair of wings appeared. They stretched out in magnificent deep blue with a sea-green tint, and she drew both near, giving her the look of an Amouni as much as the Great Phoenix.

But she did not transform, instead reaching out to pluck two long feathers from her wings. "This will probably hurt, Never. Do you still want to try?"

He let his own dark wings free and stepped closer. "A little pain is no price to pay compared to what others will suffer if we can't stop Oleksan."

"I thought you'd say something like that," Ayuni said as her wings vanished. But the two feathers remained and she lifted them, one in each hand, quills poised as if to strike. "Forgive me if this is worse than I'm predicting."

"Of course," he said.

Ayuni reached up and jabbed her feathers into his wings, twin spikes of discomfort following.

She stepped back. "They fit perfectly."

Never flexed his wings; they seemed just as strong, just as responsive... and yet, there was a new warmth. But the warmth grew to a burning, and then a searing pain. He stiffened, clenching his jaw.

"Never?"

"I'll be fine," he gritted out, yet his wings felt like they were afire.

The searing heat lashed its way down his shoulders and into his spine, growing worse. It drove him to his knees, and he hunched over – hands clenched to keep from hollering, and though someone called his name and seemed to draw near, he could not tell who. The sense of a vast, ancient benevolence brushed against his mind and in that moment the pain vanished.

And then it was over, leaving only his harsh breathing. Never wiped away the sweat upon his brow, ignoring the tremble in his hand. "I think... it worked."

"Are you sure you're all right?" Rikeva asked.

She stood over him, Ayuni and Biyo too, but he nodded as he rose, keeping his wings unmoving for now, and drew one of his blades. "Let's do a little test."

"You'll be careful with the garden, won't you?" Biyo asked.

"I will." Never lifted the blade and set the point to his skin, then stopped. Was the crimson-fire somehow nearer, easier to sense? Could it be called without—

A globe of bloody flame sprang up around his hand. "Well. That's one change. Let's see what else I can do."

In the quiet that followed his words, he reached for the faint trace of the Phoenix, of Ayuni, and without any more effort, the flame turned blue and green. The additional heat and power was obvious but as with the crimson-fire, his skin did not burn.

Never let the fire fade with a grin. "Just one more test."

***

Morning light once again fell across Ayuni's table where they gathered in her study, and despite the strain it put on his still tender back, Never leant over the table's surface and slid a slip of paper away from the other pieces – all written with words they had gathered at Rikeva's request.

Oracle.

"This I think we can set to one side, considering the source," he said, glancing at Ayuni, who nodded – her opinion of their father had not changed. A relief.

Rikeva slid the piece of paper marked 'Holy Fire' to its own space, adding the one for 'Barrier' with it and 'Imperial Forces'. She glanced around the small group. "These are linked as far as I can see."

"Agreed," Never said. "Leaving Jardila, her priests and the soma in another group."

Rikeva made the adjustments.

Ayuni leant over the table, sliding the names of the Amouni books together. "What of these?"

"Perhaps nothing," Never said. "We do not know where *The Origin* can be found and neither *The Forgotten Ones* nor *A History of the North Spear* hold answers to defeating Oleksan. Or the Stone Plague. They might hide some secrets yet... but I'm starting to wonder, can we afford to search for them any longer without solid leads?"

"You know my feelings on that, Never," Rikeva said.

"Then you still need to test the Fires of Heaven. And with the *forasa*, it wouldn't take long," Ayuni suggested.

He nodded.

Rikeva rested a finger upon 'Soma'. "What if Jardila cannot find a cure? Who else can we ask?"

Never retook his seat, muscles still unhappy. A good sleep in a nice bed would have been welcome. "Perhaps Elina's grandfather."

"Elina, the Hanik Queen?"

"Yes. Olivor has long been seeking and preserving knowledge of the Amouni. Perhaps he can help." And more so than Father's chamber. Olivor might even have been a better first choice.

"Then let's visit him before we return to try your fire," Rikeva said.

"All right. There is one more worth seeking – The Bleak Man," Never said, going on to explain when her expression suggested she did not recognise the name. And the longer he spoke, the more he realised another mistake. "I should have thought of him sooner. He is probably old enough to recall *something* we can use."

"Then he's on the list too," Rikeva said as she leant back in her chair. "When do we leave?"

Was it so far from noon? "Let's eat first." He didn't add that the thought of moving now, and possibly having to fly soon after, did *not* appeal.

"No objections here, the sweet pods are amazing."

Ayuni smiled. "I'll call for Biyo–"

"Please, let me help," Rikeva said as she stood.

"As my guest, I really should..." Ayuni trailed off, tilting her head as if listening to an unheard voice. "Never, there is someone nearing that wishes to see you."

"Outside?"

"No. It is Mukatagami... he has been travelling from the south for some time now," Ayuni paused to close her eyes. "Ah. He brings a stranger... and she has travelled from even farther."

Rikeva glanced at Never as she whispered. "Is she listening to this Mukatagami speak from afar?"

Never nodded. "Is Muka all right, Ayuni?"

"He does not say, only that *she* seems unwell – and has travelled from Vadiya to find you... they will arrive this evening..." Ayuni opened her eyes. "I have lost contact, sorry."

Never stood and started to pace, as much for his stiffening back as his concern. Could it be Sacha? Afflicted with something her traces of Amouni healing could not defeat? Could she have known to travel to Kiymako? "She would have needed to leave *before* knowing I'd even come here," he murmured.

"It sounds like someone needs your help," Rikeva said.

"Can you wait until they arrive? If not, I can take you to Jardila if you want to check on her progress," he offered. "Or to your tribe?"

Rikeva hesitated. "The *forasa* do make travel easier, but someone needs your help. I'll help too if I'm able."

"Why don't you make your final decision after that meal?" Ayuni asked.

"I can't argue with that suggestion."

Together, they left for the larger, central kitchen the village used to feed visitors and pilgrims, but Never followed a little more slowly, pausing by one of the winding waterways.

Who sought him?

Was it worth using an opal? Did Ayuni even have one at the shrine? He did not call ahead to ask. After all, Muka would have left already. Flying toward wherever Muka had last been was probably out of the question. Even a *forasa* couldn't place him close by, he'd be back to flying.

He sighed and continued on. "Exercise a little patience, whether you like it or not, fool."

After the meal, Never and Rikeva helped Ayuni with simple tasks, lifting and carrying or rearranging smaller boxes or items and he found himself watching Rikeva often, the game of tira-tra coming to mind once more. So often did he find himself imagining... specific things the game might have led to, that by the time evening fell, he had his fair share of minor bruises.

Worse, his spine was afire once more. Not the 'Holy Fire' somehow attacking him within, but his own choices. After the shock and pain at gaining the new fire, continuing to work had been a mistake. Now, his muscles and bones were screeching at him to stop, to finally rest, and ignoring the warnings earlier had a price.

So he skipped the evening meal, made his apologies and crawled into the bed Ayuni had arranged for him where he lay very still, closing his eyes and waiting for sleep to claim him.

Chapter 20

"Not what I imagined I'd be waking up to," Never said as he frowned down at the press of corpses that crowded the wooden gates, spreading in a mass of tangled limbs beneath the wall – thousands easily, a mass of gaunt flesh and mud-caked bones, skulls grinning up in perpetual silence, lit by the faint moon.

Having been roused by Rikeva hours after seeking his rest, he'd followed her, Ayuni and Biyo back down the mountain passage. It had been expanded in places, and Ayuni's voice echoed as she explained the threat.

And when they'd reached the Vale of Lights, Never found that the old festival platform had been turned into sturdy walls with a solid gate, along with new homes and fences, farming plots and other structures.

In the village, monks in their dark robes, pilgrims too, men and women alike all stood armed and ready where they had gathered beneath the wall. Murmurs and calls of relief and gratitude rose when Ayuni neared, her expression determined.

"What's the plan?" Rikeva asked, glaring down at the army.

The only sounds that reached them were faint clacking of bones and old weapons, though once again, not every figure held a blade and no-one bore armour. What clothes did remain were often ragged and threadbare.

"I'd be surprised if I had enough blood to burn all of them."

Ayuni braced her hands upon the parapet as she glanced over. "I was not convinced of this wall at first. I want people to feel free to visit us but now I find myself glad."

Sister Sikoka joined them from farther along the wall, where other monks stood, bows in hand. She had not changed, grey-haired and thin, but she was almost smiling now. "Your wisdom is clear, Great Phoenix."

Ayuni smiled, a faint change to her lips only. "That almost sounds like you're mocking me, Sikoka."

"Of course not. I, too, feel the same relief."

"Can you stop them, My Lady?" Biyo asked. "So far from the Shrine?"

She nodded. "I am at my limits, I admit, but Mukatagami is drawing near. I must clear the way. Never, Rikeva, could you deal with any poor souls that remain?"

"Of course," he said, but hesitated. "Are you truly able to do this?"

"I am." His sister took a step back from the parapet and without ceremony, raised outstretched arms.

A mighty roar followed as twisting blue and green flames shot up into the sky.

Punishing heat emanated from the enormous barrier

and while Never, Rikeva and the monks shielded their faces, Ayuni did not so much as flinch.

When she lowered her arms, the inferno fell away and shadows returned as she gripped the parapet once more. "I'm sorry, Never, but it's not easy this far from the nest. There shouldn't be many left, at least."

He squinted down at the sea of ash barely visible in the starlight save for smouldering embers winking up at him. "No, that was perfect." A few dozen corpse-creatures stood at the edges of the once impressive army, but they did not seem particularly troubled by the Phoenix fire.

In fact, they were already beginning to turn to face the road.

Ayuni didn't answer – she had slumped against the wall.

Sikoka and Biyo started forward, but Rikeva was already at Ayuni's side, lifting Never's sister easily. "I'll take her back. Will you be able to handle things here?"

"I will," he said.

"Be careful, Never," Ayuni whispered.

"Always," he replied with a smile, though it probably wasn't the truth precisely and his smile did not last. Would Ayuni recover? So far from the shrine? He knew so little.

"I'll hurry back," Rikeva said as she started toward the stair, joined by Biyo.

Sister Sikoka stared after them.

"Is she going to be all right?" Never asked.

"She will need to spend some time in the nest first, but yes."

"Good." Never let his wings free. "Can you look after the gates when Muka nears?"

"Certainly."

Never took a running leap and cleared the parapet, gliding down, Amouni blade ready. Crimson-fire was already blazing in his hands as he hit the ground running, having missed most of the ash.

Half the creatures turned to him, one lifting a bow as others charged.

Never raised a hand, flames flaring. The skeleton let loose an arrow – only for it to be consumed by flame.

A thunder of hooves from the forest drew near.

The remaining figures charged the tree line, where what appeared to be a black carriage, barely discernible in the starlight, had emerged. But the horses did not slow; the driver was going to scatter the corpse-warriors.

Not every skeletal figure had turned away from Never; the nearest dove at him with hands outstretched.

Never shot another globe of crimson fire and his enemy burst into ash. He let twin streams free now, and swung them across the road to incinerate the remaining skeletons as the whinnying of horses echoed across the night, wheels rumbling to a halt.

The carriage had been fitted with coverings, heavy blankets placed over the windows and the door, and the figure sitting in the driver's seat bore hints of silver in hair and beard, barely discernible in the starlight.

"Found you at last, Never," Mukatagami said.

"I didn't know you could drive a carriage like that," he replied.

The man extended a hand, the hilt of his *sisan* visible when he leant down. Never accepted the help and settled into the seat next to the warrior monk. "Sorry about the unpleasant welcome."

"Those things have plagued us for days now," Muka replied, voice calm, as though he mentioned an inconvenience only.

"Us, meaning you and my visitor?"

He nodded. "I've barely seen her this whole time, since she has to rest during the day, but when we camp at night she protects us from the ancient warriors."

"Illya."

"That's her. She wants to warn you about something – a patrol found her travelling across the Southern Reeds. She sailed from Vadiya, alone somehow."

"She's a nekromant; I'm not actually sure of the extent of her abilities."

"Well, she brings a dire message, though you can no doubt guess at least a part of it."

"The Burnished King and his undead warriors."

He nodded. "Only she said something a little more troubling before she explained it all to me." A hint of worry had entered his voice. "She said that the dead were arguing over whom to side with."

"Side with?" *That* was an unpleasant sentence, more so due to the fact that it made little sense. "The dead? Between whom?"

"You and Oleksan, Amouni and Malecaphera."

Chapter 21

Ayuni's library was lit only by dying starlight beyond the windows. Illya sat in her white feathered vest, hair faintly luminous. As she spoke, the vivid blue of her eyes seemed to see beyond those gathered, though the now-recovered Ayuni had been most fascinated by the black feather tattoos that ran down the nekromant's cheeks.

"Is the lamp in the hall too much?" Rikeva asked as she returned, angling the door after her as Never translated.

"Perhaps a little more," Illya said, and he translated her answer too. "Forgive me, but only the stars and the moon are tolerable."

"Of course."

Never waited for more darkness to fall across the room. "I know not everyone will be aware of all that Illya can do, and I'm not either, but she is one of the few people that can speak with the dead."

"And they have a message for Never," Muka added into the hush.

Illya closed her eyes and Ayuni's study dimmed a little

further. She rubbed at her temples. "There has been chaos. Sometimes their voices are too loud, too scattered, too many. And despite the truth of Never's words, we cannot always communicate – there's so much fear and desperation."

"Of what?" Rikeva asked.

"Life. Or at least, a return. That's what Oleksan is promising the God Arkenon will deliver, should he be restored and allowed to cover the lands in his decay." Illya glanced around the room. "That is part of why the dead sent me to find you, Never."

"The dead knew he would be here?" Ayuni asked.

She nodded. "Both those that wish to help, and those who seek to hinder."

"Then are the skeletons that have been attacking us acting on their own desires to return to life? Or are they being driven by the Burnished King?" Rikeva asked.

"In a way, both," Illya explained. "While he is still marshalling his power, he can only deceive the most desperate of the dead. Until he breaks the Seals and is fully restored, he is forced to act mostly through surrogates."

Rikeva sat back. "That was a *lot* of desperate corpses back there."

"Assuredly; the bitterness of death in war knows few bounds."

Another passage of silence fell over the table. Never opened his hands, only the faintest hints of scars now; his Amouni healing. Illya's words brought little comfort. Legions of the dead supporting him? A war of the fallen... To tear the dead from their rest to fight the Burnished King?

And to hear Illya tell it, some of the dead did not or *could not* rest.

Of all the mistakes he'd made so far, had not actually seeking out Illya been the worst? Even without her skills as a nekromant, she'd been the one to explain the threat of the Burnished King. Had an inflexible reliance on the Amouni legends sent him astray? It was... disappointing to discover that there was no immunity to the Amouni hubris, simply because he was among the last.

"How can we stop Oleksan before it comes to that? A war of the dead," he added.

"Destroy the Temple Trivium."

Never straightened. "Then it still exists. Beneath the Lakes?"

"Yes."

Ayuni turned to Never. "That name is familiar."

"I can describe the legend, if you like?" Illya offered.

"Please," she replied.

And while Illya had shared something of the Burnished King's legend back in Vadiya, she had not mentioned the Temple Trivium.

The nekromant settled into her seat. "Never, you may know some of these details – considering the Amouni role in sealing The Burnished King in his own Temple."

"Only what I learnt from the Guides, which was not much."

"Then for everyone's benefit, let me begin with the Legend of the Burnished King as I learnt it in Vadiya." She paused. "I will not share every detail, as I know the hour grows late. The dead do not tell this tale, though it marries well enough with what Oleksan is seeking now.

"As a young warrior priest, Oleksan of Vadiya fell into the clutches of Arkenon, fooled by promises of a power able to stamp out injustice. Oleksan's boyhood temple was razed by a neighbouring city-state, and his desperation for justice all too swiftly became lust for revenge, making him an easy target for Arkenon.

"He built his power by leading on the battlefield and using the clever words of Arkenon to woo leaders of the city-states, and over the next four years, he eventually unified much of what we call Vadiya today. But by then, battle-lust had changed Oleksan, and he began to see insult, insubordination and the threat of betrayal everywhere. In the glitter of every smiling eye, he saw only daggers."

"We have a not dissimilar tale here," Ayuni said. "Asaji of the Shadows."

"Only defeated by a bitter betrayal," Muka added.

Illya nodded. "Oleksan's story bears no happy ending either. His time as glorious ruler would fade swiftly, after a bright day beneath plum blossoms in the courtyard of his keep, the Burnished King lay the reprehensible seeds of his new plan; a madness courtesy of Arkenon. It started with the slaughter of his outer vassals, fuelled by lies about traitorous alliances with Hanik.

"And yet, what followed was enough to turn the stomachs of even his most staunch supporters. Oleksan ordered the bodies of men, women and children, of animals and foodstuffs, possessions, homes – everything – to be burnt down to ash and mixed with droppings and rotten fish and spread across the very lands. When asked, he claimed it was for such a bleak compost to help the land begin anew; he had become obsessed with returning the lands to a supposedly pristine time."

Never paused his translation to glance at the others; even

in the darkness their horror mirrored his own.

Illya continued. "When it was done, Oleksan turned his attention to all those who opposed him, and some who had not. In time, he turned east, looking to Hanik and beyond, claiming that repeating the process across all lands was the only way to ensure a golden future. Yet only those he had chosen would survive to see this new land."

"But the Amouni intervened when he tried to move on Hanik?" Ayuni asked.

"Perhaps their first steps were taken sooner," she replied. "They likely knew of Arkenon's influence, and marshalled their forces, raising an army and a vanguard of Ascended warriors to strike back and in time, Seal the Burnished King and his plague hammer."

Rikeva exhaled. "So, Oleksan is going to use his powers to slaughter just about everything, then use the bodies as fertilizer for a new world, and we need to raise an army of Amouni to stop him?"

"In essence."

Rikeva turned to Never. "How many more like you?"

"One."

"Only one?"

"That I know of. A man named Cog. His blood line is not the same as mine, so he cannot do all that I can," he said. "And capable as I know he is, we are but two."

"Can armies be raised, nonetheless?" Muka asked.

"I want to avoid that much death at all costs," Never replied. And something Illya said had caught his attention, not just the phrase 'Ascended warriors', which was not one he'd heard before, but mention of the Seals. "How does the Temple Trivium connect to the Seals?"

"According to the dead, Oleksan needs it to break the final Seal. That will supposedly allow him access to Arkenon's power – enough to achieve his goal of a new world."

"Final? He's already broken the second?"

"So say the dead; it lay within the temple itself."

He leant closer. "If the first was located at Mount Siyapol, and the second in the Temple, where is the third?"

"In the northern reaches of Marlosi – the Amber Isle."

Chapter 22

"Illya, I want to ask the dead something," Never said after most of the small group sought their rest. "More than one question, actually."

She stood in an archway that led to connecting rooms, one of which had already been fitted with heavy black curtains for the coming day. Her pale hair seemed to hold a hint of the blue glow from her eyes. "I think I can guess at least one of them," she replied. "It is not always like this, but so vehement are the disagreements that I have been able to learn much simply by eavesdropping. And there *is* something seeking you... but few of the dead seem to understand it. Most are afraid."

A chill followed her words. "Wonderful."

Best to leave Kiymako as soon as possible, to avoid putting Ayuni and the others at risk, at least until the thing sent to hunt him had been dealt with. Rikeva too, remained in danger the longer she stayed by his side. "What about Oleksan himself? Can the Holy Fire stop him, does anyone know?"

"That is more a question for the past. The dead see the world today very well, but not yesterday and not tomorrow. But considering he has sent something to hunt you, it seems clear you are a threat."

"That's what I hope," Never said, and maybe it shouldn't have been a surprise. "Then he is in the Temple Trivium, beneath the Lakes now? Trying to raise it?"

She nodded. "Though none seem to know specifics. Many remain overwhelmed by the gifts offered; the urge to return. They can be difficult to question in that regard, unlike the stakolin for example, since some of those returned to living death simply do not answer me at all."

He paused to rub at the back of his neck, weariness creeping over him once more. "Illya, of those who came to you – do they know me somehow? Are they people *I* have known?"

"Not that I am aware. The dead do not always have much sense of self. They recognise you only as Amouni," she said. "I have probably made them seem too organised, but to be honest few seem as much. I suspect that only Oleksan creates cohesion in those he deceives, and the others seem simply to be rejecting him – perhaps as they might have in life."

Her words offered some measure of relief. "Ah. Thank you, that is mostly good news, I think."

"Was there someone specific you sought?"

He hesitated. *Was* there someone? Snow who had been much in his memories of late. Perhaps Mother... And yet, what would he say to either? Was it worth calling back Father, just to curse him? A childish notion.

"I cannot guarantee anything, Never, but if you think of

someone you wish for me to seek, let me know and I will try," she offered.

"I appreciate that," he replied, but no name came to mind.

She nodded. "Now I must rest, the dawn approaches."

"Can I help arrange the coverings?" Never asked.

"That would be kind, Never," she said as she turned to the nearest room, presumably a place where Ayuni rested after study. At the doorway, Illya paused. "There is one more thing."

"Another message?"

"Just a suspicion. The dead see mostly what they want to see, or what they are afraid to see. Some are more aware, and believe there is something Oleksan fears, other than you."

"Do they know what it is?"

"No. Only that this mysterious thing exists," she replied, and though it was not close to light outside, she was beginning to squint. "I will share details should I learn more."

"And I am sorry to have kept you so long; I hope the light hasn't been too painful."

"Not unbearable, but I am glad to rest now," she replied.

"Thank you again," he said as she shut the door.

***

It was noon before Never stood with Rikeva near the shrine garden's *forasa*, Ayuni, Mukatagami and Sister Sikoka nearby.

"Take care of each other," Never said after he embraced his sister.

"We will," Muka replied with a nod. "Although, Ayuni protects us more so."

Ayuni smiled. "We depend on you too."

Muka hesitated then, hand on the hilt of his blade. In the light of day, it seemed there was a touch *less* grey in his beard, perhaps even fewer lines upon his face. "Are you sure you do not wish for me to raise arms here? Wanatek and others will meet the threat."

Never shook his head slowly. "No. Better to gather them to protect your homes – ready them in case the Stone Plague reaches your shores. Take the precautions we spoke of earlier."

The warrior sighed. "If you are certain."

"So little seems certain, but I won't risk so many lives when I can stop him myself."

"Isn't it better to accept all the help you can while we're unsure?" Rikeva asked.

"As a rule, yes," he replied. "But no armies need set sail unless as a last resort. If the dead rise here once more, who will protect the people if the best warriors are in southern Marlosi?"

"Then you have a plan, I hope?" Sister Shikoa asked. "Not going to fly off into the Burnished King's lair alone?"

"Something better than that," he said. "I think it's time to focus on the cure first, now that I can use the Heaven's Fire."

She nodded.

"Are you sure you need nothing else?" Ayuni asked, a trace of sadness in her eyes – no doubt he bore something of the same look. It *was* hard to leave his sister, harder this time when it was a parting unfettered by bitterness.

"Rikeva would probably carry off your entire supply of sweet pods if we let her, but I think we're fine," he said.

Rikeva glanced away. "I didn't know liking food was a crime."

Laughter filled the shrine.

"Best to shield your eyes, everyone," Never said as he reached for the web of *forasa*, their buds, names and images taking over his vision, but this time, he tried to hold on to the scene before him at the same time – and it worked.

Ayuni was waving as the light grew and swiftly covered her, and he raised his own arm but couldn't be sure she'd seen.

***

Once more, Never delivered Rikeva to the Marlosi plains – his back and wings seeming fully recovered now. They were near enough to a village where she might find a horse and be able to check upon her people before heading for Hanik. "Want me to fly you the rest of the way?" he asked as she rearranged her pack, kneeling in the yellowed grass beside a twisting road.

"No need," she replied. "I won't be long and the quicker you learn about Jardila's efforts, the quicker we can act, whether it's to use her cure or to visit City-Sedrin."

"Right. Where will I meet you?"

Rikeva hoisted her pack. "East of here."

"I hope you find them well, all things considered."

"Me too, Never," Rikeva said with a small smile, then set off for the village at a jog.

Never watched her leave before striding off into the fields, avoiding folks who toiled there as best he could before tracing the symbol over his chest – without blood, as a test – and blessedly, the silver glow engulfed him.

When Never landed back in the darkened shrine, he was already reaching for the *forasa* symbol in Isacina. The light blazed once more, and this time he arrived upon the plain beyond the walls instead of in the fountain. He leapt forth immediately, dark wings sending him sailing up and over the city with ease. Shouts of panic and awe followed him from the gates, but he ignored them as he flew across the city, shooting for the pale wings of Pacela's Spire like an arrow.

Some of Rikeva's impatience was obviously wearing off on him.

This time he didn't land atop the Spire, for scores of yellow-robed figures moved about in the square, whether between tents or to show citizens to and from the stalls – and amongst them all, the proud figure of Jardila.

Never banked and swung around to swoop down behind a nearby building, startling a beggar at the mouth of an alley as he did. The young man's eyes were wide as he scrambled back, snatching after a small bag of possessions.

"Sorry, friend," Never said, flicking a silver coin through the air as he strode off.

The man's startled thanks followed Never as he neared lines of people at the square – and almost before he noted the rigid movements, it was the murmuring panic that told him the Stone Plague had reached the city.

He quickened his step once inside the square, approaching Jardila who directed her people to and from the pavilions, many carrying vials of soma in small boxes. It was a welcome sight; Jardila doing something to combat the fears she held during the invasion, fears that Pacela's chosen had withdrawn too far from the people of the city.

The High Priestess caught sight of Never before priest or patient could question him, her expression one of surprise. "Back already?"

"I feel like I should be more surprised," he said, looking around at patients being shown to tents. "You've already found more *hizre*? Or a complete cure?"

She sighed. "No. We have only been able to improve its potency by over half, but it is not enough alone. We will not stop searching. And combined with Pacela's Breath, we are making a difference..."

"You don't sound convinced, but improving the soma that much buys us more time."

"We are also helping the Empress in her search," she replied. "There is concern that we cannot locate from which building or well the Stone Plague is spreading. It is not easy, since few in the poorer quarters trust the soldiers. Or us, I am ashamed to admit."

"Oh." If it was in the water already... "At least it spreads slowly if it's in a home."

"And what of you, then?" she asked as she nodded, her expression not holding out a lot of hope for his prediction.

"I can use the 'Holy Fire' now, and I mean to test it soon, but I think there's one more place I need to visit first. It might help with the cure."

"Then go with Pacela's Grace, we need your speed."

"Fast as I can," he replied.

***

Rikeva's tribe, the Doerin, had camped perhaps half a day's travel northwest from Red Ridge, and not too far from a nameless, sparkling stream that ran swift but not wide.

Their wheat-coloured wagons were still loaded with possessions and provisions, one carrying caged chickens with another holding sheets of canvas stretched over frames, used to paint and then read the stars. And while the dozens of tents were double-pegged and faint paths were forming between them, the hints of permanence to the place were offset by the lack of stone or wooden structures.

Fewer horses than expected were visible, but if needed, the tribe could leave swiftly enough. Perhaps that was true even in part due to the smaller numbers of the Doerin, perhaps only three score, including the children. How many had been robbed of life by the Stone Plague?

As he'd landed, sentries called to one another, but no-one brought bows or seemed ready to cast their daggers – Rikeva had obviously warned her people, and while he received nods, a few smiles and even the occasional greeting as he walked between the tents, most folks in their leather and constellation-patterned beads were busy with small and important tasks: fetching water, preparing or preserving food, mending clothing or attending to their mounts.

A young woman, or perhaps an older girl, met Never and offered to take him to Rikeva. Her wavy blonde hair and freckles suggested an innocence that did not match the weapons at her belt.

She also bore a pair of tattoos upon the backs of her hands, a custom he did not recall from his youth. The patterns were of the stars. "Rika is with Alena and Kardi. She told us to expect you, Hero," his guide said, speaking Quisoan.

He answered in kind. "Thank you, but you can call me Never, ah..."

She smiled, and there was something familiar about it. "I'm Haya."

"Thank you, Haya. I like your tattoos."

"Do you? My friends and I are all getting them," she said. "We got the idea from the other tribes but I think ours might be better."

He returned her smile. "How does your tribe fare?"

Her cheer faded. "No-one else has died yet... but my sister, Kardi can hardly move now. And she's not the only one. We're keeping them in those tents but it's hard." She pointed to a row of five tents set a little way apart. "I hate seeing them over there, cut off from us. They can't even share our meals at the fire."

"Rikeva and I will find a cure."

Haya nodded, still sombre. "So say the stars... but we don't know if it will be soon enough."

"They do?"

"We'd believe in Rika even if they didn't," Haya replied, and then paused before the first of the tents which had been separated from the camp, and lifted the flap. "They're in here. I'm not supposed to go inside, just to be safe."

Within, Rikeva knelt beside two women who lay beneath blankets, their features similar enough to be sisters; wavy blonde hair alike, and though they were both younger than Rikeva, they were older than Haya.

Kardi shared Rikeva's blue eyes while Alena's were grey... but more obvious finally, was that they were *all* family, from Rikeva to Haya.

Kardi lay propped up, water beside her – near enough for Alena to hold it to her lips, and Kardi's voice was strained when she thanked her sister. But she still looked to Rikeva, head moving only a little, to ask about Never. "So this is your handsome friend who's going to help you save us?"

Rikeva smiled. "I don't know if I described him like that, did I?"

"Maybe you did."

"Did she at least mention that I fly her everywhere without complaint?" Never asked with a smile.

"That's at least half-true," Rikeva replied, then turned back to her sisters. "We will return as soon as we have the cure, I promise."

Alena nodded. "We believe in you – just hurry, won't you?"

"We will," she said, then led Never back outside and sent Haya off to help with food preparation, her high spirits fading as they approached the stream. There, she bent to fill her flask. "This has to work, Never. There are four other families counting on me, and who knows how many others across the land by now. How did things go with Jardila?"

"They've improved the effects of the soma significantly, but it's still not a cure."

"I see." She took a long drink.

"Haya thinks we'll succeed, according to the stars."

"She does; it's a popular reading but I cannot rely only on those predictions."

"You have me," he said.

"I do." Rikeva rose with a small nod. "All right, take us to Hanik, Never."

Chapter 23

City-Sedrin contained more *forasa* symbols than Never had expected – within the city and the palace, along the outskirts of the city too – and most seemed extra responsive, giving accurate impressions of their location.

One offered a view of bluestone towers stretching high above the walls, flags of green, the silver tree upon their centre; the images seemed more current compared to some of the other locations he could have travelled. Another symbol would have taken them to stone piers, filled with river craft, the impression of white sails and rigging strong.

But the symbol he deemed best included a view of the towers and central domes of the palace, graceful balconies and walkways stretching between like works of art, the sparkling tops of each dome threaded with quartz.

The view from Olivor's tower? Hopefully.

Yet the more Never focused on the *forasa* with his mind, the more an unseen force seemed to rebuff him. Yet not with violence, it was more of an urge. It wanted him to wait?

"Found one, yet?" Rikeva asked where she paced beside

him, steps echoing in the cool, dark of the shrine.

"I believe so…"

"But?"

Never opened his eyes and again, kept half his attention on the map of *forasa*. Indistinct shapes interfered with his vision but he was able to see Rikeva well enough. "It feels like the *forasa* wants me to wait."

"All of them?"

"No, just the one that I've chosen."

She sighed. "And it's truly a better option that the others?"

"It puts us right in the palace, which is quicker than –" Never stopped. The block on the *forasa* was gone. He held out his arm. "We can leave."

Rikeva took his hand and the bright light blazed.

When it cleared, they stood within Olivor's tower – the same comfortable armchair overlooked a window, which in turn offered a view of the rest of the palace and its quartz domes, along with a huge courtyard below.

The same cluttered table and shelves greeted Never. Rows of vials and pots and delicate instruments that may or may not have been connected to the Amouni too, and a chandelier that he hadn't noticed from his last visit hung from the roof which, oddly, had been painted black.

"I hear footsteps," Rikeva said.

From beyond the door, the sound of slow footfalls descending reached him. Had that been the reason the symbol couldn't be used? Someone in the room, standing on the *forasa*, perhaps? Never strode to the door and opened it to call into the dim stairwell, the nearest window obviously hidden around a bend.

"Olivor, is that you by chance?" he called in Hanik.

The footfalls stopped and the man's scratchy voice rose – but it was also the twin voice Never recalled from their escape from the palace, a soothing, agreeable undercurrent. "Reveal yourself."

And despite the power in the man's voice, Never could have answered in any way he chose. Of course, there was no need to attempt deceit but his Amouni lineage was obviously enough to resist. "Olivor, it's Never. I need your help."

A moment of silence followed then his voice echoed. "Never? How... No matter, I'm on my way."

"We'll be waiting."

"We?"

"Yes. I'll introduce you to Rikeva and tell you all about the plague we're trying to stop once you get here. Save us shouting to each other."

The footsteps quickened a little. "I'm not a young man anymore, Never – but I'm hurrying, I promise."

"I can lend you a hand?"

"Nearly there," Olivor replied as he drew near, and soon enough, his kindly, wrinkled face came into view, white hair longer than before, combed quite neatly too. He wore the same long-sleeved grey robe, but now a new, simple symbol of Clera was more prominent upon the front – an open book.

The man was grinning as Never admitted him into his own tower and made the introductions, translating for Rikeva as he explained how they'd arrived, along with a few details of the truth behind the Stone Plague.

"Please, let's all sit," Olivor said, taking the armchair but waving for Never and Rikeva to draw stools closer. "And tell me more, if you would, about the plague. As much as I am curious about the *forasa* and ancient Amouni travel methods, I will do my best to help in whatever way possible."

Never began, once more translating for Rikeva, and by the end of the explanation, Olivor held her last vial of soma up to the light, frowning at the pale liquid.

"Can you help us?" Rikeva asked.

He nodded as he rose with a small groan. He began to search his books, arranging his vials and instruments, hands swift and sure, murmuring to himself as he did. Within moments, he'd made a small stack of books and started writing a list, using the stack as a writing surface.

"Forgive the short delay, and I don't want to raise your hopes... but based on what you've told me about this soma and the possible minerals found in the mines of Marlosi and even here, I believe I can prepare something within two days, maybe even sooner. I just need to contact an associate in the city regarding the *hizre* and something I believe will be far better." He paused to glance at them both. "Can you wait that long?"

"We can," Rikeva said.

He smiled as he strode to a hatch in the wall, signs of his fatigue vanished. "Leave it to me, young lady." He placed the list inside a box within then pulled a lever, and the box descended soundlessly.

"For supplies?" Never asked.

"Indeed," he said as he returned to the table and started to make more space to open the books. "I admit, the magnificent view from a tower is not the compensation it once was when I have to deal with all those stairs at my age."

"Understandable."

"Why don't you both head to down to lunch in my stead?" Olivor said. "It was meant to be Her Majesty and some old friends, but you'll be a welcome substitute, I've no doubt."

"We are sorry to interrupt," Rikeva said when Never translated.

He waved a hand. "I assure you it is no bother. And it'll be more fun than watching me work, I'm sure."

"Then we'll send you some food," Never said.

"Very kind of you," Olivor said, though he had already started flipping pages of one of his books.

Never closed the door behind them and led Rikeva down to ground level and then through halls lined with detailed paintings and bronze statues of kings and queens, to the palace courtyard, where he came to a stop. "I should have asked *where* they were eating. It didn't sound like a formal meal, at least."

"Ask one of the servants," Rikeva said, pointing to a pair of boys crossing the courtyard, arms laden with linen.

"I doubt they'd answer a stranger."

She shook her head. "Of course."

"On the other hand, I'm sure they'd send for someone if I mentioned that Never, the so-called Winged Hero of the War, would like to see the Queen."

"Let's find out."

Chapter 24

Night had fallen and Elina, Luis and Tsolde were still smiling and laughing, something they'd been doing since Never surprised them in the private dining hall. Now, seated in armchairs in a sitting room decorated by scenes of nature – forest glades, flowerbeds and a hidden waterfall – Never's own cheeks had grown a little sore from grinning.

Rikeva too, seemed to enjoy the stories they told, even when some took a turn toward more sombre moments, like with Karlaf or the stories of Snow...

Luis, who now wore a thin beard to go with his moustache, put his cup down. "There was also the time when Never nearly got us drowned."

Never offered an exaggerated sigh. "Aren't I lucky to have such wonderfully forgiving friends?"

Tsolde reached across from her chair to point at him. The lamplight lit her strawberry blonde curls and she seemed, even before the meal and wine, to be truly happy – a more relaxed air about her. "You are, indeed."

"But so are we," Elina added with a smile. She still

wore green and black silks, appearing composed even half-slouched in her armchair, but earlier she'd hitched up her skirts to demonstrate a series of complex dance steps she'd been obliged to learn easily enough. "And despite how much I've enjoyed this, I think I need to turn in."

"Your meeting with Vadiya dignitaries?" Rikeva asked.

"At dawn, no less, since they have to be back on the river by noon," she said with a sigh as she rose.

Luis stifled a yawn. "Might not be such a bad idea for all of us to get some rest."

"I can show you to your room, Rikeva, if you wish?" Elina offered.

Rikeva stood. "Thank you. It's not every day that I have a queen as escort."

"I'll do my best," she said with a smile as she led her from the room.

Never hauled himself out of his chair to follow, but Tsolde stopped him. "Never, I wanted to ask you something."

He turned back to where she and Luis were grinning at him. "What's happening, you two?"

"You seem to be staring at Rikeva an awful lot," Tsolde said.

Luis was nodding in agreement.

Never raised an eyebrow. "A comment on my manners?"

Tsolde rose and crossed the room to stand before him, *almost* swaying on her feet. "Of course not. But I'm really happy for you, Never."

Luis joined her. "Me too. I used to worry that you'd be lonely forever."

"I... wait, you think I'm lonely?"

"Not anymore," he said, placing a hand on Never's

shoulder as he left. "See you in the morning."

Tsolde gave him a hug and wished him goodnight before catching up to Luis.

Never did not follow at once.

How long had they seen him so? Was it true – or maybe, *how* true? After all, seeing Ayuni again, Muka too, and now his oldest friends... halfway through the meal, he'd found himself wishing time would pass slower. Found himself glad that Rikeva was enjoying their company...

"Well then." He strode into the hall and started down the carpet, passing yet more paintings and statues until he reached the nearby guest wing – and found Elina returning.

"I forgot to give you this," she said, holding up a key. "Seeing as you didn't drink as much as Luis and Tsolde, I'm sure you can find your room without too much help?"

"I think so, yes," he said.

Elina paused, key held between them in the soft lamplight. "Never, I have been thinking."

"Oh?"

Her green eyes grew serious. "We all know and appreciate how driven you are. We know how important you consider the role of protector, and we owe you so much."

"This sounds like the sort of compliment that has something less pleasant lurking behind it."

Elina smiled. "Perhaps it is. Just make me a promise, will you? You don't have to miss out on something wonderful just because people are in danger. That won't ever change, so think about what I said." She pressed the key into his hand.

"Are telling me to sleep late?"

Elina started back along the carpeted hall. "Maybe I'm telling you not to sleep alone."

For just a moment he wondered... but no, Elina wasn't talking about herself. Idiot, it was someone else. Maybe the queen was trying to offer her suggestion in such a way as to let him save face. He took half a step after her. "Sometimes it's hard to believe that there can be time for both," he said, and a defensive note had crept into his voice.

She turned, her face half-shadowed now. "I imagine it seems like we've all conspired against you tonight, Never... and maybe it's an unusual way to show that we care, but I know you believe the most bitter regrets come from chances not taken, right?"

And then she turned down a different corridor, on her way back to her own rooms to rest and prepare for her duties as the leader of a nation.

Never stared after her, unable to answer – a rush of gratitude had robbed him of speech... but he *would* thank her.

In his room, he lit both lamps and paused before the square mirror, running a hand over his jaw – enough stubble to suggest a shave was in order. Especially if he really had decided to call upon Rikeva. Yet still he hesitated, frozen in place. Why such trepidation? Would she truly reject his advances? There had been no shortage of signs, and maybe more that he had missed. "Go, you fool."

Never undressed then strode to the adjoining room with its brass bath, pulling the lever that sent steaming hot water pouring from the brass pipes. He sat on the edge of the bath, letting steam warm his back while he waited, and when he finally submerged himself, it was with a welcome sigh.

And yet, he did not linger.

Once clean, he stepped free to towel himself off. Next, he dressed in the cleanest clothes from his pack and rummaged around in a cabinet for a bowl and razor, then returned to the mirror.

The blade clattered to the bowl.

A pale figure stood by the bed.

Never spun.

The room was empty. He reached for the razor, and once more – the same indistinct shape in the mirror. Standing closer now.

Its body flickered faintly, limbs slipping in and out of human proportion, a milky colour brightening. There was even a scent, something... the chill of dirt at midnight? Strong enough to sting his airways too.

Never made a small incision and crimson-fire bloomed in his hand.

The intruder vanished.

Something impossibly heavy caught his shoulders. Never strained against whatever force held him, and though the crimson-fire flared, he could not move even a finger and worse, there was no target.

The pale thing appeared in the mirror only, its blob-like head resting on his shoulder.

"Get off me," Never growled, but that was all he could manage – he couldn't even flinch. Oleksan's assassin, striking at last? How to break free? His heart rate doubled. None of the usual Amouni tricks would work if he couldn't even twitch!

Its maw opened in a jagged line and hung in silence.

Soil filled Never's mouth.

He gagged.

Air vanished. No matter how hard he tried to cough or spit, the thing simply sat upon his shoulder, its entire weight bearing down on him like a mountain, made all the worse by the inability to fight back.

Sweat formed as even the red glow began to fade, leaving only inky shadows.

***

In the darkness there came a warm light, snapping on in a mix of gold and green, as though little suns hung above a canopy of slithering vines, green dripping down to hiss and sizzle upon a path carpeted by pitted bones. Most were arms, legs and ribs, but the occasional dome of a skull or shadowy eye-socket stared up at him as he walked in the only direction available.

A drop struck his arm and he swatted the moisture away, but a stinging pain lingered.

Not a welcoming place, wherever he'd wound up.

A patch of shadow waited ahead; beyond it was a large chamber, vines entwined as they stretched up into a high steeple, the golden light less overbearing here, beams falling down to the bones.

And in the centre of the room, a throne made of leaves.

Beneath the vines and leaves – some smooth and shiny, some like daggers of green and others a more muted yellow – stone may have waited but the mess was so dense that he could not see the arms or the back either, just the shape. The vines even encircled small berries of black and red, their skin unnaturally shiny.

Someone sat upon the throne but not the pallid thing that had attacked.

It was a hulking form, skin seeming polished to a dark, golden sheen, an unnatural brightness simmering beneath. And there was something stakolin-like about the man, not just his size or the clawed hands, but significant elongation of arms, hands, legs... and face. The thing's face was almost beak-like, only the maw was made of golden flesh too, lined by white fangs.

Three eyes watched him approach, irises white and pupils yellow.

Somehow, it was almost beautiful.

And when it rose to spread both arms, there was naught but grace to each movement, even the tilt of its head.

"Welcome, Tekavesa."

Chapter 25

"That is not my name, Oleksan."

The creature's lips stretched over sharp fangs in what could have been a smile as he settled back down, perched upon the throne. "Never, if you prefer, then." His voice still bore a profound unpleasantness but face-to-face, what had become overwhelming was an aura of beauty and grace, despite his form remaining quite unlike what Never might have called beautiful.

"What I would prefer is not something you'd enjoy," Never said from between clenched teeth. The mesmerizing force of the Burnished King grew and it was enough to slow his movements as he lifted a dagger and made twin cuts, blood snapping into crimson globes. His wings burst free and the light flickered blue and green.

Oleksan watched without reaction, one arm rested across his knee.

Never lifted both hands – and nothing happened.

The fires of heaven did not shoot forth in unstoppable streams, they did not even flare or crash against an unseen barrier, they simply did not appear at all.

"Confused? You are not actually here, Amouni."

"What?"

"You are collapsed in your room in that which you call the Silver City; my servant has conveyed your awareness to this place."

He lowered his arms, fire fading. "You sent an errand boy instead of an assassin?"

"When you fail to wake, then I suppose the *belsete* will have been both."

Never glanced around the green and gold of the chamber – no windows and the only escape seemed back the way he came. But was that truly an option? "Why bring me here?"

"You are aware that the Seals are falling like brittle leaves in the throes of autumn."

"One remains."

"Hmmm. So it does."

"I won't break it for you."

The Burnished King rose, almost sliding down to the ground to stand over Never, a good head and shoulders taller, golden gaze bright. Impossible to look away and up close, a sweet scent was strong enough to make Never's eyes water. "I do not need you to."

"Then why have your pale dog drag me here?"

The Burnished King spread his hands. "That is not accurate. Rather, I have come to witness your demise."

Never glared at the demi-god.

Oleksan returned to the throne and almost before he sat, he was beginning to fade. "I must add, I do find it faintly amusing that you did not come to recognise the darkness within your companion before the end."

He folded his arms. "Then you came to lie to me."

"Did I?"

The Burnished King was gone.

"Bastard." Never turned back to the passage... little chance that escape would be so simple as walking back the way he came.

And Amouni gifts were powerless.

Or at least, his fire was. But what of the *forasa*? Were the branches out of reach? He drew the symbol over his chest... and nothing. "Bastard."

Never strode to the wall of vines and gave it a kick. Solid as the stone it probably concealed. Nor did even a single vine budge when he gripped a tendril and wrenched, the jerking motion doing little but hurting his shoulders. He glanced up to the top of the steeple. No gaps wide enough to break through, even with the golden light streaming down.

And yet, if everything he saw was an illusion, did it matter what his eyes told him?

He strode to the throne and sat.

The vines were hard and cold enough to be real... Yet Oleksan's claim about being stuck back in his room at City-Sedrin rang true, even if it was hard to imagine actually lying upon the carpet, unable to breathe.

Never closed his eyes.

Was it even possible to break from a dream? To force wakefulness?

"Focus." Did details from the room in the city possess any kind of anchoring power? He reached for the cool weight of the bowl or the hard edges of the mirror, the smooth surface of the bathtub and all to no avail.

Never opened his eyes with a sigh.

And caught a gasp.

Chill light of soft blue and green fell into an empty hall, fluted columns half-visible in the shadows, little else clear. A throne of dark stone rested beneath him, carvings of wings on the arms.

He rose and found dead leaves beneath his feet.

Never.

A voice drifted to him from afar, but the darkened hall was empty. "Hello?"

The speaker did not appear. Instead, he blinked at a white feather that floated down from above, gentle and soundless.

Never reached out and the throne room vanished the moment his fingertip brushed against the feather.

More darkness followed. But this time, Illya appeared before him in her vest, the tattoos on her face somehow making the blue of her eyes brighter. "Finally," she said. "Welcome back to the land of the living, Never."

Relief washed over him. "It's a little darker than I remember."

She smiled, a faint change of expression. "I'm sending you back, now that I've dealt with the White Clamp."

"The White Clamp? Is that really what it's called?"

"*Belsete* is the ancient name," she said. "But I am glad to say, more importantly, that it will not be returning. Though it was not something I expected to encounter while listening to the dead, and to be honest, neither were you. It might not have seemed so, but you were close to death."

He shuddered. "I'm in your debt once more, Illya."

"Yet it is I that will owe you once this is all done," she replied. "Keep fighting for us."

And then she was gone, her voice and the darkness replaced by soft sheets and a pillow, by the warm colours of his room and a certain weight to his limbs that had been missing in Oleksan's prison.

Curls of strawberry blonde moved into view; Tsolde's worried expression becoming clear, then easing into a smile of relief. She pushed herself from the bed then strode across the room to open the door, where she called into the corridor. "He's awake!"

Never sat up. "You sound like a proud parent."

Tsolde returned, hands on her hips. "We were all worried, you fool. It's been three days already, what happened?"

"Three days? Truly?"

"Yes."

"Oleksan attacked," he said, explaining the *belsete* and its appearance in the mirror – which now remained blessedly empty of pale things. Tsolde turned her own gaze to the mirror, a little hesitant, and he smiled at her. "I don't think you'll be Oleksan's next target, thankfully."

"I suppose so."

Never slumped back down, staring up at the ceiling. "Three days isn't so bad."

She sat beside him. "It is if you're worried about someone."

"I meant for the cure, but I know what you mean." He reached out and patted her hand. "Sorry to have scared you."

Tsolde sighed. "Luis probably took it the worst, you know. We've all been taking shifts here."

"I'd feel the same way about him, or you, if our roles had been reversed."

She offered a small smile only, and it didn't seem that she doubted him. Something else was troubling her. Tsolde swallowed before she spoke. "Never, I'm not sure how to say this."

He sat up again. "What's wrong?"

Tsolde shook her head. "No, it's just that with everything you've told Elina about this plague... When Luis and I passed through the blighted parts, it was early and things could have been worse. But how long will that last? I'm afraid. Afraid for myself and Luis most of all. Isn't that just so selfish of me? To worry about my own future first, about those closest to me?"

"No."

"But –"

He smiled. "I still say no, Tsolde. Why *wouldn't* you want to protect your family?"

"Even when others are suffering?" She took a deep breath.

"I'll stop the Burnished King. Elina knows what to do if the Stone Plague reaches the city – that's what all that smoke to the north is for, I suppose."

"Even that..."

"I know," he replied softly. "But Olivor finished the cure while I slept, right?"

Tsolde nodded, some of her concern fading. "He did, and he's pretty confident."

"Then Rikeva and I will test it to make sure."

"So, you're feeling well enough to travel?" she asked. "Rikeva seems to think that the soma will last a little longer still."

A rumbling echoed from his stomach. "Apparently I could use a meal first."

"Good idea."

He rose. "How about I cook, since I owe everyone at least one meal after the worry I've caused."

"Have you improved that much?" she asked.

But he only grinned. "You be the judge, Tsolde."

Chapter 26

Once again, Never found himself having bade goodbye to old friends – friends he would have welcomed on the rest of his quest – but relief outweighed regret. They wouldn't have to face the dangers ahead. And the threat of the Stone Plague in Hanik was enough to deal with.

More, the golden, stretched face of the Burnished King lingered in his mind as he half-listened to Olivor give Rikeva instructions about the cure.

Would the Fires of Heaven be enough?

Rikeva nudged him where they stood within Olivor's tower, sunlight streaming through the window. "Never?"

Olivor was waiting, having handed over the heavy bottle of lavender-coloured liquid.

"Sorry, I missed that last part."

"I said that the final ingredient is now exhausted, but I will procure more on the assumption it will work. So if your test is successful, please let me know."

"We will," he promised.

"Ready, Never?" Rikeva asked.

He nodded, placing a hand on her shoulder as silver

light began to glow. It soon covered Olivor's kind face and once the light faded, it revealed the all-too-familiar darkened shrine. Never started for the tunnel at once, climbing into the cold stone opening.

"Are you getting a little tired of this too?" Rikeva asked from where she crawled after.

"I actually am, yes."

"Not that I'm ungrateful, but I'm starting to wish we had a symbol nearer the camp."

Never climbed out to the mountainside and its clear air and let his wings free. "Remind me to try making one," he said.

"So that's possible?"

"Probably, but I'm happy to fly for now."

Once again, after a somewhat more graceful take off, he and Rikeva took to the skies, gliding down the mountain and across the plains toward the Doerin camp, and when they landed at last, Never couldn't keep the anticipation out of his steps.

Even so, he couldn't match Rikeva's pace as she strode along trodden grass between tents. She waved or returned greetings as she headed for the tents on the edge of the camp, but did not stop, only saying that she would have news to share soon. A few of the horses were stamping and snorting. Restlessness or something else? The two men adding vegetables to a stew nearby did not seem too concerned.

"I want to visit Bhi and Oramo first – their little boy can no longer move," Rikeva said, the bottle of Olivor's soma in hand.

"Do you want to dilute it with a little water or test it first?

Olivor thought we'd get more use from it that way."

"You actually heard everything he told us after all?"

"I did."

She shook her head. "I think we should see what it can do first."

"Rika!" Haya ran toward them, pigtails flying and a big grin on her face. She leapt with arms outstretched just as Rikeva turned, crashing into her big sister.

The bottle of soma flew through the air.

Never lunged but the cure hit the ground, glass shattering with a force that seemed to echo across the entire camp.

Haya froze, eyes wide.

But Rikeva was already kneeling by the shattered bottle. Olivor's cure had splashed across a small rock and a wildflower, its blue and purple petals obscured by the pale lavender liquid, which was fast soaking into the earth – unnaturally so. One corner of the bottle remained intact, a little of the cure within, but Rikeva had not reached for it.

"Haya, carefully salvage what you can, but don't worry." She reached up to the ribbon in her hair as she spoke.

"But I ruined it!" her little sister said, voice rising almost to a wail.

"Everything is fine, just do as I say. It will work out."

Never smiled down at Haya, despite his own worry. "It might take a while, but I can easily get more."

Haya knelt to collect the remaining cure, taking shuddering breaths as she did, but still Rikeva focused on the wildflower and its arching petals. She wrapped the ribbon around the flower's stalk, fingers moving quickly as she tied a loose knot.

Then, she held both hands over the plant and fell still.

"Rikeva?"

"I'm Weaving."

He moved a little closer. "I know that but, how do you know the flower will be able to be used as a cure?"

"I don't." She slowly lifted both arms. Beneath her palms, the plant began to grow, stalk and petals rising, expanding as the flowers brightened. New shoots grew from both the stalk and the ground all around the first wildflower. "But I still *feel* like this will work."

"Can I help?" he asked.

She stood, lifting just one hand now, and the wildflower grew more quickly. It was almost chasing her; the Weaver's gift transformed it from a single flower to a waist-high shrub as he watched. "Yes, once I'm finished here, I'll likely collapse. Carry me to a tent then figure out a way to prepare the flowers to save my people."

"Wait, how long will you need to rest?"

"A day or two. Maybe only overnight." Rikeva pushed back a sleeve and removed another ribbon – and she had so many it was as though bandages wrapped her forearm. A clever way to store vitality without risking too much of her current strength in one Weaving, but far more than he'd expected to see. She took each ribbon and tied it around the smaller stalks to repeat the process, pausing long enough for each to grow and then raising them up one by one.

Haya was watching on in awed silence, a faint smile on her face where she held the remnants of Olivor's cure.

Rikeva did not stop – in fact, she worked harder, sweat soon forming at the small of her back as her shirt darkened. With each ribbon she tied, now taken from her other arm, she was able to coax several stalks from the earth, and before long an entire grove of wildflower plants stood before them. Some were taller than Rikeva herself, stalks more like slender trunks, and the weight of the blooms caused more than a few branches to droop.

"I think that's all," she said, then lowered herself to the grass.

Never turned back to the tents and lifted his voice, calling for a healer. Had she given too much, even with her store of ribbon? He knelt beside Rikeva and slid an arm around her back. "Which one?"

She had already closed her eyes, each breath coming slower. "Not far, at the edge here."

Never lifted her and strode to the pale tent, not too far from the separate row of five, glancing to Haya as he did so. She nodded as she followed, cradling the cure in her hands.

Inside, Never set Rikeva down upon a bedroll that rested between a small stand with a handful of recipe books and maps on one side, and neat piles of folded clothing on the other. She was already in a deep sleep, her chest rising and falling steadily. It didn't seem she was suffering at least; no worry lines on her brow, no frown or murmurs.

She was at peace.

"Are you staring?" Haya asked from just outside, and it seemed she hid a smile when he joined her.

"I suppose I was," he said. "Will she be all right?"

Haya nodded. "I haven't seen her Weave so much before, but the last time she worked on a crop of carrots for half a night, and she was fine the next evening. You just have to store up enough ribbons in the lead-up, is all."

A man with streaks of grey through his hair led several

tribesmen and women over, his expression one of concern, and though he did glance at the new grove of wildflowers, his question was about Rikeva. "She pushed herself too far Weaving?" His voice was quite commanding. He was removing fragrant herbs from a leather satchel.

"Yes."

"Inside?"

Never nodded and the Healer entered the tent. To the others gathered, he explained the wildflowers. "Can you harvest some so we can test them?" he asked.

A younger woman nodded. "We'll start right away."

"Can we go see Kardi and Alena now?" Haya asked.

"Your sister wanted to visit Bhi's son first."

"Oh, that makes sense," Haya said, then started toward the row of five tents. "Let's hurry, then."

A small family rested inside; the faces of both parents dark with smudges of shadow beneath their eyes, movements weary. Bhi stroked her young son's forehead while the father cut up an apple where he knelt upon a rug, a thin stone table resting across his knees.

A large tapestry of the Twin Constellations hung above two bed rolls.

Their son, whose name Rikeva hadn't shared, lay upon pillows, skin totally grey. Where he ought to have been able to move via his joints, like his neck or elbows and even his fingers, all were covered in pale dust. Even the whites of his eyes were dark and dull.

The soma was the only thing keeping him alive.

For this young boy, everything hinged on Olivor's cure.

Never greeted the parents after Haya introduced him, explaining the cure she held.

"Please, we will try anything," the father said.

Haya looked to Never but he smiled down at her. "You'll be fine. Just pour the cure between his lips, keep your hands steady and don't use too much at once."

"All right." She knelt beside the boy, whose eyes continued to stare at nothing. She extended her arms over his mouth, tilting the remnants of the broken bottle gently. Lavender liquid flowed into his mouth, a little spilling across his bottom lip but Haya tipped the glass upright and paused, arms still extended. She'd used only half of what was left.

"We can use more if we need to," Never said.

Haya sat back and everyone in the tent held their breath, the father leaning in, clenching and unclenching his hands.

"Did it work?" Haya eventually asked.

There *was* new colour blooming, climbing up the boy's throat and spreading across his face – the awful grey of his skin fading, and then his breathing became visible in the movement of his chest.

And finally the boy turned his head, tears flowing as he spoke.

"Father? Mother?"

Chapter 27

The healer was pleased to have patients in separate tents, since it meant he could more accurately test the effect of the scent, the petals, the pollen, the seeds and nectar from the stalks – and while it did seem that the wildflowers, or arch-blossoms as Never had been informed, were curing the tribe, they did not work so fast as the liquid form that represented Olivor's efforts.

In the grove, another Weaver was working carefully to create more shoots as other folks dug holes or hauled water or planted seeds. And despite the rapid growth of the grove, it would take a *lot* of arch-blossoms to fight Oleksan's corruption.

Yet other Doerin, including Rikeva's now recovered sisters, were working on a celebratory feast and so the rushing and the hard work did not seem at all desperate, but joyous.

Everyone was smiling now.

There was only one lingering problem – Rikeva's recovery. Or perhaps it was not a *problem* so much as a concern.

And so while he helped with water or swung an axe to split firewood, or worked to set up long tables built from wicker and twine, and as the day wore down to night, a faint sombreness grew within him.

Rikeva was missing out on all the cheer.

Over the meal of spiced poultry and fried potato slices he dimly recalled from his childhood, Nikalem the healer assured Never that she was in no danger. "Sometime tomorrow, she will be awake and ready to continue fighting soon enough."

"That's a relief to hear," he replied.

"Is it now? I've told you twice already, Never," Nikalem said with a chuckle.

"So you have. It seems I'm quite accustomed to worrying."

The Healer handed Never a fresh drink, a cup of citrus water. "Well, for tonight at least, you don't have to be."

The feast continued and fresh toasts were given, for Rikeva, for Never, for those who had recovered and whose faces seemed perpetually streaked with happy tears. But despite the bright mood, Never soon slipped away from the tables. He moved off to stand beyond the edge of the firelight where he could stare up to the glittering stars – a riot of twinkling lights, small but plentiful.

In the relative quiet, he rubbed at his temples.

A ridiculous time to be restless, truly.

Nikalem's advice was more than sound. Why not take a moment to rest, to enjoy the feast properly? The happiness that poured from every person at each table. But it seemed that the very moment one problem had been solved, his feet started to shuffle, leading him on to the next one – Oleksan and Heaven's Fire. Would the fire be enough?

Could production and then delivery of the cure happen at the same time?

"You two seem a little alike, you know."

Kardi stood behind him, smiling as she neared. Her eyes, which had been grey before, were actually grey in health too; there were just more faint flecks of green and brown to be seen in the firelight, and when she folded her arms beneath her breasts, it was not in frustration.

"Me and who?" he asked.

"My sister. She's always ready to take on a new task or visit a new place," Kardi explained. "Once, at a young age – too young probably, she travelled all the plains to the coast, just to see the ocean she'd read so much about. Father was so furious when he finally caught up with her a week later... but when he saw how excited she was, splashing about in the waves, he wasn't able to punish her as he'd intended."

Never smiled. "What did he have in mind, and what did he settle on?"

"He was going to have her cook for the entire tribe for the rest of the year but instead, he took her back and made her map the paths she took, so that all could benefit from her curiosity."

"He sounds like an interesting man."

She nodded. "He certainly was. So, what happens next, Never?"

"Next, I need to see if I can burn the plague as it creeps across the land, and break into the Burnished King's stronghold. And then destroy every trace of him – the essential things."

She placed a hand on his shoulder. "Then set your mind at ease about the cure. We will call more Weavers to expand the grove and others will make sure it reaches those in need. Go with our hopes and do what you must."

"That does help to hear, thank you."

***

"Let's go, Never."

The voice woke him but he did not rise from the bedroll all that swiftly, eventually recognising the faint, lingering scent of arch-blossoms – they'd been placed in all tents as a precaution, perhaps in hope of some sort of immunity. The light cast the speaker in silhouette, mild morning air entering the tent with her words.

"Rikeva?" His mouth was dry enough to make speaking a little unpleasant, so too, the fog within his mind. How long had he actually slept? It had been a long night after speaking with Kardi, since he'd not sought his rest at once.

Instead, he took cuttings and blossoms to Olivor, to Jardila and even west to Vadiya, where he delivered them to Sacha, whose deep weariness had not been entirely banished by the good news. Keeping his visit short had not been easy either, considering the stranglehold the Stone Plague had on the southern reaches, but Sacha urged him to leave. "Go, Never. Deal with the source, I can handle the cure."

But he blinked away the memories and rose to a half-sitting position.

Rikeva was smiling down at him. "Good guess."

Waking to welcome news was a nice change and it seemed the flutter from his heart agreed. He reached for a nearby water flask and soothed his throat, drinking half the bottle. "You're feeling better, then?"

"Close enough," she said. "I've already wrapped new ribbons, so you don't have to worry about me failing to hold up my end of the bargain."

He started to gather his things, sorting through a cloak and knives, Amouni blade, water and cold meat leftover from the feast. The morning didn't seem old but it was already quite warm. "You mean, about offering me the use of your gift? It's probably better spent on the grove."

"No. I meant the Burnished King," she said. "I'm coming with you." He stopped and before he could object, she climbed into the tent, expression intent. "You kept your side of the deal, let me do the same for you."

"I..." A too-familiar worry gave him pause. Would it ever ease, the fear of losing others? Unlikely. Yet, her sincerity actually helped make something clear. Always trying to decide things for those around him, to decide *for them* the risks they were willing to take, it was ridiculous. Even cruel – and Rikeva wasn't a child. "All right. I don't know what will happen. He's not like anything I've faced before."

"Finally admitting it, are you?" she asked with a smile.

"What?"

"That you're worried. It's at least part of the reason you've visited all of your old friends. Just in case we don't succeed. Am I right?"

He hesitated, then shook his head with a soft laugh – at himself. She saw what he had not. "I didn't actually realise it, you know. But I'll keep my word too. I'm not going to stop until he's defeated."

"Then let's go see what that Holy Fire of yours can do."

"Right."

She leant closer then, one hand moving up to his cheek – and she drew his face near to press soft lips against his, just for a moment, before she drew away. "Come on. Time to find one of your fancy *forasa* symbols."

Never stared after her, then smiled.

Chapter 28

"You chose quite the place to test the Holy Fire," Rikeva called, gripping his hands as she stared down at the mist-shrouded wall of decay encircling the blue of the Evache Lakes.

"I know. But this wall is probably the closest I can get to him," he said, angling his wings and circling closer to the withered earth below. Once again, he had to expend a little extra effort so that Rikeva would be able to drop safely to the grey dirt.

"Is it safe to walk here?" she asked as he beat his wings, stirring dust.

"We have the arch-blossoms. And we've both taken the cure on top of that. I don't think we'll need to stay here so long." He paused. "I can set you down within sight of the wall, instead?"

"It might not hurt to know if the cure works to prevent the Stone-Plague too."

"Are you sure?"

"I am," she said. Rikeva let go and landed easily.

Never followed, glancing around at the empty land, the piles of grey leaves and diseased-looking stone and logs, most of it only half-visible within churned earth. Even the soil had faded almost to ash.

"If any of our friends appear, I'll hold them off you," Rikeva said, staff in hand.

"That would be most welcome," Never replied, turning his gaze to the towering wall of... Stone Plague and its sentient mist. So far, it didn't seem to be attacking. Just what was the reach of the tendrils? He called the crimson-fire, this time by snapping his fingers. Just as pertinent a question, what was the range of his own fire?

"Showing off there?" Rikeva asked with a grin.

"A little," he said. "But I'm enjoying not having to use a blade, to be honest."

"Not quite as dramatic though."

"True." Never lifted both arms and urged more heat and power into his hands, the blaze a restless mix of blue and green now, enough that the heat reached him, in a way that it did not do so with the crimson-fire – not painful, but definitely present.

Rikeva had already stepped back. "The two feathers Ayuni gave you are glowing. Will they be enough?"

"Let's see." Never sent twin streams surging forth.

Both blazing lines of Heaven's Fire struck the wall easily, despite the distance. The mist vanished, seared away, only to be replaced by steam, and where steam rose from the wall in great clouds, the undersides were tinted blue and green. Almost beautiful. But he narrowed his eyes – was the wall withstanding the onslaught?

He did not let up.

"I think it's working!" Rikeva called. She'd circled around to find a better vantage.

Never let the fire die away then joined her – and there, becoming clear as the steam faded, twin holes stood in the enormous wall. Each large enough to crawl through. Glittering blue was visible beyond. Never clenched a hand. Success. The Holy Fire was certainly powerful enough to burn away the Stone Plague. How would the Burnished King fare against it?

"That's enough for me," he said.

A rumbling echoed from the wall, enough to set the very earth to trembling. Never tensed as he urged the flames free once more. Rikeva had braced herself too, staff in hand as she watched the wall.

Something moved beneath the surface, straining against the darkness, and it was large. Easily the size of an entire building.

"Do we really want to meet whatever that is?" Rikeva asked.

"Probably not."

A small piece of the wall spurted forth to splash across the earth and the hissing that followed reached them easily. It continued, a second and third piece and then finally, *something* huge and blocky and unwieldy broke free, first step like thunder.

The heavy frame was a similar colour to the wall, and as each new leg burst free with a sharp crack, Never stumbled back, hands clamped over his ears. It already had a dozen limbs, how many more? The thing bore no discernible head or face, but it still charged directly at them, its speed far belying its size, feet tearing at the earth as it closed rapidly.

He flung Holy Fire at the creature.

The bright flames cut through several legs with barely any sense of resistance and sent the thing spinning off to one side. Unbalanced now, it could not right itself and tipped; the thunderous impact sent him flying, even from a distance. Never wrapped his wings around his body as he hit the ground, rolling to his feet and whirling around. Rikeva was also rising, her own eyes wide. "Time to fly, right?"

"Very much so." Never leapt into the air, wings pumping.

Rikeva had already started running from the creature, arms outstretched.

He banked sharply, swooping after her. Their arms met with a smack and she kept hold as he hauled her into the air. Never beat his wings fast enough to lose a few feathers, not slowing until he was certain he'd put enough distance between them and the wall, after which he circled back enough to witness the many-legged hunk of Stone Plague climbing back to become one with the barrier.

"I wonder why he didn't come himself," Never called over the passage of the wind.

"He has to be busy in the Temple," Rikeva replied.

"Probably."

She looked up at him, blonde hair flying across her face. "Where to now?"

"Somewhere we can plan in peace," he replied. "We could try the city but I wonder if somewhere closer might be better."

"Do the symbols give us that many options?"

There were a few to choose from but one place came to mind – not that distant from Isacina, as it turned out

– a destination he had overlooked. But it had been worth visiting since the moment the Burnished King's path out of Vadiya became clear.

Finally, it was time to discover why Oleksan turned north and east to swing around near Olecsa. Why not simply travel directly east from the mountains to the Evache Lakes? Doing so offered a far more direct route. Something important had either been within or still rested in the smaller city. And Olecsa itself was not so far from the Lake system either, making it a suitable place to prepare a proper path of attack too.

Even its name – Olecsa.

Oleksan.

Could the two really be a coincidence?

"Never, are you going to answer?"

"Sorry. Yes, I do have somewhere in mind. Olecsa – there's a symbol that should put us inside the walls."

"That sounds perfect."

Never headed for the ground, letting Rikeva leap down to the grassy plain when close enough. When he joined her, it was with a hand poised over his chest, ready to trace the five-pointed leaf once he found the right *forasa*.

"This one is in a large square," he said.

"Not in a fountain, I hope."

"Me either," he replied as Rikeva took his hand, and the glow rose.

When it cleared, they stood not *within* the square, but upon an empty rooftop garden that overlooked the square, potted plants overgrown with weeds, the door to the building barred.

"This is much better," Rikeva said as she looked down.

Never followed her gaze. Olecsa appeared to span the more modest homes of Cagila to the multi-storey inns and storehouses of Isacina, though the people who walked the cobblestones or met before garden boxes were less cheerful than those in the capital.

Every market corner or intersection visible from the roof was crowded with people huddled around small bundles of possessions, sometimes grouped together in alleyways with makeshift shelters. Not all bore the look of farmers driven away by the plague; many might have been from other towns, considering their dress.

When Never led Rikeva to climb down through the abandoned building and started to walk the streets, many of the refugees were casting frequent glances skyward. There, a muddy haze ruined what ought to have been a lovely spring day – the faint taste of ash another unpleasant sign of fires being used to hold the Stone Plague at bay.

Just how close had the Burnished King's trail come to the walls?

Equally present in the city were Imperial Soldiers, breastplates bright beneath the sun, often joined by Pacela's faithful as they moved about the place offering to help. Never found himself nodding in approval – Crisina was living up to her promises about helping the people.

Not every local they passed held the same charitable views, easily overheard complaining about rationing. One shopkeeper was so loud his assistant tried to hush the man, as more than a few customers moved away from the fruit stand.

"It doesn't look like there will be many rooms free," Rikeva said.

"I've stayed in the Golden Harvest enough times to start there," he replied, heading for the southern entrance. "But you might be right about it being difficult."

Rikeva adjusted her pack as she kept pace. "So why Olecsa, then?"

"The Burnished King took a detour this way and I want to know why."

"You think there was something here? Like a Seal? Or something we can use?"

"Perhaps. We might not learn much, but I think we deserve some rest – even if it's only enough to figure out our next move."

When Never at last caught sight of a huge barrel and its potted plant, complete with painted leaves of gold, he pointed out the Golden Harvest Inn where it rested beside a courier which boasted 'the fastest hooves south of Isacina'. The buildings may have shared a stable based on the size, larger than his last visit. "There it is. If you have a lucky charm, we still might get a room."

"Hmmm."

But inside, the innkeeper – the same young man who taken over from his father – apologised from the common room, now quiet some time after the noon rush. "Since the Stone Plague came, we haven't had a spare room – whether it's soldiers, priests or travellers."

"We understand. Any suggestions?" Never asked.

He hesitated, then ducked into a back room before returning with a key. "I don't think my friend would mind, if it's just a night or two."

Never accepted the key. "That is generous. Is your friend elsewhere?"

"Set off for the capital just a few days back. I know you'll take care of it, and I still owe you for saving my skin."

"A debt repaid, Jadeo." Never thanked him with a smile.

Jadeo's friend owned a home located only two streets across, near enough to a market to stretch the word 'peaceful' but it was clean and well-maintained inside, floorboards smooth and wicker and wooden furniture free of damage, cushions clean and plump.

Rikeva paused by the curtains above the stove, lifting the hem to examine the painted image of a pink and brown wren on a delicate branch. "Who lives here – tailor or painter?"

"Could be both," Never said as he took a seat at the kitchen table.

Rikeva joined him. "This is impressive, Never."

"What do you mean?"

She gestured to the room. "How many people are actually in your debt?"

"A nicer way to ask would be to enquire as to how many people I've helped, you know."

"You're right about that," she said with a quiet chuckle.

"A fair number, I suppose." And though he could have described more than a few others, now that they were alone, the memory of her kiss seemed more important. Especially given the scent of her hair, somehow the citrus scent was enough to set his mind to racing...

"Never, I've been thinking about the Temple. What do you have in mind? You could probably ignore that creature in the wall and leap directly inside, right?"

Not quite the same thought he was having.

He nodded. "The direct attack does tempt me... we just

need a way to see what's really going on in the Lake first."

"What if we returned to the Amber Isle and found the final Seal? Could we strengthen it somehow? Or maybe restore a broken one somewhere else?"

He leant back in his chair. Rikeva's idea was a good one. "I don't know. But if we could find out *how*, we could even try both. I know Illya said we need to destroy the Temple, but that's another problem. Will destroying Oleksan be enough to achieve the same result? And if we *can* reseal the other Seals, will that lessen his power?"

"Who would know that? Illya?"

"We could start with her." He began to tap his fingers upon the table. "We know the final, unbroken Seal is in the Amber Isle. Another was in the Temple beneath the centre lake – I don't like our chances of being able to do much there. There's also the first Seal, the one on his tomb in his temple, back in Vadiya."

"What about those strange Guides?" Rikeva said as she leant forward. "Could they help?"

He nodded. If anyone 'remembered' more, or held more knowledge, it would be the Guide in the tomb, surely. Or perhaps a Guide near the Lakes, or one of those who remained at the isle. "We may need to visit Mount Siyapol too–"

A knock at the door interrupted.

Never drew the Amouni blade as he rose, exchanging a glance with Rikeva, whose staff was already in hand. Unless it was a visitor for Jadeo's friend, no-one had reason to seek them in Olecsa.

Another knock upon the door, and this time a voice followed. "Amouni, I seek your aid."

Chapter 29

"My name is Ivadr. I am a Traveller," the man continued. "I followed you from the Golden Harvest – it is more than chance that brought you here at the same time as I."

Ivadr? The name was familiar... hadn't one of the writings in Father's chambers mentioned the name Ivadr? Never did not answer the man. There was no guarantee that whoever stood outside was trustworthy simply because they recognised him or knew of an ancient name connected to lost Amouni texts.

There was always a chance Oleksan had sent another assassin.

"I seek your help in preventing the return of Arkenon. Will you not listen to my request?"

Rikeva leant closer, whispering. "Can we trust him?"

"I don't know."

Never let a little crimson-fire free and lifted his arm to point at the door. "You offer scant proof, friend, so forgive my wariness."

"Understandable. Would it allay some of your concern to know that we have, after a fashion, met once before –

prior to Oleksan's escape?"

"Where?"

"The Young Stag in Hanik, not so long ago now. I was in the stable when you were asking after her owner."

The traveller? The only details about the fellow that returned were vague indeed – he'd been tall, and rode a fine horse. Not enough to make any kind of decision. The stranger certainly *did* possess some knowledge that suggested he was not attempting a clever ploy.

Never lowered his arm, then gestured for Rikeva to hide herself in the adjoining room. Just in case – he mouthed the words, and she nodded, slipping into the bedroom. Whether the man had seen Rikeva or not mattered little if he had come with malice in his heart – he would assume she had left.

If he did assume she was no longer in the building, then Rikeva would have the element of surprise if needed.

"One final question, Ivadr," Never said.

"Yes?"

"How do you think I can help you?"

A pause. "That is a long tale... but to move to the most recent part, I need you as Amouni to open a tomb that lies on the outskirts of the city, where I believe something of value has been hidden for a long time."

He straightened. "Such as?"

"That I do not know, but it was important enough that the Burnished King attempted to destroy it on his path to the Lakes."

Never let the crimson-fire fade and sheathed his blade. "Join me, Ivadr."

The door opened to reveal a tall man; a rangy, bearded

fellow wearing a long braid. Like Rikeva, he carried a staff tipped with iron, but his weapon bore spiral carvings along its length. He wore a dark cloak over brown tunic and pants, his belt bearing similar spirals.

And while he *was* the traveller from Tsolde's inn as he claimed, there was little else to be discerned from his appearance.

He could have been Marlosi or Quisoan, perhaps even from one of the eastern islands but any more than that, Never could not guess. There had been a faint trace of an unfamiliar accent too, but only on certain words.

"Let me introduce myself formally," the traveller said, his expression serious without being stern perhaps, almost as though he was preoccupied with something troubling. And if his claims were sincere, his concern was understandable. "My name is Ivadr and I am a traveller whose people have sought to locate and eradicate traces of the Malecaphera and their foul God since the days following the Amouni. We are few now, a mere three families scattered across the lands. I am the forty-third child of Ivadr and I come here now to request your assistance."

"I am Never," he replied. "Please sit."

Ivadr did so, and Never joined him at the table. The man glanced around the home. "Will your friend be joining us?"

Rikeva moved back into the room and leant against the cold stove. "I am Rikeva of the Doerin Tribe."

"Also their leader and a powerful Weaver," Ivadr added. "Your assistance would be of great value also, and I hope you both come to deem me worthy of it."

Never exchanged a glance with Rikeva. "You have our attention."

"Thank you," Ivadr replied. "Where would you like me to start?"

"With the tomb," Never said.

"It has long been buried not far beyond the city – our stories told of something here, hidden since the time of the Amouni but we have not been able to locate it. No surprise, I suppose, with such scant details."

"Probably difficult to start digging up the countryside without drawing attention."

A nod. "But we always considered it possible. The stories even claimed that the very name of the city was changed to serve as a reminder, to guard against the Burnished King's return."

Never kept Ivadr somewhat in focus as he checked the branches of the *forasa* symbols – no sign of one just beyond city. But with several options available inside Olecsa's walls, that fact alone did not mean much. What waited in the tomb? If it existed. While Ivadr did appear trustworthy, there was still a chance of deceit.

So far, that had been Oleksan's game as much as anything else.

"If that's truly what the ancients had in mind when naming the city, then we definitely need to get inside this tomb... if it exists," Never said.

"I can take you there," Ivadr replied.

"Whatever's inside could be related to the final Seal," Rikeva suggested.

"Final of which Seals?" Ivadr asked.

"Are there others we need to know about? More than the three Oleksan needs to release Arkenon?"

Ivadr nodded. "We believe there were five. Two reserved

for both the tomb of the Burnished King and the former man himself, placed somewhere on his body. Three to unleash the destruction of Arkenon; one in the Temple Trivium, one hidden in the Amber Isle and a third beneath the city of Isacina."

Never straightened. Five Seals? Oleksan had lied to him in the golden chamber of vines – could *two* Seals actually still be intact? Five Seals might have explained the *forasa* beneath the palace dungeons. And a Seal on the demi-god himself? That must have been well-hidden. "What is the Seal on his body?" he asked.

"Then what's in the tomb nearby?" Rikeva asked at the same time.

Ivadr almost smiled. "Our hope is something to use against Oleksan himself, or perhaps at least information about the Seal upon him. It is actually a point of contention amongst the families as to whether the word Seal is appropriate for Oleksan. Some believe it to be a *mark* placed as a fatal weakness."

Never exhaled. "If all this is true, I can't help wishing we'd crossed paths a lot sooner."

"I have been in Olecsa for several weeks now," he replied. "News of your triumphs has circulated since the war but had I known Oleksan would break free, I would have sought you at the Young Stag. In fact, I nearly did regardless, but I deemed stories of the stakolin more vital."

"Oh, that's not a criticism," Never assured the man. "More wishful thinking on my part. But if I combine what I've learnt from Illya and the dead, with what you have told us, I think a course of action becomes a little clearer."

"From the dead?"

Never explained a little of what they had discovered so far, focusing on his new ability to use the Fires of Heaven. "Some texts call it a Holy Fire but whether that's true or not, I know it can definitely break through the wall around the Lakes."

"As I'd hoped," Ivadr said, his shoulders relaxing a little where he sat.

"You knew of the Holy Fire?"

He shook his head. "Only the notion that your blood would burn through the darkness. And now, the decay that has built around the tomb will be no obstacle."

"We still have plenty of daylight left; let's seek this tomb now," Rikeva said as she straightened.

Never stood, his urge to rest and consider and plan now brushed aside at the chance of something that could help destroy the Burnished King. "What say you, Ivadr? Ready to rob a grave?" If the tomb existed, it would be a good test of Ivadr's true intentions. On the surface at least, he seemed sincere.

The man joined them. "I am, though I did not imagine I'd be doing such a thing with this much anticipation."

"Strange times, aren't they?" Rikeva observed.

Never chuckled. "They're probably going to get stranger, since after this we still need to kill a demi-god hidden in a sunken temple."

"Then you've got some more ideas?" she asked.

"Not really. I'm hoping the tomb will help with that."

Chapter 30

The afternoon was still warm as Never rode along the empty highway, Rikeva on one side and Ivadr on the other as they left the city and headed for the mysterious tomb. Above, the haze of smoke seemed to trap the heat, though it wasn't so thick as to blacken the sky – even if it remained a screen, covering the pale blue and casting a murky tint over the occasional cloud.

It was Ivadr who broke the silence. "Oleksan was said to be striking against 'Amouni conceit' with his grand rebirth, but to me it always felt like hubris of his own making," he said as he kept watch on the quiet road.

Never's own mare was good-tempered, but the horse they'd purchased for Rikeva was more skittish, judging by a bit of head-tossing. Rikeva did not seem worried, patting the horse's neck and murmuring to calm the steed. "It sounds like your family is somehow connected to the Amouni, or at least shared a common purpose?"

"If our histories have been passed down correctly, then I believe so," Ivadr replied. "Just like there were those in Hanik said to be favoured, we were existing allies. Not so powerful nor plentiful, but we banded to the Amouni banner to stand against the Malecaphera."

"Does your family have many stories about Oleksan?"

"Few that deviate from what histories remained but during my time digging through Vadiya libraries, I was able to confirm one that might be relevant to us."

"You must have had the ear of someone powerful there," Never said.

"It was thanks to my ability to shadow-run, actually. Something other than the name that was passed on to me from my father and his before."

"What do you mean by shadow-run?" Rikeva asked.

"Something akin to leaping through *and* between shadows," he said after a moment of thought. "My body changes. I have so rarely had to explain it, I'm sorry I cannot be clearer. But there are limits and I do risk being lost within them."

Ancient and powerful magic indeed.

"That still sounds useful," Rikeva said.

"It can be, especially for sneaking in and out of libraries," he replied. "My Vadiyem is not perfect but one of the scrolls seemed to match a story about Oleksan. It claimed that he had made armour *of* himself."

Never frowned. Another hurdle. "Let's see how well it holds up against the Holy Fire."

As the road became more prone to cracks and sharp depressions, to swirling dust or the stench of blackened fields and a dozen other signs of the swathe Oleksan had cut through the land, Rikeva offered Ivadr some of their store of arch-blossoms. "Possibly as a ward, but if not it definitely works as a cure."

He held the flower in his palm, examining it with a softening of his expression, and Never realised the man's eyes were somewhere between brown and black. "You grew this?"

"With help," Rikeva said. "We're expanding the grove and sending the cure everywhere we can."

"That is wonderful."

Never pulled back a little on the reins, slowing his mare as a crater appeared ahead. Gently sloping sides led to a sharper drop, earth darkening on the way down. It was perhaps four, maybe five storeys deep, where a stone slab stretched wide enough to reasonably be the floor of a house yet whatever waited within the crater was not fully visible – a pool of decay covered most of the slab.

The same earthy brown as the wall around the Lakes.

What force had the Burnished King used to dig down and expose the roof of the tomb?

Rikeva was frowning at the pool. "What if another of those things appears?"

"If it's small, I have my Amouni blade."

"And if it's as big as the last one?"

"I thought the Holy Fire worked well enough."

She nodded. "And after that?"

"We take whatever we find inside to use on Oleksan, then infiltrate the Temple Trivium – there's more than one *forasa* in there. Or we can check the Seals first, but I'm starting to wonder if we aren't running out of time. The Burnished King hasn't come to taunt me for a long while.

He might be close to launching an assault on the final Seals."

"It will be impossible to defeat him with all Seals broken," Ivadr warned.

Rikeva turned from the decay. "We could still reinforce the Seals that remain."

"Maybe we should." Never rubbed at the back of his neck. "I've been thinking about ways to enter the Temple, and how to see inside before we break in. If the Guides have nothing, then we'll ask Illya to seek help from the dead and if there's little risk, then they could be our spies. We might be able to find out everything we need to know."

"I like the sound of that," she replied. "We'll still have to solve the problem of breathing under water, though."

"That's something that still stumps me." He let his wings free, the relief a little less palpable now that he'd been flying so often. "Everyone ready to see what's inside?"

Ivadr stepped back, and Rikeva moved out of his path as he made an incision and let his blood burn to blue. He could have simply called the crimson fire first, but it seemed more ritualistic to let some blood first, a vague urge he did not understand.

He let fire surge forth with a faint hiss. It struck the plague barrier and steam rose, quickly sweeping the remnants of the poison aside. He kept the flames blazing longer but didn't push so hard that the heat became overwhelming.

When he let the Holy Fire die away, the tomb was clear, and thankfully, he'd shown enough control that the stone had not melted.

A large symbol remained upon the roof, not dissimilar to the *forasa*, only three angled lines passed through the leaf here. And it did not glow silver or gold; it was more a sinister red. Or maybe just vibrant? In fact, it brought the colour of crimson-fire to mind. Perhaps just a little blood would be enough to gain entry.

"I had not imagined it so," Ivadr said softly.

"Time to dig in," Never said with a smile as he started down the slope, boots stirring faint clouds of the terrible plague-dust, though by now he had little reason to worry. Either his Amouni heritage or the arch-blossoms were enough. He stopped at the edge. "I'll fly us the rest of the way down. One at a time, I think."

He carried Rikeva first, then flew back up to Ivadr, who held on a little tight, but overall, the man might have enjoyed floating down, since he did not complain.

Never stomped on the slab. "Rock-solid, at least."

Rikeva hung her head with a sigh but made no further comment on his attempt at humour.

"Do you think you will be able to open it?" Ivadr asked.

"Only one way to find out." He knelt and placed his palm upon the symbol; the remaining traces of his blood caused a flare of crimson light. Was that why he'd felt the urge to use a dagger? The grinding of stone on stone followed as a centre panel within the symbol slid away, revealing a staircase that spiralled into shadow.

Never 'lit' a finger, and with a breath, started into the darkness, red glow lighting their path.

Stone walls had all been carved with five-pointed leaves and eyes similar to what he'd seen on the painting in Father's chambers. Amouni traces continued along their descent and he kept half his attention on the stair and half on the walls, as it seemed the patterns were responding to the crimson-fire.

Would a little blood help with whatever the walls seemed to be trying? One way to be sure.

"How deep do you think this will take us?" Rikeva asked.

Never touched the wall, letting his blood soak into the pattern. "Hard to say." Light bloomed all across the surface, banishing shadows as it raced down the stairwell and he smiled, a touch of relief following. "That's convenient."

At the bottom of the tomb, Never led Rikeva and Ivadr into a wide chamber with fewer patterns upon the walls, though the stone still offered plenty of red glow. In the centre of the pale, tiled floor rested a chest-high, circular podium. It was quite broad, and its quartz top reflected the light, obscuring the contents.

But as Never neared, it revealed its purpose – a coffin.

An older man lay preserved within the quartz, Amouni robe with its flared sleeves and five-pointed hem. The whole scene within had been arranged neatly, colours bright, untouched by time.

The symbol on his chest was unfamiliar however, appearing as a hollow spearhead. His grey hair was receding but brushed to a sheen; stern features still held enough colour to suggest he was merely sleeping.

A small silver box was clasped in one hand while the other gripped a dagger carved from bone and decorated with an eye set in purple ink.

Never could not take another step.

Here, before him, an actual Amouni.

Frozen in time. Preserved. Hidden for hundreds and hundreds of years, entombed beneath the earth... but of course, the Amouni could tell no tale. Could not have helped Never's search for answers during the years spent wandering.

Could not help now either.

Even so, an irrational sense of missed opportunity weighed heavy.

Had the Amouni chosen himself to be guardian of whatever lay within the tomb? Or perhaps, the silver box since nothing else resided in the chamber. Was *he* the one that was supposed to give up some secret that would defeat the Burnished King?

Unlikely, surely.

"Never?" Rikeva's voice was soft.

"Let me check something first." He turned to the empty room and raised his voice slightly. "Guide."

A robed figure appeared, arms bare, head of an unfamiliar animal with a wide bill and soft fur, not quite a duck or a beaver. *Master.*

"What have I left here?" Never asked, as behind him, Rikeva was explaining to Ivadr what was happening.

You left yourself and the Jewel of the Sun, the Guide replied, voice predictably flat.

"To be used against the servants of Arkenon."

As you instructed.

"And I am free to retrieve the jewel now?"

Of course – you and only you can retrieve it, Master.

"What does it do?"

Banishes the darkness.

"Specifically, Guide."

A pause. *It banishes the darkness of Arkenon.*

"How?"

You need only to carry it to them.

Never thanked the Guide. "One more question – I must see inside the Temple Trivium without setting foot within. How can I do so?"

I may know if you speak to me at the Enyaon Lakes.

Perhaps the answer, hopeful as it was, should have been no surprise. "That is all I need."

Yes, Master.

The Guide vanished.

"Are there such spectres in all places?" Ivadr asked in the silence that followed.

"It's unlikely," Never said as he turned back to the quartz coffin. "But the ones that have survived have proven extremely useful."

"How can you reach the Jewel of the Sun?" Rikeva asked. "Does the Guide expect you to break this man's coffin? That seems a little callous, doesn't it?"

"Maybe I won't have to," Never said. He pushed against the quartz – and stumbled a little when his hand met scant resistance. Instead, he might have reached down through water. His fingers met the silver box and a shiver ran through his body. The Amouni's grip released, and Never lifted the box free.

"Thank you, friend."

Rikeva touched the surface after, and as the Guide promised, her hand did not penetrate the quartz.

Never turned the silver box over but found no clasp. Despite the lack of even the suggestion of a seam, he was able to open it like any other jewellery box. A ring of silver lay upon a bed of velvet, set with a golden stone shaped as a triangle – the Jewel of the Sun. It gleamed but seemed no more spectacular than any other gemstone.

Still, if it was needed to defeat the Burnished King, its appearance did not matter.

He slipped the ring onto a finger and waited but no burst of power became available, no glorious golden light, no sense that a single thing had changed at all, for better or worse.

"Anything?" Rikeva asked.

"No, but I suppose that the real test won't be until we face Oleksan himself."

Ivadr nodded. "Until then, I pledge my life to protect yours."

"That isn't necessary, please."

"However, I offer it to you, Amouni."

"Ivadr, I –"

Rikeva punched his arm. "Let him, Never. It's obviously important enough for him to make such a promise. Don't insult Ivadr by trying to refuse."

Ivadr's expression remained stoic.

He turned to the traveller. "You have my thanks, Ivadr." And though he meant the words, was he even worthy of such devotion? Rikeva was obviously right, based on the way some of the tension left the man's shoulders. More, there was no need to insult Ivadr even without intent; he was a relatively new ally, but that did not mean that the man was not just as concerned as anyone else who had chosen to fight the Burnished King.

"Where to now?" Rikeva asked. "The Seals or back to Illya?"

Both choices seemed just as necessary, but there was no guarantee Illya would still be in Kiymako, making her a little harder to find. There was something to do before any decision was made. "I want to seal this place first. The Amouni deserves peace, now it seems he's fulfilled his role."

"Can we help?" Ivadr asked.

"Keeping watch while I work should be enough," he replied, glancing at the quartz coffin once more. "Let's head back."

Chapter 31

Clouds had formed overhead as the afternoon became evening, resulting in a drop in the temperature; perhaps made more noticeable when he eased off on the crimson-fire.

But his work was good enough.

The interior of the stairwell had melted enough to collapse in on itself and so he moved to the opening in the slab and touched his palm against the symbol, then stood back as it slid into place.

Sealed anew.

Next would be burying the slab and symbol itself, but that had to wait. The *how* would have to wait also, since he wasn't going to run off to find a shovel, but at least the traces of decay that remained might keep the curious at bay.

"That will have to suffice for now," Never said. His voice seemed almost too loud in the quiet evening. He hadn't used as much blood as the ascent on the Stair of Wind, but it was no small amount either. "Let's stable the horses and get some sleep. In the morning, we can decide where to go next."

Rikeva nodded.

"I will meet you then," Ivadr said. "I have commitments at the Golden Harvest."

"Ready your horse for a long stay while you're there," Never said.

The man hesitated.

"There are travel symbols we can use," Never added.

"Ah. I wasn't sure how you could fly us all everywhere."

Never smiled as he moved to his own mount. "Only for a short distance."

The ride back to Olecsa did not seem so arduous, but once they'd stabled the horses and left Ivadr, the few streets back to their borrowed accommodation was surely twice as long as before, and every streetlight was itself a small, blazing sun, each drunkard's call a roar.

By the door, he was stumbling.

Rikeva caught him. "What's wrong?"

"I don't know." He drew in a deep breath. "I was tired after using so much blood, but I've used more in the past. A lot more. Doesn't make sense."

"Where's the key?" Rikeva asked. She supporting him with her arm now, as he'd begun to sway upon his feet.

Never fumbled through his pockets then handed it to her, movements far too slow.

Once Rikeva guided him inside and to the bed, she sat beside him. "Is it the Stone Plague somehow?"

"I don't think so."

"And it's definitely not just blood loss?"

"It can't be," he said with a groan, lowering his head into

his hands. "I learnt my limits. Even taking the Holy Fire into account... it has to be something else."

Rikvea had kept her arm around his shoulders, and she pulled him closer. "Never, show me the ring."

He looked up as he raised both hands. In the dim room, the jewel was a point of light – not blazing or bright, just a noticeable gleam. "You think..."

"I do," she said when he trailed off. "Try taking it off."

Never gripped the ring and pulled – it slid free easily. His exhaustion vanished, leaving behind a general heaviness to his limbs, a welcome weariness only. He straightened. "Well, that's a shame."

"Why? You seem better now."

"I hoped I'd bear it better, to be honest." He shook his head, then turned to her – her face was quite close, traces of freckles visible on the bridge of her nose. "But thank you."

"Of course," she said with a smile, then rose. "Do you still have that silver box?"

He withdrew the box and placed the ring inside before returning the Amouni relic to an inner pocket. "Let's hope this works."

"I'd offer another game of tira-tra," Rikeva said as she moved to kneel before her pack, unlacing one of her boots. "But why don't you take the bed this time."

He smiled, not willing to object, and lay back. "I appreciate that, since I don't think I could actually win if we played again."

Rikeva chuckled. She had moved on to arranging her bedding, and once she was settled, she sighed. "We forgot to eat."

"I can wait until morning if you can."

"I suppose I could." She sat up with a mischievous grin. "Tomorrow, we can play for who makes breakfast."

"You'd still have the advantage."

"It doesn't have to be tira-tra, Never. We could play any number of childhood games to decide."

He smiled. "Same problem. I don't remember."

She lay on her side, resting her head upon her hand as she faced him. "Your Quisoan is pretty much perfect. How long did you live on the plains?"

"We left when we were fairly young," he said. "Our village wasn't large. Not everyone liked us – probably because of my father, at first. But whatever the beginning, it was enough to attack us sometimes. I do have a few fond memories, though. We were able to do the things that most children do; laugh and run, swim in the river, make up stories about figures we shaped from clay, and everything else. But sometimes our blood... well, after a time, I was glad to leave."

"I didn't know."

"It was long ago." He closed his eyes as he continued. "And it wasn't fair to expose people to such a threat. But what would have been better than fear and distrust would have been if they'd helped our mother."

"When you say 'our', do you mean your brother?"

He nodded.

"Elina and Tsolde told me a little more about what happened, while you were trapped by that thing," she said. "It's hard to imagine. If I lost any of my sisters..."

"It leaves a hole." And the feelings that rushed in to fill that hole were sometimes as bad as the loss. "Do you want to check on them before we leave? It wouldn't take long."

"No, I can rely on them to take care of each other."

"Let me know if you change your mind."

"I will, Never." She shifted onto her back. "Sleep well."

"You too."

Chapter 32

An impeccably clean series of chambers waited below the capital, more tiled floors and walls, though this time there was no red glow. Here, white had been joined by columns of wide, silver tubes that climbed from floor to ceiling, along with similar shapes made from glass.

All empty, all without an opening.

What many did contain however, was light. Somehow, each column must have been drawing light from the surface, that or some other Amouni ingenuity was responsible.

Up close, the glass columns bore a faint blue tint – Amouni symbols covered them, words written *inside* the glass. But though he'd recognised the language, the words themselves were indecipherable, and even the long strings of numbers included were empty of meaning.

"Hard to imagine what this place was used for," Ivadr said as they walked, footfalls loud. By his slight wincing, he was still recovering from his first use of the *forasa*.

"Agreed." Some rooms were empty, others contained more tubes, and a few bore silver tables beneath openings in the ceiling that may have once been skylights but offered only darkness now. The tables were not so purposeful in shape as what he remembered from the Awakening Chamber but they surely had a specific purpose in the past.

Perhaps equally unusual were the empty rooms, spaced at regular intervals between the others – why build such empty places? They may have once housed furniture or other items, but none now remained, offering no clues.

And that same lack of clues extended to an absence of dust or debris too—

"Do you hear that?" Rikeva asked as she came to a halt.

Never paused. A faint crashing sound reached him; regular and unrelenting, for it did not ease or pause the longer he listened, nor when they drew weapons and continued forward. "We might be too late," Never said. "Let me lead."

He called the crimson-fire and twin globes engulfed his hands as he strode forward; it even ran along the Amouni blade, which had remained quiet. That fact alone might have given him pause but the Seal had to come first.

The Jewel of the Sun did not burst into blazing sunlight and so far, his strength had not flagged. How much had the Amouni artefact been responsible for his earlier exhaustion and how much had been the loss of blood?

The crashing sound, which was growing louder, echoed twice as fast now.

Never shifted into a run, tubes flashing by, and when a wide corridor appeared ahead, this time the white tiles were no longer clear. Hunks of broken stone, tiles, dirt and dust lay scattered across the floor from an opening in the wall, dark tunnel beyond.

The debris continued across the floor, fragments leading

to the source of the sound – a golden figure was hurling itself against an Amouni symbol that covered the wall. Not the five-pointed leaf, but a jagged series of vertical lines cutting down through a single rune, the swirling Amouni letter that corresponded to the Marlosi 'A'.

And it was buckling under the onslaught of its attacker.

Like a human-sized Oleksan, its golden limbs flashed as it charged forward to swing overhand blows at the Seal. The creature didn't appear to be Oleksan himself, perhaps another surrogate, and it did not turn when Never flung a ball of crimson-fire at its back.

Never let his wings burst free as he charged, crimson turning blue and green. He hurled more flames at the creature and this time Oleksan's surrogate flinched as it spun, beginning to thrash beneath the onslaught of Holy Fire.

The creature fell to the tiles and Never caught a glimpse of fangs and three golden eyes before the Fires of Heaven engulfed its torso, spreading across the faltering limbs and burying the head.

Finally, it grew still.

Never sheathed his Amouni blade as the surrogate continued to burn, soon little more than a pile of ash at his feet. He lifted the Jewel of the Sun, but neither diamond nor ring had changed, no light had burst free. Had it made any difference? Would he only know when he faced Oleksan in the flesh?

"Look," Rikeva said.

He lowered the ring. The grey ash was shifting, spreading out to form words upon the tiles.

Too late, Amouni.

The Seal.

A large crack ran through the letter – and it continued to widen, coloured tiles, silver and stone peeling to crumble down. Some of the pieces were large enough to break the floor tiles when they hit.

Never kicked at the ash.

Only one Seal remained now – hidden somewhere within the Amber Isle.

"Never, we need to go," Rikeva said. "He might already be attacking the final Seal."

"I know."

"Wait," Ivadr said from where he knelt near the remnants of the ash. "I didn't notice this."

The Traveller pointed to a deep groove in the floor. The tiles were cracked and even warped, revealing stone beneath, the furrow leading to the wall... as though something had charged across it over and over, many thousands of times.

"How long was he attacking the Seal?" Rikeva asked.

Never smiled. "I think we can take heart from this; Oleksan must have had his servant at work for a *very* long time."

"But what if he's already had a surrogate at the isle?" Ivadr asked. "And *this* was actually the last Seal?"

Never's smile faded. A fair, and troubling question. "Then I'll have to ask one of the Guides for help. We could always return here to try repair a broken Seal, if it's possible. It wouldn't take me long to check the Lakes first. If the Temples have risen, we'll have an answer, but I think we should try the Amber Isle next."

"Either way, we want to restore *or* strengthen a Seal, don't we?" Rikeva asked. "And if we need a Guide for that, then let's hurry to the isle."

He nodded as he extended both hands. "Hold on, folks."

***

There was no Seal within the Amber Isle.

Or so it seemed.

Never paced the faint chill of the corridor near the sleeping quarters they'd chosen, lamp light throwing shadows. Despite his impatience, their search had not been fruitless.

Oleksan was nowhere to be found. No *forasa* led to some long-concealed chamber containing the Seal and several ostensibly important rooms had been ruled out; nothing in the altar room, the mural chamber nor beyond Javiem's resting place above.

The Guide *had* assured him that while a Seal couldn't be repaired without a dozen Amouni, tracing a Seal with just his blood would reinforce one – yet not even the Guide could describe *where* within the isle it was located.

At least the sea-creatures had not troubled them, though their role at the isle was somewhat more suspect now, perhaps. Were they more than sailors and treasure hunters transformed? Had some instead once been guardians left behind? Sailors and seekers had been drawn to the isle for a long time... but just how long? Had some of those come for something else? To break the Seal?

"Hmmm." Never moved a little further from the camp, keeping it within sight, and with his watch not quite over, he called a Guide.

The golden robes and stag head of the Guide appeared. *Master?*

"What purpose do the sea creatures serve?"

Sea-Creatures?

"They guard the isle and are a meld of fish and man."

That is unfamiliar.

"But guardians exist here, do they not?"

Yes.

"In the jewel pit. Where else?"

The stag head nodded. *All around.*

"I see. What do they guard?"

The isle.

"And the Seal?"

Yes.

"Guide, tell me again, where exactly is the Seal?"

In the Northern Isle.

The exact words from their last conversation. "Am I standing near the Seal right now?"

You are.

Never sighed. Again, the same answer – only last time, he'd asked it from the altar room. There had to be a better series of questions to ask. "Where do the guardians of the isle wait? No, instead tell me, where can I find a Guardian in the altar room?"

In each cell.

Slightly better. "Can they be seen?"

By you, Master.

"And what actions will they take if the Malecaphera come?"

They will attack, most ferociously, as per your instructions, Master. Is this still suitable?

"It is. Tell me their form."

It is not a set form, Master. You have created them incorporeal.

"Why?"

So that they will inhabit invaders and eventually turn them upon one another. In that sense, they can be said to be corporeal as well.

Progress! And maybe it offered something of an answer to the sea-creatures, yet even if they were still able to perform their duties, it was not likely they'd stand a chance against Oleksan. "I will strengthen the Seal come daylight. I expect you to meet me where I must draw the first part of the symbol."

Of course, Master.

Never dismissed the Guide and returned to the camp with a little more confidence, though the morning would either crush or confirm that confidence. He woke Rikeva, who rose with less grumbling than he had offered when Ivadr roused him earlier. "Anything?" she asked from the doorway.

"No, but wake me if anything happens," he said.

"I will."

Never removed his boots but didn't bother with anything else, settling into his bedroll and closing his eyes. At first, the lamp seemed too bright and he could have turned away from it but a welcome heaviness to his eyelids soon followed.

Yet sleep may or may not have fallen, for white feathers appeared within the darkness, a pale figure with twin points of vivid blue resolving into a familiar face.

Illya.

"Finally!" she said. "Never, I've been trying to find you."

His heart skipped several beats.

"Forgive me – you are not dead, if that's what you fear. Only asleep. I can reach you, like before, but our time is limited."

"My relief knows no bounds."

She smiled, but it did not last. "Never, the Temple Trivium is already rising but if you can protect that Seal, there is still a chance."

The bitter taste of failure followed her words. "Then the one beneath Isacina was all he needed?"

"It seems for the temples, at least, but the dead are just as restless as ever. Many are growing excited, even. There is just one Seal left between Oleksan and his foul God now, and so the dead believe their time is near."

"I will strengthen it," he said. "And then I will stop Oleksan by my own hand."

"I have another message that may help with that," Illya said. "Oleksan cannot raise the corpses that surround the isle and so he is trying something else – he has dredged up something from the depths of the ocean, instead. It is not swift, but it will reach you tomorrow."

What by all the gods, vanished or otherwise, did that mean? "I'm no longer comforted, Illya."

"I know my warning sounds dire, but you can turn it away, Never. Simply use the Jewel of the Sun."

"It's been a little reticent so far."

She smiled. "Try a little blood."

"Ah." Fool! "Of course. Do you know anything else about what's coming?"

"It is not dead, so I cannot be certain. But any creature from so far beneath the ocean would not abide such light, of that much I am certain."

"Right. What about your message?"

"Oleksan is stretched thin, with the creature and the temples especially, but also the wall – even the Stone Plague will fail in time, as the cure continues to spread across the lands. And there is more in our favour; the Burnished King must manage his servants from moment to moment, and even now he sends another surrogate north since he cannot act himself. You must take this chance to strike."

A second little copy of the demi-god himself? Then so it, too, would burn. "I will. Is the message from the living? From Ayuni? Or Sacha?"

"No, though I am still in Kiymako for now," she said, then paused. Her image began to fade but then solidified.

"Is something wrong there?" he asked.

"We are under attack. Ayuni and I are holding them off, but I cannot stay with you much longer."

"I'll be there right away," he said, almost before she finished speaking.

"No, Never. We can hold them at bay," she said, and once again she was fading. "This is a diversion; Oleksan wants you distracted."

"But what if –"

"You know that we can manage this, Ayuni especially, and I must finally share the message before I rest. Trust your sister."

Not racing to Ayuni's side did not sit well... but Illya was right. Ayuni could take care of herself *and* protect the others. And she was hardly alone. "Of course, tell me. And thank you."

"I will be watching over your friends," she assured him. Her voice was growing faint. "The message is from the dead... I cannot offer my advice on whether you should trust it but it *feels* trustworthy."

"Someone I know?"

"His name was Ecanseja and you must return to him immediately." Illya's form faded yet further, only her blue eyes remaining. "That was all he said, and to be honest, I could not at first decipher the words."

"I do not know any by that name."

"It sounds like you have met this Ecanseja at one time or another," she replied, her voice but a whisper now. "Even to my ear, the name sounds like it might be connected to the Amouni. I am sorry I cannot offer more but do not worry about us, Never. Focus on the Seal."

And then she was gone.

He did not wake but the name rang within his mind even as it drifted back toward sleep: Ecanseja. It likely *did* have an Amouni ring to it, just as Illya guessed.

And if so, that meant only one man, surely – the Amouni frozen in quartz.

Chapter 33

Never led Rikeva and Ivadr to the easternmost point of the isle in time to see the sun rising over the ocean horizon, casting its shining light across the waves. The morning air was clear and cool, and had he not already woken without even a trace of lethargy, the temperature would have done the rest.

He frowned at the Guide and its expressionless stag head. "This is where I begin?"

Yes, Master.

"There is no Seal here." It was getting harder to keep frustration from his voice, since the threat of two enemies closing in remained, one of which was imminent according to Illya. Rikeva and Ivadr both held their own weapons ready, though it was probably out of habit or for some sense of comfort since the creature from the depths was likely to be monstrous.

There is, Master. You set it yourself.

He hung his head. "Very well. Tell me exactly what I did the last time I strengthened the Seal." It was the question he should have asked earlier, but if it worked, he wouldn't bother taking himself to task.

You flew high enough to take in the entire island, then used your blood to repaint the letter A within the Binding Rune.

Never blinked before bursting into laughter.

At last everything made sense – no wonder the Guide kept insisting that the Seal could not be found in a single room, that it was within the isle, or that it was of the isle.

The *entire* Amber Isle was the Seal.

It also explained why the Burnished King had sent a monster to help his surrogate, since breaking an island-sized Seal was obviously going to require colossal force.

"Thank you, Guide," Never said. "Please send the Guardians now."

At once. The golden robes flickered from sight.

"Is there time before the creature arrives?" Rikeva asked.

He nodded. "I think so. I won't be flying too high but I'm sure I'll see it approach."

"Right." She leant against her staff. "Try not to splash us while you're up there."

He grinned.

"Will those sea-creatures really help defend the isle?" Ivadr asked.

Never freed his wings as he made two incisions, one in each palm – again, he could have called the crimson-fire without doing so, but the ceremonial approach was appropriate now. "They have to be better than nothing, at least."

He leapt into the air to circle the isle, fire in hand.

It was not a small island.

But he'd placed the Jewel of the Sun back into its case and if he kept the stream thin, his blood would last. Hopefully.

Never beat his wings and swung around to swoop across the stone and isolated shrubs, a stream of crimson-fire painting the first line. He wheeled at the far end of the island and left another searing trail of blood, passing Rikeva and Ivadr once more.

After his third and fourth pass, the symbol was beginning to take shape, though the swirl of the A was a little ungraceful. Even so, the Seal had changed, a sense of the Amouni power rose up like a fierce call, stronger now.

But when he at last settled upon the earth once more, Never was breathing hard as his own strength was tested. He moved to one of the larger rocks and sat as Rikeva and Ivadr joined him. "It worked. Now we wait for the thing from the depths."

Rikeva handed him a flask and he drank deeply, thanking her.

Ivadr had turned back to the sea. "I don't know how we help with what is to come."

"I guess if you don't mind carrying me back to shelter after. If the Jewel of the Sun isn't enough, then I'm not sure what else would work. There is always the option to flee and hope the Seal holds long enough for us to destroy Oleksan in the temple."

"Should we take that risk?" Ivadr asked.

"It's approaching," Rikeva said before Never could answer. She was wrapping a ribbon around her staff, face set in determination.

Never rose.

Still distant for now, the sea was rippling as something neared, surface darkening rapidly. A tail broke free with a fountain of churned water, like a whale-sized serpent... only larger.

He almost took a step back.

The creature burst from the ocean once more, and this time a giant head was visible. Flat, broad, and turtle-like, the face bore a ring of sharp fins, all ragged and similar to those found upon the glimpses of its undulating body. The eyes were dark pools, easily the size of grand windows upon the royal city.

Strangely, a golden talon had been embedded within one – clean and glittering.

When its maw opened, rows upon rows of green fangs were revealed, pitted and aged, covered in slime. They did not match the golden bone, a mark of the Burnished King, surely.

The serpent shrieked.

Never clamped both hands over his ears. Rikeva and Ivadr had done the same, and the behemoth continued to bear down on the island, water spraying from the force of its approaching bulk, casting sea-creatures and fish aside in its wake.

Whatever ships and boats that still surrounded the isle would be dashed to tiny fragments – would even the stone itself hold?

Hurry, fool!

Never ripped the ring from its case, jammed it onto his finger and called the crimson-fire as he held the weapon high.

Blazing light burst forth. It blinded him for just a

moment, then narrowed into a bright beam. The lance flashed across the water.

Light struck the serpent between the eyes.

The creature thrashed back and the scream that followed cut through Never's skull, driving him to his knees but not before catching a glimpse, through tears of pain, as the ancient creature writhed up from the water and hung for a breath, only to fall, crashing against the surface with a mighty crack.

A bare moment of respite from its cry followed – and then a wall of water bore down upon them.

He could not even call a warning. There was no shelter to take.

No way to survive.

Something caught him. "Take a deep breath!"

It had been Rikeva's shout but he could hardly answer – for the water crashed across the isle. It surged like a storm, tearing at his limbs with a muffled roaring, the chaos of charging water endless, but somehow unable to break Rikeva's grip.

Something dark flashed by, too fast to recognise as the wave continued to tear at him.

And then it eased, dumping him with a splash.

Rikeva released his arm and he sat up, gasping for air.

She lay upon the stone, still holding the base of her staff, which she'd driven into the isle. Her Weaver gift had saved them twice over. Not just her ribbon-covered staff, but her strength too – Rikeva's muscles had grown; shoulders broader, arms bigger, her entire torso and legs too. But even as he watched, Rikeva was changing, her body steadily returning to its regular proportion.

"I can't believe that worked," she said from where she lay. But it had.

He laughed as he sat up, clothing squelching. "I'm certainly glad it did." He paused. "Where's Ivadr?"

Chapter 34

Never flew across the ocean, keeping close to the isle but there was no sign of Ivadr in the water and the occasional body always turned out to be a sea-creature, green, bloodied forms bobbing between countless wooden fragments that littered the surface.

Any number of horrible fates could have befallen the man.

Somehow, it was of only a small comfort that the behemoth sent by Oleksan was apparently not returning.

And maybe creeping exhaustion was to blame; but each wing beat burned now. He found himself dipping too close to the waterline, always at times not of his choosing. "Gods be damned," he snarled.

By the time he returned to the isle and the *forasa*, Rikeva had already emerged from Javiem's cave, her own weary gaze revealing her failure. "Any traces?" she asked.

"Nothing."

Rikeva turned back to the ocean. "Is there anything else you can do?"

He nearly answered that he could not, but there *was* something he hadn't attempted. He raised his voice. "Guide."

The robed servant did not appear.

He tried again.

"What's happening?" Rikeva asked. "Shouldn't it appear right away?"

"Usually, yes." Had something gone wrong during the attack?

Cracking stone echoed from beyond the cliff. He spun as a pair of golden limbs slapped down upon the edge.

Never tore his Amouni blade free as three golden eyes with purple irises and a beak-like mouth appeared; a smaller, human-sized surrogate of Oleksan climbing up to stand before them on level ground. "Stay behind me," he told Rikeva, who did not answer.

He glanced at her; she was glaring at the servant, breathing hard too, but otherwise seemed frozen.

"That's far enough," Never called as the graceful thing drew closer. Even the surrogate was captivating when it moved. Would the Amouni sword be enough to hold it back until he could summon more crimson-fire, or did he risk using the Jewel of the Sun once more?

What cost if he used the relic twice in close succession?

"Then we disagree," the surrogate said as it flashed forward.

Never swung his blade but the weapon struck only a taloned hand, flying from his grip with a burst of blue sparks. The surrogate caught him by the throat, lifting him easily. "You should have tried the ring – it might have killed you, of course, but you would have stopped my surrogate, Never. Then you could have gone to your grave satisfied with the illusion that you'd struck a decisive blow."

Before he could answer, Never was hurled through the air, Rikeva's cry following.

He sailed beyond the Isle and plummeted toward the waves, but somehow without panic. He wasn't falling, he was being *carried*. The surrogate tore across the waves, brine spraying from the force of their passage as it flew toward the mainland.

And its speed was inhuman. Pressure that built and built until Never was barely able to keep his eyes open, or cling to awareness as colours flashed by in unnatural streaks and curves – not so different from travelling a river with a guide.

Aside from the fight to stay conscious.

His vision dimmed. He could not manage even a single word or protest, much less fight free.

And then nothing.

***

Never awoke immersed in cold, breathing the lingering damp of the shadowy air. Within the stone he sat upon, vines bound him and their leaves rustled as he strained to move.

A Throne of Leaves.

The same as in Oleksan's strange, dream-like hothouse. Only now a far colder light poured in from above. Darkness still waited beyond its limits, beyond hints of tall columns too. Darkness and silence. He was alone.

The Temple Trivium?

Possible, but proving so would be difficult, bound and alone as he was. It made little sense why the Burnished King had captured him when every other encounter had been to torment or kill.

Something had changed, and not for the better.

Oleksan wanted blood. Amouni blood.

Never called the crimson-fire and tore the vines free, most of each tendril seared to ash in his hands.

Disturbingly easy.

He stepped down to the stone floor and found that, wherever he was, there were no puddles, no clumps of lake-weed or drowned fish, of silt or shells or other debris. Instead, more vines and other plants pushed through the stones, most of which bore patterns of wings and unfamiliar combinations of runes. All dry. Chill, but not appearing to have recently been freed from the bottom of a massive lake.

His Amouni blade was missing, as was the Jewel of the Sun.

Not surprising, yet they had to be recovered.

But Oleksan had bound him to the throne and left him unattended for a reason. If something had changed, and the Burnished King now wanted blood, or something else, then handing it over by rushing after the ring was madness. Even an obvious if unclear trap could still be sprung by haste.

Was the theft of the Jewel of the Sun the bait?

Or was it the urge to explore, to attempt to take down the temple from within?

"You gleaming bastard," Never muttered. Hard to take a step without knowing which one could spell disaster. Some comfort remained; Rikeva was probably safe enough on the isle, and there was even a slim chance she would be able to find Ivadr. Hopefully.

He turned back to the Throne of Leaves.

"Why here?" Nothing in the way of an answer came to mind. Never raised his voice somewhat. "Guide?"

No robed memory-keeper appeared.

Another turn of events that was entirely unsurprising. Oleksan would have repurposed, banished, or hidden any hints of the Amouni that might be helpful. Just as his surrogate had seemed to have done at the isle. Above all, there was one assumption that could be made. Whatever the Plague-King wanted, he could not simply take.

It was obviously not a matter of simply draining blood either, or he would have done so.

Time to find answers.

Never moved into the shadowy hall, watching for threats, soon reaching an arched exit – it led to a corridor with three exit points; directly ahead, a large, sealed door, or two paths on each side that led around the throne room... if that was the room's function.

Skylights lit both paths, and so it mattered little which he chose.

Left had him crossing more tiles, these too a clean white. The walls were unadorned by art or statuary, but halfway along the hall he found an engraving, gleaming words set in silver.

"In you the world is created; its only limits are your own."

He couldn't help but frown at the message. Who exactly

was 'you' in the message? A message so important as to be enshrined upon the walls of a temple? Echoes of Father, even of Snow's desperation to change the world were clear...

More evidence of the Amouni conceit that so many had come to fear.

He walked on, eventually reaching a large room empty of furniture, with empty crates of steel beside a stairwell at the far end. No light waited below, so he called the crimson-fire and let it burn bright enough to act as a torch. At the bottom, another passage behind a closed door that swung open on silent hinges. Still no signs of decay or rust, of anything that suggested the place had once been submerged.

And no attack either.

The new passage led to what might have been an enormous storeroom, one that stretched wider and longer than he was expecting. Just how much temple was hidden below the waterline?

But more disconcerting was the storeroom's contents.

The huge chamber had been divided by silver bars – creating a spacious cell, and one that contained scores of prisoners, people of all ages within. They even had small areas of partial privacy, with blankets strewn on lines.

Not all people were caged. Guards moved about carrying trays of food and water... though 'servants' might have been a better word, since none were armed, and their clothing was in no way uniform. Much like the prisoners themselves; fisherfolk wore water-resistant smocks for the most part, farmers in more muted, earthy tunics and both town and city folk alike bringing a little more colour. But in addition to the Marlosi, other prisoners were present – Quisoan, or Hanik and Vadiyem too.

And while expressions were hardly joyous, there was an absence of panic or visible despair.

Everyone seemed at least comfortable, they were obviously being provided for when it came to meals and shelter, having plenty of space in their massive cell. And while there were clear 'sections' of folk from the various nations or cultures, they did seem to be communicating, sharing, helping the younger ones, cooperating with the servants.

And yet, all remained prisoners still.

He approached a young Marlosi woman at the bars, hailing her but she did not respond. Up close, it did not even seem that she saw him, since she simply fidgeted with the hem of her bright yellow tunic without reacting to his presence in any way.

No one else seemed bothered at his approach, either.

"I am Never," he introduced himself to her. "What happened here? I can free you."

Her gaze did not change. She sighed and turned away from the bars but leant against them.

Never frowned as he reached out to touch her shoulder. "Can you hear me?"

She turned her head slightly but did not react any further... she was not choosing to ignore him, nor did she seem to have trouble hearing. It was clearly something else. Oleksan's dark power? Never took a few steps, nearer a pair of older men who spoke together softly – they were worried about 'Erabiam' who had not been captured.

Neither answered when spoken to.

"Hey!" Never shouted but earned no reward. He waved his hands before them, even stretched into the cell and gave one man a fair shove, but the farmer only righted himself and kept speaking, his fellow not even acknowledging the interruption.

"Do you actually believe that thing?" the man was asking.

The second man scratched at his beard. "No, but he hasn't hurt anyone yet. I don't know what to make of that."

"That's not really true, is it?" said the man Never had pushed. "What about the three soldiers?"

"Well... we don't know where they are."

"Exactly."

The bearded man frowned. "So, what are you saying?"

"That we have to keep watching for a chance to escape."

Never moved on with a frown of his own. As easy as it would have been to cut through the bars, there was no way to rescue even a single prisoner if he could not lead them. And setting everyone free to wander aimlessly, trapped in the temple, would that be dangerous? What Amouni devices remained? Had Oleksan taken other measures to keep them in place?

Just what power did the Burnished King possess?

The demi-god had placed some magic upon the room. Or upon the people directly. The mystery was impossible to unravel. And perhaps a more pressing question, how many had Oleksan stolen away to save from his plans for slaughter? There was every chance that more prisoners resided in the other temples.

He found another passage and door at the end of the room but it did not open – not even in response to blood, and there was a sense that once again, the Burnished King had a hand in the changes.

Never strode back across the prison, pausing at the stair to glance toward the people. Were the prisoners somehow part of the trap? There had to be a way to free them... but it was clearly impossible so long as Oleksan lived.

"I'll be back," Never told them as started back up the stairs at a jog and resumed his search of the long-disused halls, where finally he found a window.

Across a short stretch of brilliant blue water waited a second temple, the hint of a third visible beyond it in turn, both gleaming white structures that stretched up toward the sky, surely too tall to have been hidden by the lake.

Smooth walls were streaked with veins of quartz, three lines of rose pink ascending, more colour faintly visible in runes above arched windows... numbers to denote floors! Each window was tall enough to walk through – and modest landing pads protruded like sturdy discs.

Functionality was not the only consideration, for the windows rose in graceful spirals, though that too might have had a practical purpose, avoiding visitors bunching up in any one area... assuming the Temple Trivium was such a busy place that dozens and dozens of Amouni were flying in and out all the time.

The entry was not visible from Never's position, but the peak was – three rings beneath it, the centre being the widest. From below, they might have been something more than decorative, but he could not guess their purpose.

Hard to imagine anyone building something similar in Marlosi, or anywhere else for that matter. He stepped onto the landing platform before his own window and reached out to touch the wall – even the way the tiles connected without hints of seams seemed impossible to reproduce. Here, the lines of quartz were amber and above, only two rings.

He turned back to the centre temple.

Oleksan would be waiting within, his hideous plan no doubt taking shape, but whether something had changed or not, there were still no answers. Only more questions. Chief among them, the purpose of his capture.

"What is your game now?" Never muttered. "Why bring me here?"

Chapter 35

"Tired of wandering?"

Never spun.

Oleksan stood behind him, his golden frame just as compelling as before, towering but somehow not purely threatening, the three orb-like eyes simply watching. As before, his beak-like mouth was full of fangs and the polished surface of his body revealed no hints of where the Seal might rest.

Though it hardly mattered without the Jewel of the Sun.

"Why spare me? Why bring me to the Temple?"

"So that you might see that the changes I bring will not mean an end to humanity, that is all."

Hardly a compelling answer. Never narrowed his eyes. "That is a lie – you need me for something else, don't you? The Final Seal holds."

Oleksan spread elegant hands. "I admit that you have caused some inconvenience but you cannot believe that I have only relied upon a single method to achieve my goal? Aside from which, there are relics of your people in the temples that may well result in a far more expeditious path to my dreams. I have found them most interesting."

Never smiled; having his guesses confirmed was a relief, even in the face of an equally troubling possibility raised by the monster before him. "Your candour makes for a nice change, but that doesn't mean I'm not going to kill you," Never replied as he stepped away from the window to free his wings. Twin balls of Holy Fire blazed blue and green in his fists.

"Then you should attempt same," the king replied, yet he did not attack, did not even move a limb; there was but a slight stretching of the beak like mouth – a smile or a sign of some craving?

Never flung a hand of fire forth.

The flames split into trails across an invisible barrier before the creature. Oleksan's voice was clear over the crackle. "I believe you should consider my offer, Amouni."

A second blast did not reach its target either, instead splashing against and searing the pale walls. Never cut the flow but kept the flame bright in his fists. There had to be a way to break the barrier – other than the Jewel of the Sun.

"Thinking that you're outmatched? No shame in that, Never," Oleksan said. "After all, I now possess everything you need to defeat me, and you can dash yourself against my form all for naught, and lose your life and then soon after, lose every single person you care about. At the very least, you will be spared witnessing such horrors. But you also have another choice – you can listen to my words. That will cost you nothing."

"I think we both know what your words are worth."

"Do you?" The Burnished King leant against the wall,

three orbs glowing. "Since you cannot harm me, I will share them anyway."

"Let me share something instead," Never replied. "When I return, it will be with the means to grind you beneath my heel." He turned to stride back down the hall; there was a *forasa* within the entry.

Once he escaped, he could locate the mysterious Ecanseja, or rescue Rikeva and find Ivadr first.

Oleksan appeared before him, blocking the exit.

"Perhaps you will. But you cannot leave unless it is by my grace," he said, a hint of displeasure entering his voice. "And to do so, you will consider my offer."

Never folded his arms. "Speak."

"Better, Amouni." Oleksan straightened. "You have seen people that no doubt appear imprisoned here, caged by a sense of calm, or even resignation, but that is temporary. Those I have been collecting will be set free in the new world, a world which approaches all the more swiftly now that I have found the unfinished Jalen Khasom."

"They are caged by your power." But for all his defiance he could not help doubting. What was the Jalen Khasom? In Marlosi, it would have been the known as the Turning Gaze or perhaps the Eye of Hours. Was it related to the Sea God's Eye?

A weapon?

And more, why was the demi-god sharing so much of his intent? Was it to create a false sense of confidence? Was the Eye of Hours yet another deception? The creation of a false target for Never to strike at?

"And it is my power that will shelter all from the most riveting abandon of the coming storm," Oleksan continued.

"Your friends are offered as much. You can choose as many as you like to not only survive, Never, but to flourish when I have cleansed the lands. They will be afforded all their hopes and dreams, they can – if they choose – grow old and quiet, contented together, or live long lives guaranteed to uncover wonder after wonder."

"I am no monster to make such choices," Never snapped.

"Yet make them you must."

"No."

"This is no lie. Those I save will have a future for there is hardly any joy in ruling over a vast emptiness."

"You have my answer."

The Burnished King shrugged. "Then that is its own choice, and you will die and have saved no-one. But go now, clutch at what little straws remain," he added, and a malicious glee now seemed to seep from his words. "I will welcome you when you are ready to concede. Just be sure you do not dawdle, for I am making great progress here, Never, great progress indeed – lo, the very mountains seem small compared to my stride."

Oleksan vanished.

Never spat after the demi-god, and strode on to the hall, picking up his pace until he reached the *forasa*, coming to a halt with a growl.

How dare the Burnished King make such an offer?

"I am not so selfish," Never said into the dark, emptiness of the entryway – certain that if Oleksan had cared to listen, the demi-god would hear. He raised his voice. "Don't be so eager for my return – it will herald your destruction!"

Chapter 36

A miracle had occurred during his absence.

Ivadr sat with Rikeva around a campfire in the same chamber they had chosen for a camp, shadows dancing across their smiles. Rikeva crossed the chamber, a fierce relief that she seemed to be holding at bay discernible in her gaze. "I thought the worst, Never."

"So did I, at first," he replied. "But I'm glad to find you both alive."

"It wasn't easy. What happened with Oleksan?"

"Well, it's not much of a story," he said as he sat, going on to explain Oleksan's offer. He described a little of the temple, and the worst of the news perhaps, the loss of the Jewel of the Sun. "If the Jalen Khasom, the Eye of Hours, can make his nightmare come true sooner, then we need Ecanseja more than ever."

"Should we call on Illya?"

Would it actually make communicating with Ecanseja easier? More concerning, could Kiymako afford her absence? Could Ayuni, Muka and the others? Illya herself? "Maybe. But they're under siege, remember?"

"A logical target," Ivadr said. "The Holy Fire is a threat and all the better if he can distract you also."

Never nodded.

"Then how can we speak to this dead Amouni?" Rikeva asked.

"I have something that might work, but let me think it through first," Never said. He glanced at the white flesh cooking upon skewers over the fire. "That's not sea-serpent is it?"

She laughed. "No, just regular fish – hake. There was more than enough of all kinds washed up after the attack."

"And it hasn't returned? No trouble from the sea-creatures?"

"None."

"Wonderful," he said as he helped himself to a few skewers. "Now it's your turn. Ivadr, tell me how you survived."

The man nodded. "Of course. You recall that I believe my ancestors bore some link to the ancient Malecaphera?"

"I do."

"Part of that burden includes the shadow-run, like leaping from shadow to shadow if you recall my description?"

Never nodded, his mouth full.

"So long as I have shadows within my sight, it means I can pass from one to another – whether cast upon water, wood, stone or steel – anything really, though this was the first time I had to test the ability while underwater."

"I found him soaking wet, gasping for breath on the beach," Rikeva added.

"And I am thankful that you did. I have never had to shadow-run for such a sustained period. I may have simply slipped back into the water, without you."

She smiled. "We've been planning a way off the isle since, but even with the extra debris, there didn't seem much hope of making a good raft. No need for that, now that you're here."

"Pleased to once more provide you with convenient travel, My Lady," he said around a final mouthful. Learning more about Ivadr's hidden ability was both hopeful and concerning. Was it something to be used against Oleksan, or did it represent some hook that the demi-god could use to influence or hurt Ivadr? "We have time before nightfall if you want to leave. Hopefully our lodgings in Olecsa are still empty. We can rest there before returning to the tomb."

"Then let's leave now," Rikeva suggested.

"I would like to check on Shade, if we could," Ivadr said.

Never rose. "Back to the *forasa* then. Unless anyone came across the Amouni blade?"

"I think it fell into the ocean," Rikeva said as she collected her belongings.

Perhaps not such a bad place for the deadly weapon. And if the Holy Fire or the Jewel of the Sun was not enough to take on the Burnished King, then not even an Amouni sword would help. "Even less reason to linger, then."

***

The home of Jadeo's friend in Olecsa was still empty, and it once more became a convenient place to eat, rest and plan, though there was little to discuss, save for where to find new horses for the ride.

All else hinged on what Ecanseja had to say, and whether it could be said in blood.

By the time all was prepared and they had ridden from the still-crowded city to reach the Amouni tomb, afternoon light shone upon a deserted crater. Despite honeyed words from the Burnished King, Never had still expected some form of resistance. Was leaving the tomb clear another part of the ploy?

"He must really want you to return, Never," Rikeva said from her saddle. "Not even a single corpse to greet us."

"I agree."

"All the more reason not to rush into our attack," Ivadr said.

"Very much. Once we hear what Ecanseja has to say, I want to take a moment to plan the details. There might be a way to draw Oleksan out, since we know he wants me to return to the Temple."

"What about your blood and the tomb?" Rikeva asked.

"This time I should be fine," he replied. "No Jewel of the Sun. Which is another problem, of course," he added, then shrugged. "Ready?"

Rikeva extended her hands and he took them, spreading his wings and lifting her into the air only long enough to adjust the angle of their descent, which was swift enough. She kept a hold of his hand when they landed. "Never, before we do whatever it is we decide, I want to ask you something." Her words were quiet.

"Your family?"

"Yes. Will you promise me something?"

"I will."

"It's something that I'll promise you too," she said, and

now her voice took on more of her usual, confident tone. "If saving the lands costs me my life, or you yours, I want the other to protect their family. Will you promise me that? I offer you the same, for your sister and your friends."

"You have my oath." He did not mention that if one were to fall, it was likely because the other had already done so. And she knew as much as well but saying the words aloud would have done naught but poison the moment.

She lifted a hand to touch his cheek. "Now that's out of the way, let's both stay alive."

"I like the sound of that too," he said as he smiled, then leapt up, beating his wings hard to reach Ivadr, immediately floating back down to set the Traveller upon the stone slab that concealed the Amouni tomb.

Once open, Never knelt at the entrance to the stairwell, which was still blocked by melted, twisted stone. He glanced up at Rikeva and Ivadr. "This time I won't be as thorough when it comes to resealing this place... at least until after we deal with Oleksan. Just in case we need Ecanseja's help again."

It was time to learn exactly what the Eyes of Hours was, to learn Oleksan's new plan, and to learn what message Ecanseja had called him to deliver – assuming the entombed Amouni was the one Illya had spoken with.

Yet who else could it have been?

Never called the crimson-fire and turned it blue and green.

Chapter 37

Once more, Never stood before the quartz coffin, the chamber lit by crimson patterns, Rikeva and Ivadr nearby.

He'd already explained how his blood could take memories, but there was no guarantee he'd find the message by accident. Ecanseja would not be able to speak through his corpse, but if Oleksan's taunting was to be believed, there was no time to search out and retrieve other *nekromant*.

And even if one could be found and brought to the tomb, would the *nekromant* be able to understand the Amouni language? Illya had managed, with some effort. Perhaps the Prose of the Dead was enough.

He hesitated, a drop of red sneaking down his forefinger.

"Never?" Rikeva asked.

"In all my years, I have not sought to try this with the dead. I do not know if it will work, or even if his blood has been trapped along with his body in the first place. Nothing at all may happen. Or anything at all."

"What should we watch for?" Ivadr asked.

"Anything that suggests I'm not having a good time," Never replied, forcing a grin. "Sorry I can't be more specific than that, but the worst that will happen – I'm hoping – is that I don't learn much at all."

He reached down into the quartz, with no more resistance than water, and with one hand made a small cut in Ecanseja's forearm. Blood welled. Next, he took a breath and pressed his finger against the point of blood.

Ice surged into his veins.

The tomb vanished – replaced by a jagged wall of Ecanseja's memories as they crashed over him, easing but not removing the discomfort. Each memory was a frozen moment, colours gone, leaving only muted black and grey, stark white.

With every image came a wealth of connected emotion, thoughts, words and even scents, all pummelling his mind. Every Amouni face, every soft grove of green or blue, every smoking, bloody battlefield, every echo from underground chambers, every song, poem and bitter diary entry, every drop of wine and juice from unfamiliar fruits crashed into his mind.

Never opened his mouth to call for help, to call for Rikeva and Ivadr to tear him away.

But Ecanseja's life continued to rush into him.

So many moments! From babe to boy to man, a disordered list of each triumph and failure, tears at a snarling dog, a first victory in a game with rings on a stone tablet and war-lessons with blazing hands, romantic meals with snowstorms beyond clear windows, passionate meetings in lamplight and crushing ends to relationships, political triumphs seen from enormous white squares along with comparatively simpler moments; at rest with literature or walking sun-lit streets of paved stone and silver. The memories continued to invade.

Ecanseja was becoming too real.

The sheer number of the man's memories crowded Never, pushing his own life to one side with the howl of a raging storm. Fighting back was like sending paper missives out to face the hurricane, just as keeping a hold of his own past was becoming futile, like clutching after fish but finding only gleaming scales in his hands.

"No!"

Never shoved back – hard, harder than he had fought in a long time, a mess of panic and fury surging forth – and then more, more as his stomach constricted and burned, somewhere in the chamber, wherever his actual body lay, palms bleeding as his dug nails deep.

And then nothing but blinding white.

It filled his mind in a soothing, sweet *nothingness* and relief flooded after.

Never opened his eyes. Above, the ceiling of the chamber waited, the red glow a blessed hint of colour. So too, the blonde of Rikeva's hair and Ivadr's dark plait with its rich brown tones, their own relief visible in their eyes. "How long was that?" Never asked.

Somewhere, hurled to one darkened corner of his mind, the life of Ecanseja lurked, or at least, as much of it as he'd been able to absorb. Held at bay for now, it seemed to be less of a whirlwind and more... more a *resource*. But would vital information be part of the memories?

Or just the truth of the man, not at all without pure value, but perhaps not useful?

"It wasn't long," Rikeva said. "You started to shake and then you threw yourself back. I didn't expect it; I would have caught you..."

"No need to apologise." He raised a hand and she helped him into a sitting position. Pain erupted in his temples, swiftly settling into a persistent throb. Wonderful. Even his stomach was swirling. "I have what feels like all of his memories. If there's something there, I will find it. I just think that first... it'd be quite a good thing if I threw up."

He leant over and retched, hot vomit splashing onto the tiles in a mess of pale brown and green. He groaned, though relief came with the vomit – an easing of the headache for one.

"I'll get water," Ivadr said as he strode to Never's pack.

Rikeva placed a hand on his back. "Do we need medicine?"

He wiped at his mouth, glaring down at the hot bile. Of course Rikeva had to witness him heaving up the contents of his stomach. It seemed he wasn't going to throw up again at least, a small mercy, but an eminently acceptable one. "I'll bring some dirt down before we leave. I just need a moment."

"Take whatever time you need," she said, the worry in her gaze easing as he slid away from the vomit and accepted a flask from Ivadr, rinsing his mouth out then drinking deeply. The bitter taste lingered, but Ivadr had come prepared, it seemed – offering a honeystick.

"It is old, but should be better than nothing," the man said as he handed it over.

Never thanked Ivadr and placed it between his teeth, the sweetness faint but a vast improvement. Whether the alertness it brought would add to the lingering headache was yet to be seen but at least it hadn't upset his stomach yet.

"Do you think the message is in there somewhere?" Rikeva asked after a short while.

"It could be. After a fashion," he said, then paused – answers were simply at his fingertips as he spoke. "Ecanseja was a high-ranking Temple Guardian, present for the construction and abandonment of the Jalen Khasom. And based on what it was supposed to do, Oleksan was not exaggerating about the thing speeding up his plans."

"What is it?" Rikeva asked.

"Something that was able to turn back time for broken things."

Chapter 38

"What does that actually mean?" Rikeva asked, brow furrowed. "Does it return things to the past?"

"Only for whatever it is used upon."

She seemed to search for her next words. "Are you saying it could... fix a broken limb? Restore a ransacked city?"

Ivadr too, appeared equally troubled as he folded his arms.

"Probably. There's one of Ecanseja's memories in here," Never said, gesturing to his head, "so I'll do my best, since I can't share it – but let's move away from the vomit a little first." Never shifted far enough that the stench was no longer overpowering. "It's a room similar to what I saw in the Temple, not so different from here. There's a group of Amouni testing the Eye of Hours – it looks like a quartz eye, coloured as amethyst, about the size of a head, suspended between silver triangular points. They've arranged the Eye to face a vase of eggshell blue," he said, pausing as more of the scene surfaced, becoming clearer, as if streams and finally beads of water fell away from his view. "One of the

Amouni breaks the vase with a hammer but just enough for it to collapse upon itself, a few shards hit the ground but that's all. Then he steps away and the others... well, they do *something* to the quartz eye and the vase *repairs* itself, piece by piece leaping back up into position, movements like an exact reversal of the order it broke in. Everyone cheers, but the emotion that I get from Ecanseja... he's afraid. It's almost an overwhelming fear."

Silence followed his words.

Rikeva exhaled. "You said this Eye of Hours might be used to restore other things. Living things?" Rikeva asked. "Is that what worried him, do you think?"

"Yes, but I think my description wasn't quite accurate. Because it didn't magically restore the vase, it somehow changed time for the vase. It returned the vase to a time in the *past* when it wasn't broken."

She shook her head. "How?"

"I don't know, but... oh." More memories rose, as if pushed up from somewhere within this time. "It costs blood, a lot of blood, to work its magic."

Ivadr stiffened. "Then the prisoners are fuel for Oleksan."

"It's likely," Never replied, one hand clenched. "Or maybe they really are meant to be saved – some of them. He told me that there was no joy in ruling over a vast emptiness, but that doesn't mean the slaughter of thousands and thousands of *others* that he's planning to undertake won't be used for the Eye."

"Will the blood of those innocents be enough?" he asked.

"He wants me for a reason he won't reveal," Never said. "Even if it's not my blood, I don't have an unlimited supply. I think we have to assume that he's found some other way to use the Eye of Hours to transform Marlosi and all the lands to a time when people did not yet exist."

"We're assuming that, aren't we?" Rikeva said, though she didn't seem to think it was a poor assumption.

"We have to assume the worst."

She nodded.

And it was a chilling possibility; to suddenly wipe entire nations off the maps, to crush each and every life, dream and hope – the depths of depravity and the monstrous ego it took for the Burnished King to believe he could start over and do better. It was not unlike the Amouni.

"It's still a trap, even so," Ivadr said.

"I've been thinking of that too," Never said. "But let's go over the details somewhere that doesn't smell of fresh vomit."

***

"A night raid, then?" Rikeva asked from where she added fuel to the campfire, their bedrolls open to the mild spring air. The stars above burned brighter than usual, not a single trace of clouds to cloak them. Instead, it was treetops that surrounded their camp and obstructed parts of the view.

And below their camp, beyond the wall and floating upon the silent surface of the central lake waited the Temple Trivium; three pale spires darkened, no hints of light visible within.

But Oleksan would be waiting.

"Night means we can take advantage of Ivadr's shadow-run. And I don't know how much longer we can afford to wait."

"He'll be expecting this too, won't he?" Rikeva asked. "After all, he wants you to return."

"I'm gambling on whether he'd expect us to wrest control of the Eye of Hours and use it on him – he might not know we're even aware of it."

"Will that work?" she asked.

"We have to try," he said. "At the least, I want it to weaken or distract him enough for Ivadr to find the Jewel of the Sun. Oleksan won't attack the Jalen Khasom itself, since it's so important to his plans."

Ivadr was nodding along. "This could work, but there is still at least one problem we must solve."

"He has hostages," Never said. "A lot of them."

"And we'll be adding ourselves to the list if we're captured," Rikeva added.

"I know," Never said as he nudged a burning log back into the centre of the fire. "It will end in a stand-off if we can only threaten the Eye of Hours while he holds the prisoners."

"We need another surprise, another trick, another advantage," Rikeva said as she rose to pace. "I doubt that growing more arch-blossoms is what we need, so I'm not much use. What about the relics in Pacela's Spire? That silver man?"

Never blinked. The silver man... it was a Diving Skin, and while Ecanseja knew exactly how to apply and use the skin to explore beneath the waves, it could not help them. "I finally understand it, but I don't know if we need to breathe underwater," he replied. "Let's keep thinking; we have a little night left."

Rikeva came to a halt. "Someone's approaching."

Never rose, blades in hand.

A shadowy figure neared, bringing with it a faint swish of grass as the stranger reached the clearing's edge. But before the man reached the light, a sense of familiar blood reached Never. "Welcome, Cog."

The plain-faced man smiled, his customary scarf and grey cloak in place. When he raised a hand in greeting, Never made the introductions. "Cog is like me," he added.

"Not quite, *Davishca*. But I appreciate the kind words."

"You've been watching the Lakes?" Never asked.

He nodded, seeming happy enough to leap directly into the problem at hand. "Save for trips away for supplies. I followed the trail of decay here soon after it appeared. Few people escaped before the barrier came. Those I did not bury described a golden figure that offered them solace, one which they could hardly look away from. But it was the apparent... kindness of the creature that seemed to trouble them most."

"Your own kindness will be remembered by those you helped," Ivadr said.

"I hope it so."

Never sat by the fire, gesturing for Cog to join them. "We're breaking into the Temple soon. Want to join us?"

"Perhaps I should."

"Are you sure?" Ivadr asked. "It is a great risk."

He nodded slowly. "The Temples stir something within me... but it is vague." He spread his hands. "There is one thing that surprised me. That poisonous wall allows people to enter. Some simply appear from the plains, as if drawn here, and they are each admitted."

"Oleksan must be calling them," Never said with a frown.

"So it seemed to me."

"Did they respond to you?" Never asked, mentioning the prisoners within the temple and their inability to hear or even acknowledge him.

"I tried to stop a few, but they would not listen. Some became frantic and all too soon, the mist started to attack whenever I approached." He reached into a pocket and withdrew a small animal skull, probably from a rodent. "One man dropped this, but I have not been able to discover its purpose – yet if you hold it, you will see why I've kept it."

Never took the skull and a strong urge to stand up and leave the clearing, to head for the wall and then the temple, fell across him. Strong as it was, it could not compel him.

"It cannot force us," Cog continued. "But for some, the lure is obviously too much. There are scores of bones littered at the base of the wall."

"Oleksan likes to use animals as messengers."

"I don't think we can use that against him in any way, can we?" Rikeva asked.

"It doesn't seem likely," Cog said. "I'd hoped to learn more but now that I have finally crossed paths with Never, I am relieved. What is our plan to attack?"

Never smiled. "You know what they say about plans – no matter how good they seem, what matters most is how you react in the moment."

Chapter 39

Midnight had barely passed and Never already taken his rest, all that remained was to storm the temple. In truth, 'storm' was probably not the right word for a force of four.

But so long as four returned.

And Oleksan was oddly lacking in bloodlust... on the surface.

His efforts to lie, confuse and sow doubt could not be ignored. Did he actually want to save a few handfuls of people for his empty future? Were they more than a supply of blood for the Jalen Khasom? Never made a fist where he stood watch, back resting against a tree trunk. Oleksan had to be destroyed – to the very last scrap of golden skin.

"Never."

He looked up to find Cog standing nearby, a glowing pipe in his mouth, shadowed by the smouldering campfire where Rikeva and Ivadr still slept.

"It's nearly time," Never said.

The man nodded and did not speak at first. "There is something that still troubles me."

"About our plan?"

"No, it is sound – perhaps all that we can do with what we possess, your descriptions of the layout of the temple itself, of the *forasa*, it is all well. We can only fight until our last."

"Somewhat fatalistic of you, Cog."

"Indeed. But I have a request, which I suppose is related to the very same view I have just now offered."

Never straightened. "Should I be worried?"

"In a word, perhaps." His mouth was set in a firm line, resolve clear. "I wish for you to use the *Hor Pyrilh* upon me."

"I..."

"Your brother taught me enough. I am confident that, with your help, we can ensure a successful transformation."

Never had no answer, he could only stare. Cog's request was *not* what he had expected – he hadn't known what to expect at all, but it was *not* the Human Maps. A dangerous request surely, and wrong to even attempt such a thing. Snow's folly. How close his brother and his mistakes seemed now.

"I believe it necessary."

"Cog, if it doesn't work... I don't even understand how. Or the risks. What if you don't survive? Or something worse happens?"

"Remember, your brother helped me with my gifts when it comes to smoke and other deceptions. We will be building upon what he started."

There were too many reasons *not* to do such a thing. And following in Snow's footsteps... No. It was not a path to be trodden by another. Failing to destroy the book after the war had been a mistake. And even if he attempted such a thing, what if the transformation did not work? What cost to Cog? "I don't want to be the one that causes you more suffering."

"What if this is the only way to stop a demi-god? He is not so far removed from you or I, after a fashion," the man replied, his voice gentle.

"We're not—"

Cog raised a hand. "I know what you will say, and yes. We are not precisely like our ancestors but I have no Holy Fire. Allow me this. I want to make a difference."

"That I understand, but why the *Hor Pyrilh*?"

"For one, it will bring me peace."

Never met the man's gaze. Peace? How? And yet, what right did he have to deny Cog?

"There is one more reason. If you need it," the man added. "The Burnished King is moving."

"How?"

Cog led Never to the opposite edge of the clearing, through the trees to where the grass sloped down eventually to the Lakes, and pointed to the Temple Trivium, which had moved to new positions upon the water.

More, a quartz eye now hung suspended above the peaks... the temples themselves formed a triangle that supported the Jalen Khasom, one that was far, far larger than that which Ecanseja knew.

Never swore.

"Have I convinced you, Never?"

He ran a hand through his hair. "How long will it take?"

"Not so long at all, especially with the *forasa*."

"Cog..." He glanced back at the dark quartz, the Eye of

Hours suspended, a looming threat. Oleksan had to be stopped; there was nothing else so important. "It's how we react, right?"

Cog finally smiled. "So it is."

Never hesitated still, one hand held at his chest, about to draw the symbol. "Watch over Rikeva and Ivadr, Cog."

"I will."

Never drew the symbol and its light carried him to the nearest *forasa*, but he didn't stay long, reaching for the next *forasa* beyond Isacina's walls, arriving on the same patch of land as last time and immediately launching himself into the air.

He flew up and over the walls, crossing the city at speed – and when he reached the home of Pacela's faithful, he wheeled around to what he estimated was the right stairwell, hovering before the window. Was anyone inside? He paused a moment, listening as best he could, then called the crimson-fire with a snap of his fingers. He sent a stream forth to cut into the stone, creating the outline of a door, then pushed the wall and window frame inside with a crash.

He climbed after with a wince. Steam rose from the half-melted steel and stone as he stepped over the mess and started up the stairs. "Sorry, Jardila," he murmured.

Only lamplight joined him on his climb, no priest or acolytes to startle this time, and when he reached the locked room of Amouni relics, he once again used crimson-fire to break in, leaving the door functional but no longer secure.

Inside, he strode to the desk and snatched up the *Hor Pyrilh* in the faint light, bypassing the silver man, before returning to the door. There, he paused. Just to be safe, could it be returned to some sort of shape, or at least, be melted enough to seal entirely, until he could return?

Never stuffed the book under his arm and used his fire to lock the door.

No time to wait for it to cool.

He drew the symbol over his chest and again, before the light faded, he was reaching for the next *forasa*, landing in the plains of southern Marlosi with a sigh. Time was running out but was it the right thing to do? He lifted The Human Maps and turned a few pages – Amouni runes with notes added in Marlosi, Snow's careful handwriting in the margins.

Above, the stars still shone. The night was not near to ending but he could not stand lost in memories.

Never took flight once more.

The camp soon appeared below, dark trees and pale wheat sliding by, while off to the southeast waited the Temple Trivium and the Eye of Hours, purple quartz gleaming in the night. What exactly did Cog have in mind? Plans had to be changed; Ivadr could still seek the Jewel of the Sun, which meant Oleksan had to be kept occupied... perhaps while Rikeva freed the prisoners?

He descended to where Rikeva and the others waited around the muted flames of their campfire. Each rose as he landed, a certain tension to their movements. Anticipation mixed with... impatience in the case of Rikeva, though Cog was calm as ever. Ivadr seemed his usual sombre self but his arms were folded again.

"Here it is," Never said as he raised the *Hor Pyrilh*.

"Thank you, Never." Cog began to remove his clothes.

"If you find the entry for Mineral, you will see the runes required."

Never flipped through the pages. And while both Rikeva and Ivadr turned away for Cog's sake, it seemed that the scars at his neck drew more attention than his nakedness. The man bore other long scars too, in addition to what seemed to be old burn marks, one for each limb, and clear on his torso too.

Just what else had Cog suffered at the hands of Prince Jenisan's father? Or after, courtesy of Snow?

"I have it," Never said when he stopped on the page for Mineral – of which there was only one note in his brother's hand, otherwise three sets of runes waited, each bearing the same six symbols in various combinations. Snow's note suggested the second to last be used... yet there was a question mark. "Which set do I try? And how?"

"The blood of the Ascended, *Davishca* – you only have to draw the runes upon my skin."

"Is that all it takes?"

"Much of the pain required for this to work has already been endured," he replied. "And there is the matter of choosing correctly."

"What if I get it wrong?"

"It is unlikely I'll survive."

Never lowered the book. "This is too great a risk."

"Greater than letting the Eye of Hours free? We're all taking risks by entering the temple; I accept my fate."

Never closed his eyes a moment before nodding. He lifted the page and stared at the runes again – and Ecanseja knew which set to use. Snow had been close, but it was the row of runes above his handwritten question. Painting the symbols upon Cog would alter the man, much as he had been altered before, granting him some ability or property related to minerals...

Vague, but what else could be done? The book offered nothing and Ecanseja's memories did not extend beyond recognition.

Never drew a dagger and pricked his finger, painting the first rune on Cog's arm – avoiding the earlier burn site.

"Thank you, Never," Cog said, even as his face twisted in pain. The rune glowed crimson and the scent of burning flesh filled the camp. "I did not expect another chance like this, before the end."

Rikeva and Ivadr had turned back now, still silent but appearing no less concerned.

Never frowned as he painted the second symbol on Cog's other arm. More burning. "The end?"

"No change is forever."

"Wait." Never stopped, bloody finger poised before Cog's chest, a creeping suspicion coming to the fore. "Are you saying you'll end up like Andramir?"

"I am. Even now, I know my time is short."

He did not resume painting.

"You *know*, Never." Cog's smile was not sad; it was a hopeful expression. "I have already told you, you are giving me a gift. Please, continue."

Still, he didn't draw the third rune – a pain was growing; admiration mixed with fear, with regret. "You are asking me to paint your death sentence."

"Better that I face it on my terms."

"This isn't right."

Cog only waited.

Finally, Never raised a hand that he could not stop from shaking, and made the third symbol. It was not so neat as the others but it was accurate. Then he moved on to the man's back, where half a dozen burns already existed, and finally Cog's legs – each rune burning then settling into the flesh.

But when he finished and stepped back, a numbness spreading through him, Cog did not collapse.

The man turned and replaced his clothes, traces of pain gone from his face, a spark within his eyes. It was probably the most animated Never had seen him.

"It worked, didn't it?" Rikeva asked.

Cog lifted a hand and paused – it was changing, becoming clear, with sharp edges tinted pink and purple, like quartz. "Thankfully. And with a little practice, I believe I can destroy the Jalen Khasom from within. I simply need Never to fly me there."

Chapter 40

Never hovered over the enormous quartz eye, a purple gleam somewhere within the gemstone rather than being a reflection of starlight. Cog was growing lighter in his arms, the man's body somehow treading a line between mineral and smoke.

"Is this close enough?" Never asked. The practical question was not precisely the one he wanted to ask... but Cog had made his decision.

Cog nodded. "It is just right, Never."

"I don't suppose you can guess how long you'll need?"

The man chuckled. "No, but I'm certain you're the only one who can buy me enough time."

Never hesitated, then spoke once more. "Ready?"

"I am."

Never released Cog and he slipped into the Eye of Hours without a sound.

The man was gone... he had chosen his own fate. Would it work? At every step it seemed they gambled. A moment longer Never watched, then turned to dive back down toward the water where Rikeva and Ivadr were rowing across the lake's still surface.

Already more than halfway to the moorings that waited before the central temple, it would not take long to arrive. Lingering guilt had Never shaking, but it wasn't the boat they'd borrowed from the abandoned villages... He glanced back to the quartz once more, and then it was time to land.

He beat his wings in a flurry, stirring Rikeva's hair and sending ripples across the water, but managed to touch down without capsizing the longboat. "Any problems here?" he asked.

"None," Ivadr replied, but even in the starlight, his eyes were troubled.

"Are you sure?"

The man paused at the oar, and Rikeva did the same. "Seeing Cog's likely sacrifice has given me pause. It is a matter that I ought not burden you both with, but I am having misgivings about what is to come. I hesitate to admit, but I am almost looking forward to this."

Never laughed softly. "I was expecting bad news, you know."

Ivadr smiled. "It is simply that, after a lifetime spent searching for traces of the Maleecaphera, for warnings that they may return, and growing accustomed to failure, to knowing that failure actually meant all was well, I had convinced myself I was custodian of knowledge only. Now that is no longer the truth and I am somewhat uneasy with my desire to face this struggle."

Rikeva put a hand on his shoulder. "No, that makes sense to me."

Never nodded. "Let's make your ancestors proud."

"And both of yours," Ivadr replied as he took up the oar again. "Thank you."

On they rowed, and when the boat brushed up against the moorings before the towering white of the Temple Trivium, Never climbed onto the wharf and tied them off. He extended a hand to Ivadr, Rikeva already climbing fee, and together they paused before the stair, grand double doors cast wide, darkness within.

"I will return with the Jewel of the Sun," Ivadr said. "I swear as much."

He flickered into a silhouette, streaking toward the entrance, sliding from shadow to shadow – an easy, fluid motion beneath the stars.

"Let's hurry," Rikeva said after a slight pause to watch, then started up the stairs.

It did not take long to reach the open doors.

No sign of enemies waiting within, no furniture or artwork here either, just the pattern of the five-pointed leaf upon the tiled floor. The interior of the central temple was equally empty – no soldiers or creatures; all cool white, leaving them alone in the carriage-sized entryway.

The same disconcerting message had been written in silver nearby and above, the windows and landing pads spiralled up and out of view.

Here, the main difference from the first temple was light and shadow. The central temple had been lit by silver lamps placed along the columns, its interior also more like a throne room than a temple, though patterns on the floor now featured wings, eyes and runes of protection. Each column offered small, curved alcoves, perhaps the size of a child, and while all stood empty, a sense of watchfulness lingered within.

And there *was* a watcher, perched upon another throne of leaves – this throne decaying, crumbling into grey.

The Burnished King.

He stood upon the throne and spread both arms. "Welcome once more."

And while Rikeva gripped Never's hand, staring as she did, he remained less enthralled, less disturbed by the golden creature after yet another meeting, as though the effect had lessened due to exposure.

Instead, something the other temples did not hold had caught Never's eye – and it was not a smaller Jalen Khasom – but another coffin of clear quartz, exactly like the one that protected Ecanseja.

"Ready?" Never asked Rikeva.

She nodded and released his hand. Never called crimson flames and let them quicken to the Fires of Heaven, bright blue flickering, green pulsating.

"Such hostility is not necessary; you and your... familiar friend are not to be harmed."

"But you are," Never replied, his words terse. Why did the Burnished King continue to insist that Rikeva was not to be trusted? What was the implication that she was somehow known to him by some vague 'darkness'?

The lie was pathetically obvious.

Again, the beak-like face stretched into something of a grin. "We have danced before, Never. You cannot harm me." He settled back down upon the throne. "Instead, there is someone who wishes to speak to you. I believe, one of your so-called Guides."

"Is this his trap, somehow?" Rikeva whispered. A litter

of ribbons lay around her feet – she'd grown again, far more muscular, taller and broader even, but still herself. Just *far* stronger.

"The Guides do not answer to any but the Amouni," Never replied, though his own doubts crept in. Why would Oleksan be so eager? What had he done?

"Call him," the gleaming creature urged.

"You goad me into summoning an ally – why?"

Oleksan shrugged. "You must find out or seek to battle me again. Of course, it does not seem likely that you can do so while protecting her, and the more... disposable of my future citizens, I'm sure you'll agree."

"We can't trust that thing, Never."

He hesitated. Overall, the plan was simple – delay the Burnished King long enough for Cog or Ivadr to succeed. Whether that was through violence or talk, did it matter? A Guide could not – would not – help Oleksan. So whatever the trap, it was not going to succeed via the Guide... and more, the coffin was a powerful tool.

Ecanseja knew exactly its purpose in creating new Guardians.

And if Oleksan thought to subvert such an event, he would fail.

"Guide."

A robed figure appeared before the coffin, deep purple cloth emblazoned with a pair of white wings across the chest. But more striking perhaps was the slender silver helm it wore – so closed up that it provided only a narrow, curved slit for vision, though no eyes were apparent.

Master.

"There is an intruder in the temple."

Yes.

"You will assist in its removal."

It is a slave of Arkenon.

"Meaning?"

I alone cannot manage such a task. A Guardian is required. Several of the Ascended may also be sufficient.

Never stared across at Oleksan as he spoke. "Is there no Guardian here?"

The Bed of Quartz lies empty.

"But I could enter it and become a Guardian?" he asked. And Ecanseja knew the answer – that was exactly the process, though it would come at a cost. The vast store of power he'd suddenly have access to would require a stasis that could not be broken.

Yes.

There was more to Ecanseja's memories – enough to reveal the possibility that even the Temple Trivium might become Oleksan's prison and in time, a new tomb.

It was also exactly the kind of power that could be used for the Eye of Hours.

Never turned to Rikeva, lowering his voice to a whisper. "I can use that coffin if we need to. Ecanseja knows more than Oleksan, but I need you to trust me."

She frowned. "What are you saying?"

"I'll be sealed in the Quartz but it I'll be able destroy the Eye and sink the Temple, to entomb Oleksan."

Her eyes widened. "Sealed? That's madness."

"Not if it saves everyone."

"There must be another way," she said, taking his arm, the grip a little painful.

"There is – the Jewel of the Sun. I'm still going to

distract Oleksan until Ivadr returns, and while I do, I want you to break the prisoners free, just like we planned," he said. "I just want to have something up my sleeve."

"Right... Of course," she said after a moment's hesitation. "But we still don't know if they'll follow me."

"Even if you break the bars, it's better than nothing. He'll probably have prisoners here too but as far as the other two temples, they'll have to wait until we deal with Oleksan."

"Trouble?" the Plague King called.

Never smiled. A flickering shadow waited between the columns. "Not at all. Guide, seal this room then destroy the Eye of Hours."

Yes, Master.

The purple figure disappeared.

Oleksan hissed as he leapt into the air. The Seal had worked. If not, he simply would have vanished and reappeared as he had before.

But when the Burnished King reached the first window, a narrow sledgehammer of black, almost spear-like, appeared in his hands. He swung *kirinth-dela*, his plague hammer, and it smashed against whatever barrier the Guide had erected in the window.

How long would it hold?

Never was already charging after, Rikeva's shout following. "Don't do anything stupid!"

Promising her as much was the right thing to do, but as he took flight he had to use his breath to call for Ivadr. And the Traveller solidified below – the plan had worked! Ivadr stepped out to hurl the silver box through the light. Never caught the box, tore the lid open and jammed the ring onto a finger.

Below, Ivadr had stumbled back, clutching at his own wrist. Had it caused him pain to carry it? No time to ponder.

Oleksan spun to face Never, three eyes blazing.

"Missing something?" Never called as he sent a wave of Holy Fire forth, and though it splashed away from the Burnished King, he followed up with the Jewel of the Sun. The blinding light won a roar of pain from Oleksan but the Burnished King fell away and the beam flew wide.

Get closer!

Oleksan continued to give ground and Never matched the creature's movements, beating his wings harder, swooping closer, more beams of light flying wide. Oleksan drew his hammer back, and Never darted forward – swifter than he'd ever flown, too fast, and like a blinking flash he'd reached Oleksan, only to crash into the creature.

And he screamed.

Chapter 41

Gripping the Burnished King was like holding blades that pierced Never from each and every joint and yet, no blood flowed. He fought against the pain, grinding his teeth as he wrestled with the demi-god, unable to do much damage and at the same time, far too close for the creature to use the plague hammer.

Never flared the Holy Fire, using his hands to claw into Oleksan's back, forcing the fire and light from the Jewel into hardened skin, and the creature faltered. But Oleksan's larger body was far too heavy. It drew them both down, the floor rushing up, even as Never clung to the blades that stabbed at him, his wings not strong enough to slow their descent.

Over the crackle of flames, the rush of air was deceptively faint. Yet it was all too fast. The fall might not be fatal, but if he could at least manage to land on –

Tiles exploded.

The shock of impact cast him into the air.

His whole body twisted and then he struck the floor again, new pain erupting as he rolled to a halt with another cry. He'd tucked his wings in, almost as a reflex, but both shoulder and collar bone were surely broken – the agony worse now that Oleksan's piercing body was no longer attacking.

Never hauled himself to one knee, gasping as each movement ripped at his torso.

Healing was already at work but it was not at all like snapping his fingers.

Oleksan lay motionless upon the broken floor, not so distant.

Never rose with a curse, and hobbled across to the demi-god, one arm hanging at his side. He still had the Jewel of the Sun, and without having used too much blood, he did not feel even close to exhaustion – a tiny mercy.

His enemy did not move. Had the Holy Fire or the Jewel of the Sun stunned Oleksan? Taken him to the edge of death already?

Never knelt with another bloody oath, but lifted the silver ring and by the diamond's light, Oleksan's weak point became apparent, a marking upon his chest. Another Amouni symbol, the hollow rays for 'Light'.

"Ready, Oleksan?"

He ground his teeth and drove his fist into the symbol.

A sharp crack echoed and the force flung his arm back, sending more jolts of pain lancing through his chest and up his neck into his skull. But something was happening. The jewel had dimmed and the symbol was blazing white, the Burnished King darkening – armour-like skin turning from gold to bronze to brown and then almost black, the colour spreading from head to toe. Yet the change had not finished, his hue soon lightening to grey and growing spotted with patterns of crawling white.

Never stood over the corpse, still breathing hard.

Had the Jewel of the Sun done its work? He lifted the ring and found a cracked diamond, no more light glimmering within.

Never frowned down at the Burnished King, now a mound of grey moss, heavily speckled with what appeared to be white spores... mould? And yet, a chance remained that it had all been a ploy. Oleksan was one to sow doubt, to seek always to deceive. What if this was the same trick now? All of it? The chasing of the Guide, the inability to break the barrier, the swift end to their battle, the death... could it be just another lie?

If so, how, and to what end?

Both Cog and the Guide were working on destroying the Eye of Hours. There'd been no need to use the quartz coffin, to sacrifice his life in order to become a Guardian. The longer he stared, the more it seemed unlikely that the demi-god could fall so easily.

Oleksan was not finished.

He had simply not chosen to spring the final part of the trap.

"Can you hear me, then?" Never asked. Little movements no longer hurt, but he was still not going to do any flying just yet. Even so, he nudged the corpse with his foot.

The Burnished King did not reply.

If it was another trick, what was next? How did drying to a husk unlock the power to use the Eye? Was there another, unconnected goal? "Do you want me focus on the Jalen Khasom for some reason?"

He turned to the entryway. No sign of Rikeva. Was she in danger?

"Never, is it over?" Ivadr was approaching from across the hall; he appeared to be straining to keep his eyes open as he stumbled forth, and even from a distance, it seemed burned skin was visible beneath the tattered sleeve of one arm.

"You're hurt," Never said as he moved, meeting the man halfway, supporting him with an arm despite the pain it caused. "The Jewel?"

"I'll recover," Ivadr said between breaths. "I didn't realise just how much of the Malecaphera lingered within me. Finding the ring was *much* easier than carrying it. At least it worked."

"Perhaps."

"But Oleksan is defeated."

Never glanced back to the bleached corpse. "You said the Jewel of the Sun was easy to take, right?"

"Yes... it was locked in a chest, but wasn't there an equal chance that my shadow-running would allow me to remain undetected in the first place, rather than alerting him to my actions?"

"And so enabling you to retrieve the ring without alerting any potential hidden guards?"

"Our plan was based upon that possibility, right?"

Never nodded. "I just find it hard to believe that Oleksan is truly finished."

Ivadr offered a weary smile. "No harm in being sure. Burn the body with the Holy Fire."

"Sound advice, Ivadr. Can you stand?"

"Go, be certain."

Never left the man and approached the Burnished King once more.

A creaking sound echoed in the quiet hall.

The corpse shifted.

Cracks appeared along the chest. One widened, splitting up the middle, then spread further as though something within pushed at both sides – something was hatching! Never freed his wings and sent twin blasts of Holy Fire forth. Roiling green and blue covered the creature and hissing steam rose as corpse and stone alike melted.

A lithe figure flashed up and out of the flames, hanging in the air.

Gold-tinted skin covered the body of a naked woman, her form still somewhat elongated, her human-seeming face compelling in its own subtle differences; wider eyes and mouth, higher cheekbones, her sigh of relief somewhat musical.

A Burnished Queen.

Never hurled more fire at her but she raised a hand and it splayed off to the sides – useless, as before. He cut the streams but did not release his hold on the Fires of Heaven. "Thank you both," she said with a smile, then flung both arms out. A wave of golden mist speared forth and it froze Never where he stood. "This is most refreshing, Never."

"Welcome back, Oleksan," he replied. At least speaking was still possible.

She spun a gown of lace from mist and clothed herself before floating closer. "Such manners, and I am in your debt."

"Was it all a front?" he asked. Had even Ecanseja been fooled? Had he in fact been guarding and protecting the ring? Keeping it locked in the quartz? "You planted stories about the Jewel of the Sun to fool the Amouni?"

She reached out to touch his cheek, letting her fingertips

slide along his jaw and to his lips, pleasant warmth following. "Not at all. The Jewel of the Sun worked exactly as intended."

"I cannot believe your chrysalis was its purpose."

"You are kind to describe me thusly, but this is the truth. The mark was placed upon my shell in the dim reaches of my past when your ancestors sealed me away. What you have done, is used to break through my armour, if you will. And now that I am more vulnerable, you are expected to finish what you started," she said. "Of course, that is *if* you can."

Never strained against the golden mist, Ivadr doing the same, but even though his muscles raged, the futility of his actions were clear.

Oleksan's face softened, her soothing voice growing sympathetic. "Do not despair; you have achieved much. There is every chance that your Amouni servant and the Prime Guide will disrupt or even destroy the Eye of Hours, given enough time, I do admit that. You are a credit to your ancestors."

"Flattery?"

She smiled and it was... strangely sincere, and all the more disconcerting for its honesty. And yet, was she sincere or was she clouding his own mind, his own reactions to her? It was hard to look away, hard to disbelieve her words. "Merely the truth. You are an interesting opponent, Never, to achieve what you have when facing me – exactly the kind of person that could be of great value in the new world."

"I cannot be part of that world."

She floated back, turning to gesture to the quartz

coffin. "Then take your chances here. Become a Guardian and protect the morally barren, rotten lands you claim to care about."

"At your invitation?"

"Why not?"

Never stumbled free of the mist – had he been fighting it the whole time? Ivadr was still trapped. "The more you offer that, the less I trust your words. You wouldn't rush to your own end."

Footsteps echoed from outside the hall, and Rikeva skidded into view, blonde hair flying. "Never! It's all lies. There are no prisoners here, just blood-soaked bones." Her voice ripped through the air, brimming with fury, but she slowed when she saw Oleksan.

"Ah, now this is wonderful. Some additional motivation has arrived." The Burnished Queen smiled.

Chapter 42

More golden mist streaked across the room, wrapping Rikeva effortlessly – and silencing her curses too.

Oleksan settled down upon the quartz coffin, crossing her legs, the lace of her gown fluttering. She stared across at him. "Should you want them to survive, you will join me here, Never."

The Holy Fire flared in his hands. "More lies."

"The prisoners? That is not true – those I have called to my side remain safe and sound within the other temples." She shrugged. "And those that your beautiful friend discovered here, I admit that they were found wanting. It *did* take time and effort for me to improve the Eye of Hours."

"And blood?"

"Yes. Not too much more than I was expecting but then, Arkenon's methods are not those of the Amouni. We require a more... full collection of materials."

Never spat. "All of your posturing about a better future and you remain just a tool of Arkenon."

She stretched, head tilted back to stare up at the ceiling as she answered. "Whatever remains of Arkenon is mine to use now but it does not bind me."

He charged.

Fire streaked forth, but her raised arm split the Fires of Heaven as it had each time before. It did not come close to touching her. "Silly of you." She snapped her fingers.

Dual screams echoed from opposite ends of the hall; Ivadr and Rikeva had fallen to their knees, whites of their eyes rolling as they flailed against the pain and the glimmering mist.

"Rika!" Never ran but he'd only taken two steps before crashing to a halt.

"Listen to me, Amouni," Oleksan snapped. "Go willingly into the Bed of Quartz and I spare them. If I have to force you, they die first."

"Don't trust her!" Rikeva cried.

Ivadr was trembling from the pain, but he managed to shake his head.

"Stop." Never glared across at Oleksan. "I will go on one condition."

"Oh?"

Both Rikeva and Ivadr had slumped forward, still breathing and hopefully no longer in pain. "Yes. Let me approach the Bed of Quartz. I need to touch it; I want to see if you're telling the truth, since we both know that deceit is your name."

"Very well."

Freed, Never strode to the clear quartz.

Rikeva's voice was soft, exhausted, urging him not to give in, but if he could just reach Oleksan, maybe there was a chance to trap her... He touched the coffin, hand passing through the surface, quite near her leg.

Never snatched at Oleksan. "Come with me."

His arms found a softer, more human body and he dragged Oleksan with him but she did not sink.

And he did.

He clung to her waist, legs dangling below, her golden form wavering as though he stared up from beneath a pool of water. "An interesting gambit," she said, and unhooked one of his arms. "But as you see, I am not permitted to enter the Bed of Quartz, even with your aid."

"I will stop you, whether I become a Guardian or not," he called back, but she did not seem to hear.

With a more dispassionate expression, she released the last of his grip and then he was plummeting, the light of the room, her body, the entire temple shrinking rapidly – too fast for how gentle his descent seemed.

Fear did not take hold – it was frustration. Ecanseja knew what to expect, and so Never knew. At the 'bottom' he would lie across a silver slab and it would coat him, not unlike the silver man in the Spire, and then the silver would sink into his flesh and bones, strengthening both, changing him, creating a new form, something bound to the coffin forever, or until his destruction.

But the new form would pose a true threat to Oleksan.

He would make the change, the sacrifice, and put a stop to her – the cost was great, bitter, but he pushed those feelings aside a little longer. There would be time to mourn what he was giving up, the rest of his life, his friends.

Rikeva.

If he was going to become a Guardian, he *had* to be

certain he wasn't playing into Oleksan's trap.

What made little sense still, was why she had been so adamant that he become a Guardian? There were no benefits, surely, if he then stood on equal footing? She had admitted to needing the power... but she could not force him to use it, not as Malecaphera.

She had not been able to reach Ecanseja either, so if that was not her game, did it leave a far more pedestrian reason?

Did the Burnished King simply want a Guardian for 'her' temple once her new world had been created?

A white feather appeared in the darkness, fluttering down toward him.

Illya?

Never reached out for the feather, heart skipping a few beats.

Was he near death already – or, as Ecanseja remembered it, the Transformation? Could Illya interfere somehow?

"Brother."

A pale figure appeared before him, piercing blue eyes, a kind smile the likes of which Never had not witnessed since their childhood.

Snow.

Snow wore a pale blue robe, unadorned by symbol or pattern, and he reached out to take Never by the shoulders, still smiling. "I did not imagine this could be possible but I am glad of this moment."

Never swallowed. Shock and regret crashed against him, relief and guilt, even fear, along with the image of the shattered Memory Trees, of bloody feathers too, all of it stealing his voice at first. "*Is* it possible?"

"You are not dreaming, and I am still dead, brother."

"How?"

"There is little time, but I imagine the nekromant would have mentioned that the dead were rallying to the Amouni?"

"She did."

"Well, thank me for that – at least, in part. I have been learning that in life, I had not discovered even *half* of the secrets of our ancestors. Nor that I could return, after a fashion. But more importantly, you have something important to do in the temple."

"Then, you're here to help?"

Snow chuckled. "You are my brother. And just because Oleksan has somewhat similar goals to mine, that doesn't mean I want her to succeed where I failed. Give me at least that much credit. Or, if you prefer, pettiness."

Never had to laugh in response. "Do you want an honest answer?"

"Not especially."

"What next?"

"Next, the temple gets its new Guardian, since I have nearly completed that process already."

Was it possible? But Ecanseja had no memories of the Transformation being interrupted in such a way. "Will this work?"

"I will find out soon enough," Snow said. "You must destroy the Eye. I will keep the Burnished Queen occupied."

Never caught Snow's arms. "Wait. You would be trapped here forever. I thought that... well, I thought that at least you had found some sort of peace in death."

Snow raised an eyebrow. "I am not sure I would go that far, but worry not, Never. I have been given a gift, now that my awareness has returned, and for you, for Sacha and Cog and for many others, I do this. And once more, it will give me no small pleasure to thwart an old enemy of the Amouni."

"You're saving me again," Never said.

"Yes," Snow replied as he took both hands and hurled Never up into the darkness "Now, off you go, brother!"

Never reached after but Snow was already a tiny figure, and light soon appeared above, surging closer and closer until he burst from the watery quartz of the coffin, landing with a thump on the white tiles.

Rikeva and Ivadr lay upon the floor now, and though they stirred at the sound of his return, neither seemed strong enough to move or speak.

"What is this?" A golden figure flowed down toward him from a window.

"You don't sound pleased to see me," Never replied.

Twin blades of obsidian appeared in Oleksan's hands as she dove toward him. Never called his fire.

A white streak crashed into the Burnished Queen.

Thrown through the air, she smashed into the temple wall – then immediately pushed herself free. Tiles and stone fell as she swung her blades with a roar.

Snow caught them on his own swords, showers of white and black sparks falling. They spun and twirled through the air, almost dancing, and when Snow landed a glancing blow, golden blood spattered upon the walls. Her own riposte sent droplets of transparent blue falling.

"Get moving," Snow called down.

Never dashed to the unconscious Rikeva and carried her behind some columns, rushing back for Ivadr, who was in a similar state, before flying to the nearest window. His wings protested with every beat but he managed to land on the ledge, only for a screech from within the temple to stop him.

Oleksan was bearing down, blades extended like a lance, Snow's transparent figure close behind.

So fast!

Holy Fire burst across his hands but Never did not send it out this time, he needed a new tactic.

Never braced himself – it had to be at the last possible moment.

Oleksan's snarl widened as she thundered closer. Behind the Burnished Queen, Snow had almost caught up but wouldn't be fast enough.

She thrust both obsidian blades.

And Never reached out to catch them, edges tearing into his hands even as he twisted.

It wasn't enough.

One blade pierced his side as the other found only air.

Blood splashed across the platform. He cried out, falling to one knee and dragging her down beside him – and she was covered in his blood. Success! Never caught her now-writhing body and pulled himself along the blade with gritted teeth, smearing bloody, burning hands across her torso, then flaring the Holy Fire.

Her scream rattled his teeth.

But even when it rose in pitch, he did not let the fire die. He would keep it burning until she was a miserable little pile of ash, no matter the cost.

White flashed, cutting off the scream.

Snow hovered above, his own swords smeared with

golden blood.

Oleksan's head lay beside her smouldering body, sightless eyes wide with rage and pain, a somehow unnatural silence following their brief struggle. More of her blood, warm and golden, was seeping from her severed neck, creeping toward him.

Never threw himself back with another cry, her blade sliding free with a new, searing lance of agony.

"Did that work?" he asked Snow between gasps, hand pressed against the warm blood seeping from his wound.

His brother stared down, and it seemed he almost smiled. "And you called me the mad one?"

Snow bent beside Never and checked his wound but had barely glanced at it before rising again with a muttered curse – Oleksan's head was sliding slowly back toward her still-burning body, even the blood was now angling for the same path.

Never straightened. "By all the Absent Gods, can we even finish her?"

Snow's still-translucent form lifted both arms, then hacked down. One of the Burnished Queen's smooth hands rolled away. He cut through her other wrist, then both feet before skewering the head on one of his blades. That, he tossed it over his shoulder.

"Snow?"

"A moment, Never." He kicked the feet and hands over next, then gestured to the body. "Think you can give Oleksan's body a little more of that Holy Fire? I'll take care of the rest but you still have a job to do."

Never grunted as he pressed his back against the wall and pushed himself upright. His wound had closed but it was by no means healed. "You mean, she'll just... put herself back together?"

"Yes. Like our healing, only more persistent," Snow replied. "I can stop it if you give me enough time but that won't matter if you don't destroy the Jalen Khasom."

"Wait, do you mean the Eye is already working? She didn't need my blood, or anything else?"

"Precisely." Snow said, blue eyes troubled now. "Oleksan was stalling because you're able to destroy the Eye, at least now that Cog has weakened it from within."

"And I was focused on the Bed of Quartz."

"That was where her ploy nearly succeeded – she gambled it all on being able to stop the Guide before you were Transformed, since the Transformation is not instantaneous. Failing that, I believe she would have attempted to somehow drain you when you reappeared as Guardian. Or, more likely, use your friends as leverage."

"Is that possible? Could she have drained me?"

Snow frowned. "I don't think we'll ever know, thankfully. Either way, all you need to do now is shatter the Quartz and this ends."

Hope surged up within him but it was tempered by reluctance. "Cog is still inside."

Snow nodded, but did not answer.

"Snow!"

"If not for him, you might not have even reached the Bed of Quartz. Don't make his sacrifice count for nothing," his brother replied. "Or mine."

"All right." Never raised one hand and sent more of the Holy Fire forth, flames taking hold of Oleksan's body, now smouldering *beneath* the skin, but oddly enough, there was no scent of burning flesh.

"Be careful of that wound too," Snow added. "Find some of that cure you and your Doerin lover are so proud of."

Never paused. "Lover?"

Snow lifted the burning body and leapt down after the rest of the Burnished Queen, but his voice floated up. "If she isn't, then maybe she should be."

Never smiled as he limped toward the night and the enormous Eye of Hours.

Chapter 43

Dawn was a pale whisper climbing above the trees that waited beyond the lake, a colour not yet realised across the rest of the darkened sky. No stars remained but something still lit the Eye of Hours from within, the enormous quartz carving hanging between the temples.

Never did not fly to it at once, taking time catch his breath, to hopefully heal a little more, despite the grave urgency of the moment.

Neither Cog nor the Guide were visible but flickering light moved within, as though the eye's pupil raced from corner to corner. Little pieces were breaking from the bulk, sparkling as they fell toward the water.

A startling lack of tension pervaded the air around the Eye of Hours.

Such calm was almost unbecoming of his task – after all, saving the entire world deserved a little more… something! And the final moment ought to have been more difficult. But the truth was, many had paid a price to get him to such a point, Cog chief among them. The man was probably *still* paying it.

Never summoned the Holy Fire and lifted both arms. "Forgive me."

Even if such an end was what Cog sought – even if Snow had echoed the man's wishes – to destroy Cog while destroying the quartz was nothing to be relished.

Fire the colour of the ocean spilled forth to pierce the quartz.

A hissing followed, reaching him at the ledge, as large shards and half-melted hunks began to fall, some spinning off with echoing cracking sounds. He swung the beams of fire and cut through more of the quartz. It was already faltering, drifting from its invisible perch.

He kept slicing and more and more quartz plummeted straight down, other pieces arcing further across the lake. Never narrowed his eyes as each piece splashed into the water, setting the blue surface to steaming. Would it harm the lake system? Power unseen for centuries, perhaps completely unheard of, was being dissolved. *Something* had to come from its release.

But nothing burst free, nothing twisted or changed and nothing disappeared either.

Had the destruction of the Eye truly had so little effect?

From above, a sharp whistling turned his head.

A huge section of quartz hurtled toward him – and something crashed into his side. The force carried him over the edge as the hunk crashed into the temple, lodging with a spray of shattered stone.

Blonde hair obscured his vision as he fell.

Rikeva! He gripped her as he spread his wings and spun to glide back up, smiling down at her.

"Great timing, don't you think?" she asked with a grin.

"Astounding."

Never beat his wings enough to hover, and together they watched the last of the Eye of Hours splash down into the lake, the enormous shapes enough to send water spouting high into the air. Soon, the only piece that remained was lodged into the temple, having obliterated the platform he'd once stood upon. Had it fallen so, or somehow been *pushed* toward him, a final attack from Oleksan?

Or was that just lingering doubts? Best to make sure when he could.

"Is that the end?" Rikeva asked. "Is it finished?"

"I think so." He stared at the Temple. "How did you get up there so quickly?"

"In short: I climbed."

"You scaled the temple interior?"

She nodded. "It's not so hard with my gift. I just punched and kicked holes. But I still think that you should be more impressed with my arrival."

"I am," he replied. "What of Ivadr?"

"He's alive, thankfully." Her cheer faded when she looked down to the water once more. "Your friend?"

Never shook his head. "I don't think so."

"Should we be sure? Just in case?"

Checking on Snow's progress with Oleksan could wait a short while. After all, there was no guarantee the falling quartz had been directed by any force, and as Guardian, Snow was a match for the ruins of the Burnished Queen. And after all Cog had done, seeking his body, if it still had a form, was the absolute bare minimum he could offer in return. "We should."

Never flew down to circle the still-warm water, and

together he and Rikeva examined the bobbing pieces of quartz, which was unusual in and of itself, though many were starting to sink. Enough had flattened out into smooth and sometimes uneven, twisted shapes, becoming raft-like, and these pieces too were somehow yet to slip beneath the lake.

It did not seem such a large area to search at first, but they found nothing until the morning sun broke free, when Rikeva pointed. "What about over there?"

Never tilted his wings and swung closer to the water. The shape was Cog... or at least, the man's head and torso, frozen in purple quartz, bobbing gently. His expression was one of peace and he did not answer when Never called.

The man was gone.

A sense of loss washed over Never, sharper thanks to his own role. First to have transformed Cog, and then to have had such a role in his death...

"Should we take him back to land?" Rikeva asked. "Does he have someone who would want to say goodbye?"

"There may well be," he replied. It wouldn't be easy to manage but nor would the task be impossible either. "I'll lower you, see how much he weighs."

Rikeva unwrapped an arm from his torso and took his hand, stretching down to reach for Cog, her fingers brushing against the quartz, but it drifted away as the force of Never's wings threw her off balance a little. "Sorry, let me try again," he said, dipping even closer.

This time her hand splashed into the water.

A ripple spread across the surface.

Cog disappeared.

All the quartz, the bubbles rising from the still-settling

pieces somewhere below, even the heat was gone – instead, just a pristine, cool blue surface, as though the Eye of Hours had not existed.

Rikeva flinched, pulling him off-balance, his own shock causing him to miss a wing beat and together, they splashed down. The cool lake closed over his head, bubbles surging, but he kicked up to break the surface right away, finding Rikeva beside him treading water. "Never..."

Droplets of water ran down her hair and cheeks, one even dripping from the point of her nose as she stared up at something behind him. Her voice had been soft, traces of confusion and awe, rather than fear.

Never turned, a clumsy sloshing, but was barely able to keep afloat himself, once he saw the central Temple Trivium and its strips of amber glistening in the sun, its white wall undamaged, the chunk of quartz vanished.

And more... dozens of figures now flew through the air.

Winged Amouni in coloured robes and cloaks and sometimes black tunics flew above them, steady and measured and some at seemingly dangerous speeds, others swooping or twisting through the air as they landed or launched themselves from window platforms, many flying between the temples, others rushing up to the rings. And below, boats shaped as whales or dolphins were crowded with figures in an equally colourful array, their faces not close enough to discern details, but voices drifted to him as they passed.

Amouni words, each and every one of them.

"Never... is this...?"

"I fear it is," he said. "The time of the Amouni."

A Note from Ashley

Hello! Thanks for reading Never's 8th adventure – I just wanted to say that there will most definitely will be a 9th outing too!

When I finished writing *Spectre* (sometime in April 2019 I think), and ended that story with a plague-god on the loose, I didn't think I'd be writing *this* book during a pandemic. I hope *Throne of Leaves* was still an enjoyable story and that you're all safe.

I'd like to ask if you could help me out by leaving an honest review of the novel at your place of purchase? Long or short, bad or good, it all helps!

AND if you'd like to sign up to my newsletter (www.ashleycapes.com) you'll be the first to know when the next book is released. You'll also have first access to preview chapters and pre-release editions of the story, in addition to being automatically added into the draw for giveaways.

Ashley

ACKNOWLEDGMENTS

Thanks again to another large cast of folks who helped me with this book.

I must of course single out my wife Brooke for her tireless support but also my writing group, the Alchemists, along with my editor Amanda and also Lin Hsiang for yet another stunning cover image!

Thanks also to Shawn T King for the superb text design and once again, also to those of you who spent time with my characters!

Ashley

ABOUT ASHLEY

Ashley Capes is an Australian novelist, poet and teacher. He teaches English, Media and Music Production, has played in a metal band, worked in an art gallery and slaved away at music retail.

Aside from reading and writing, Ashley loves volleyball and Studio Ghibli – and *Magnum PI*, easily one of the greatest television shows ever made.

Visit his blogs at www.ashleycapes.com or follow him on twitter @Ash_Capes.

Fiction

The Bone Mask Cycle
1. City of Masks
2. The Lost Mask
3. Greatmask
4. The Last Sea God
5. The Raven's Price
6. Lionsheart

Book of Never
1. The Amber Isle
2. A Forest of Eyes
3. River God
4. The Peaks of Autumn
5. Imperial Towers